Pollard

Book 3 of the Banebridge Companion Novels

A Story in the Soul Forge Universe

Pollard by Richard H. Stephens

www.richardhstephens.com

Cover & interior art by: Widget Wyvern Studios
Paperback ISBN: 978-1-989257-30-2

2nd Edition: 2021

Acknowledgements

Pollard is the final installment in the Banebridge Companion Novels; bringing the stories of *Larina*, and *Sadyra* together.

While looking to fill in the time between the completion of the Legends of the Lurker series and a research trip* the British Isles, I wanted to do something different. I surveyed my amazing readers and asked them which minor character from either of my first two series would they like to see a story written about. Sadyra, the cheeky, fun loving, wear her heart on her sleeve archer from the Soul Forge Saga was the winner. She beat out notables, Olmar, another favourite from the Soul Forge Saga, and Devius Misenthorpe and Tamra Stoneheart, from the Legends of the Lurker. I thoroughly enjoyed fleshing out the backstories that explain Sadyra and Larina came to fight alongside Pollard Banebridge in the Splendoor Catacombs Guard—a division of the Songsbirthian Guard.

*Unfortunately, my research trip has been cancelled due to COVID-19, so the Rise of Grimclaw is now on hold.

On the bright side, as one good thing is put on hold, another opportunity arises. I am excited to announce the next series in the Soul Forge Universe: The Highcliff Guardians. This series will revolve around the elves: Ouderling Wys and Pecklyn Ors, filling in the history with regard to the emergence of the Windwalkers.

Within the pages of *Pollard,* there is mention of the clever craftmanship and engineering skills of the dwarfs from Sarsen Rest. As such, I have been blessed with the opportunity to come to know a man who would have made the most excellent of dwarfs. *Pollard* is dedicated to Alexander Bogue. Don't ever lose that sharp wit.

'The fate of the masses hinge on the deliberations of the few.' ~ Master Pul

None of these stories would be possible without the input of my incredible beta readers. A heartfelt thank you to: Joshua Stephens and Caroline Davidson. Your input truly puts the magic in my stories.

A big thank you also goes out to my cover and interior picture designer, Tessa Escalera of Widget Wyvern Studios.

Special credit: To honour the First Nation Peoples of North America, I chose the name Lozen to represent an Altirius Mountain Indian; a title that appears in the original book, *Soul Forge*. All incidents involving Lozen in the books: *Larina, Sadyra,* and *Pollard,* are purely fictitious, and by no means represent the real warrior, Lozen.

A brief, unverified history of Lozen.

A famous warrior and prophet of the Chihenne Chiricahua Apache, Lozen was the sister of Chief Victorio.

Born in the 1840s, her brother once said, *"Lozen is my right hand...strong as a man, braver than most, and cunning in strategy. Lozen is a shield to her people."*

Lozen used her spiritual powers in battle; calling on the favour of the gods to discover the location and movement of the enemy.

She participated in many fights on the San Carlos Reservation in Arizona. During those fights, she helped many women and children escape the hands of the enemy and avoided capture herself.

A warrior named Kaywaykla, once said, "She could ride, shoot, and fight like a man; and I think she had more ability in planning military strategy than Victorio."

Lozen fought alongside Geronimo in the last campaign of the Apache Wars.

Going forward.

As in my last series, The Legends of the Lurker, I will be searching for new and unique dragon names. If you wish to submit a name to be added to my list, please connect with me on my Facebook Author Page: RichardHughStephens

Credit in the form of a personal thank you, in the foreword of the book in which the names are used, is my way of giving back to you, the reader. (Including your real name in the acknowledgements will only occur with your permission.)

Zephyr
The Unknown Sea
Mt. Cinder
Mt. Gloom
Cliff Face
ALTIRIUS MOUNTAINS
DRAGONFANG PASS
THE SLITHER
PEDFIRE PATH
ZEPHYR FLATS
Fishmonger Bay
Thunderhead
Storms End
FRITHE RIVER
Madrigail Bay
Castle Svelte
SAROS' SWAMP
The Forke
WEST CASTLE RD.
Carillon
RING LAKE
MILLSFORD
MADRIGAIL R.
Millsford
CANOROUS RIVER
St. Carmichael's Shrine
ALPHEUS' ARCH
Riad Ocean
THE SPINE
SPLENDOUR FALLS
MADRIGAIL LAKE
Songsbirth
THE MUSE
CLEFGRITARN RD.
GRITARN HILLS
Ghost Island
TORPID MARSH
Gritian
TREACHER'S GORGE
UNDYING WALL
FORBIDDEN PASS
THE GULCH
LOWLAND GRASSLANDS
NORDIC WOODS
REDFIRE PATH
Nordic Town
N
THE OCEAN WAY
Apexceal
Amber Breath
PENFLOWERGRAPH

Table of Contents

To view the full colour maps in the Soul Forge Universe, please visit: www.richardhstephens.com

Pollard

Book 3 of the Banebridge Companion Novels

A Story in the Soul Forge Universe

Pollard

A Distant Storm

"A distant storm is brewing on the horizon." Thoril Half-Hand's words resonated in Pollard's head as he watched the waves; a prophetic warning not to be taken lightly. If the son of Thoril the Kraidic Crusher foresaw disaster in the not too distant future, his son, Pollard, would do everything in his power to see to it that those he loved and protected were safe.

Being part giant, whenever Pollard set his mind to something, it was done quickly and efficiently. Fortifying the garrison of Songsbirth against the imminent threat required new recruits, but not just anyone would do. They had to be cut from a different cloth—endowed with the spirit of the ancient warriors who had fought and died for Zephyr in centuries past. Back to the Age of Saints and beyond.

The people Pollard searched for were more often than not outcasts from society. In his years of experience, peculiar quirks and eccentric mannerisms differentiated those who professed the desire to do the right thing and those who were bereft of the common sense that prevented them from placing themselves in the life or death situations his garrison required if the ideals of Zephyr's regime were to survive the imminent cataclysm his father predicted.

The southern ports of Apexceal and Ember Breath had netted Pollard's expedition fifteen promising trainees. Of those, he projected that less than half would prove worthy enough to become a Songsbirthian Guard. Of this fact he made no bones about hiding from the recruits. He allayed their apprehension by assuring them that any who failed to make the cut would be sent to join the Royal Guard in the king's city of Carillon.

Pollard's family's flagship, the *Crusher,* sailed clear of the Undying Wall's western isthmus jutting leagues into the heavy seas of the Niad Ocean. Three tall masts bulging with sailcloth carried the sleek, black warship over the water's rough surface—its bow plunging into deep troughs and cutting the backside of the next wave.

A cold spray washed down the main deck; its mist rarely reaching Pollard where he stood high atop the quarterdeck. He leaned on the port rail, studying the lofty heights of two volcanoes that dominated the eastern horizon, farther out to sea. Ghost Island. He had never set foot on its mist shrouded shores, but from what he had heard of its inhospitable climate, the large island was aptly named.

"All clear!" Came the call from high atop the mainmast crow's nest.

Safely through the treacherous strait separating the outer reaches of the Undying Wall and the lava reefs surrounding Ghost Island, the captain of the *Crusher* left his place beside the helmsman and joined Pollard. "Quite a spectacular sight, eh Master Banebridge?"

"Aye." Pollard flexed his back muscles—the ship's railing was not built for someone of his size. "You think anyone lives out there?"

The captain pulled on his short, pepper-grey beard. "Tough to say. Doubt it. Never seen any sign of life when sailing this way. I've always wanted to put in a lander and check out the island, but I've never gotten around to it."

"Someday, perhaps." Pollard leaned on the railing and smiled. Captain Bennek Crow had been sailing his father's ships for as long as Pollard remembered. Bennek had been a wiry, shrewd young sailor while Pollard had grown up in Storms End. The man hadn't spared much time for the son of Thoril Half-Hand, although Bennek had never been anything but fair during Pollard's youth. If anything, the good captain had hardened Pollard about the unforgiving ways of the sea—his teachings enlightening Pollard of the inherent dangers of the ocean and the men who sailed it.

"Aye." Bennek's gruff voice bore no trace of humour. "Perhaps the crew will bury me there when the time comes."

Pollard nodded. "Certainly a peaceful spot to spend out your days."

Bennek reached up to pat Pollard on the shoulder. "Get some rest, Master Banebridge. Judging by the rising seas, we've a hard trip ahead."

"Thanks, Cap. I'll head below shortly."

Bennek held his gaze for a moment, as if wanting to say something else. He flashed a quick smile and walked away—his sailor's swagger absorbing the roll of the ship.

Pollard watched the captain's progress as he disappeared down the steep steps emptying onto the main deck. Settling his elbows on the railing, he stared at the distant volcano—his mind hundreds of leagues north of their present position.

He had sent his most trusted advisor ahead on the *Half-Hand*—named after his father—the second of three warships in his family's possession. If anyone could ascertain the truth about the rogue thief preying upon the more affluent residents of Storms End, Lozen was the one for the job.

Lozen, a proud warrior from the Altirius Mountains, had agreed to take leave of her tribe to help Pollard train selected members of the Splendoor Catacombs Guard in the way of her native people. She did this to honour the memory of

Pollard

Pollard's grandfather. Her way of paying homage to Thoril the Kraidic Crusher for his role in keeping her peoples free.

With the exception of his father, Pollard valued Lozen's counsel above all others. She possessed an uncanny knack of seeing past a person's persona to discover their true spirit. To Pollard, Lozen was much more than a medicine woman and warrior to her people. Lozen was a dear friend.

Pollard grunted. As conscientious as he was about morality and scruples, his gruff personality didn't lend itself to making friends easily. It took something special for someone to be the recipient of his friendship, but once earned, he would fight to the death to defend them.

The mission he had sent Lozen on left him reeling with mixed emotions. To quell an unfounded fear, he may have inadvertently placed her in danger. Should the Storms End Watch become suspicious of her true intentions, the captain of the Watch, Danth Emerald, wouldn't hesitate to kill her for her deception.

Pollard's father had messaged him through Master Pul of the Songsbirth Council, bringing to his attention a young woman who might prove to be a real boon to the Catacombs Guard. He had called her the Storms End Lightning Bolt—a person who had eluded Danth Emerald and his lackeys for years.

The Storms End Watch had placed the Lightning Bolt high on their wanted list. Though a thief by interpretation of the law, Thoril had insisted there was something special about the rogue lock pick; claiming he had it on good authority that she was merely doing what the city council would not. Looking after its vulnerable citizens.

Thoril feared that one day soon, the upstart woman would slip up. When she did, Danth's vigilante sense of justice would spell her untimely death.

Pollard

Pollard bit his lower lip. He had purposely put his most faithful friend in harm's way in hopes of keeping a lawbreaker from being captured. Until he could return to Storms End, Lozen would have to find a way to cope on her own.

His distant gaze took in the receding volcanic peaks of Ghost Island as he reflected on his father's prophecy. If Thoril's words were true, the coming storm would fall upon Zephyr's people with the fiery fury of an erupting volcano.

Pollard

Homecoming Execution

Madrigail Bay had netted Pollard's contingent seven promising recruits; the number smaller than he would've liked, but he had wasted little time combing the major seaport. His distracted focus lay far to the north; to Storms End where he needed to see to the safety of Lozen. He had left her to deal with the Watch for long enough.

A long day's journey through favourable seas had allowed his ship to reach Thunderhead and the great inland waterway that travelled deep into The Spine.

The afternoon sun at their back, the Crusher slipped through Thunderhead Fjord, dwarfed by the inlet's lofty heights. Behind the towering walls—the tops of their banks shrouded in mist—white-capped mountains disappeared into the clouds for as far as the eye could see.

Pollard hadn't sailed this way in many years, but he knew the land like few others. Rolling moors marked the end of the fjord; a stark relief to the crags and tors along Zephyr's west coast.

He stood along the portside railing of the quarterdeck, anxiously waiting to spot the first sign of Storms End—the northern watchtower.

As the *Crusher's* bow came around a gentle bend in the fjord, Pollard frowned. The smell of charred wood wafted across the deck. Spotting the first sign—the watchtower looked different than he remembered. At first, he thought the stone along the top had weathered but as he looked closer, tell-tale blackened stone surrounded the tower's stairwell window slots.

Bennek Crow called to him from his usual place beside the surly-looking helmsman. "Something's going on."

Pollard didn't respond. Searching the unfolding skyline of the multi-tiered port city, the starboard side of town drew his gaze. Wisps of black smoke rose above the warehouses lining the shore. "Looks like a fire on Canal Road."

Bennek accompanied Pollard on the starboard rail. "Did you notice the north watchtower?"

"Aye." Pollard glanced at the southern watchtower as it came into view—its stonework uniform in colour from top to bottom. "Appears that whatever's burning, isn't the only building to be set ablaze recently."

The peal of large bells reached them across the water.

"That's odd." Pollard turned his head to listen. He knew at once they belonged to the main temple dominating the city square. "Must be a ceremony this afternoon."

The harbourfront didn't appear much different than it had the last time Pollard had made the trip home to visit with his father. The dark hulks of the *Half-Hand* and the *Pul* were tied to their private pier close to the roadway that led over the rocks to where the southern watchtower jutted into the bay.

"Furl the cloth! Man the oars!" Bennek shouted.

No sooner had word been given than pulleys creaked and oars slid into place—the efficient crew had anticipated the command as the south watchtower slipped by.

A couple of Watch stood at the lofty tower's base, waving to those aboard the *Crusher*. Pollard would have normally returned the greeting but his mind was preoccupied.

Pollard

Something was happening in Storms End. Something big. He could tell by the odd atmosphere the city exuded. Or, if he thought about it, the lack of noise. An expectant calm before the proverbial storm. Stepping away from the rail, he approached the top of the steps and located his second in command.

"Carnoch!"

The man in question sought Pollard out. "Master?"

"Have the troops outfitted and ready when we tie off. They shall accompany me into the city. The recruits are to remain onboard."

"Aye, Master Banebridge." The fit, young man nodded a clean-shaven face and began to prepare.

By the time the *Crusher's* crew had her tied off and secured, the afternoon sun had dropped between the high walls lining Thunderhead Fjord; its dazzling rays setting the waters ablaze with stunning shades of orange and red.

A group of twelve, consisting of both men and women, marched in practiced cadence behind Pollard and Carnoch. Resplendent in Songsbirthian Guard grey, the staccato of their boots echoed off the buildings built along Canal Road. Pollard gave word to Carnoch that his troops were to keep their weapons sheathed until he knew what was going on.

Usually teeming with people, the cobblestoned road that separated the waterfront warehouses and the businesses along the banks of a man-made canal lay empty. The top of the gallows platform that had been built in the centre of the commons over two decades ago provided a stark relief against the distant temple—both structures visible above the buildings fronting the canal. A commotion reached their ears—growing in volume the closer they got to the great open space signifying Storms End's central square.

A pair of Watchmen ran up from behind; slowing to inspect the disciplined ranks. Their consternation eased as they realized who led them.

"What goes on here?" Pollard asked the older of the two grizzled men.

The man bowed his head. "Master Banebridge. Welcome home. You've arrived at a bad time. We're responding to reports of an assassin murdering the baron and one of our head captains."

Shocked, Pollard could tell the men were itching to be on their way. "Don't let us detain you. We'll provide whatever assistance you require. Lead on."

"Thank you, Master Banebridge." The man looked to his companion and indicated with a nod to follow him toward the city centre. They bowed their heads to Pollard and ran up Canal Road, passing a burnt-out building farther up and on the right.

"That explains the burning smell." Pollard pointed to a pile of charred timbers. "That used to be the *Kraken's Curse* if I'm not mistaken."

Carnoch nodded. "Aye, Master. I believe you're right." Without being told, he chased after the receding Watch.

Pollard increased the length and frequency of his long strides. Behind him, the contingent from Songsbirth jogged in order to keep pace. A few, soot-smeared faces turned to watch them as they tromped past the skeletal remains of the *Kraken's Curse.*

The canal curved inland in a great sweeping arc, circumventing the wide commons that dominated the central region of the lower level of Storms End. Canal Road emptied into the city square, resuming its course on the far side.

Pollard

Pollard slowed his advance and turned to face his troops. "Let's not rush into anything. If Captain Danth Emerald has anything to do with this, it may become volatile quickly. Under no circumstances do you bare weapons except on my order. Is that clear?"

"Yes, sir!" Twelve Songsbirthian Guards answered at once.

Pollard's gaze lingered on his troops, appreciating their steadfast loyalty. Each one had been handpicked by either him or Captain Johnnes Holman, the leader of their illustrious garrison. The troops would die before they disobeyed him.

Walking around the corner of a two-story, stone building, the city square opened before Pollard's eyes as Carnoch rejoined them. The spectacle unfolding in the commons took Pollard's breath away. Not since his grandfather's funeral had he seen a crowd this big gathered outside the temple. Except today, the crowd's attention didn't lay on the ancient sanctuary, but on the gallows scaffold dominating the city centre.

Trying to assess everything at once, he noted the colours and insignia of the commander of the Watch who stood on the edge of the gallows platform. It had been several years since Pollard's last trip home. He didn't know the man by name.

He followed the commander's gaze to three people crouched on the ground at the base of the gallows with weapons drawn. A large man pointed a familiar dagger his way. A young woman dressed all in black, brandished a short blade. And, the woman whose safety he had fretted over for the last week, stared back at him.

Lozen threatened the closest Watch with her bow. As their eyes met, she dropped to a knee. "Master Banebridge."

Pollard

The large man with the dagger smiled. "Look, it's Pollard."

Pollard's breath caught. Trying to ignore the respect many in the crowd offered him by following Lozen's gesture and dropping to a knee, he smiled. It had been many years, but he would know the scruffy looking hulk of a man anywhere. Despite his smile, he couldn't help wondering what his dear friend, Gom, was doing with Lozen. He certainly wasn't dressed like one of the Watch.

Uncomfortable being treated as if he were royalty, Pollard waggled his fingers for the people to rise. With a subtle nod to Carnoch, his troops fanned out around him.

"Ah good." The commander leaned out to direct his words at Lozen, Gom, and the woman in black. "Now you'll meet the justice you deserve."

Pollard frowned. "What goes on here?"

The smugness on the commander's face spoke loudly as to the type of man leading the Watch. "Son of Thoril. As temporary ruler of Storms End, I beseech you to apprehend these people."

"Temporary ruler? What happened?"

"These three," the commander used his sword to indicate the three people on the ground who were attracting everyone's attention, "have conspired to kill the baron and a captain of the Watch."

Concerned for her welfare, Pollard started toward Lozen. "Those are serious allegations, commander. Are you accusing my warrior of this crime?"

"Well, no," the commander sputtered. "Not her, exactly."

"Then what, good man? What is her role in this?"

"She freed that man from the gallows." The commander pointed at Bear. "Lozen has also facilitated the escape of Storms End's most wanted criminal."

Pollard

Confused, Pollard studied the woman in black. "You mean to tell me this girl is the Watch's biggest concern?"

"Aye. She's committed countless crimes against the people, burned the north watchtower to the ground, and assassinated the baron and Captain Danth Emerald."

Pollard glanced at the blackened watchtower, thinking, *'so that's what happened to it.'*

He returned his attention to the commander. "The same Danth Emerald who has been terrorizing the upper tiers with his gang of over-righteous thugs? The same Watch captain who has been operating above the law with the blessing of the baron?"

"Well, I-I…Yes. This woman is the Storms End Lightning Bolt. She's eluded us for years."

Pollard cupped his chin in his hand. "Ah, yes. A person who has dedicated her young life to look after our most respected citizens. Feeding and clothing our elders and less well-to-do." He nodded, his temper rising. "The very injustice that drove me to leave Storms End. I find your accusations troubling."

The commander glared. "You have no jurisdiction here, son of Thoril. Either help us bring these criminals to justice or be on your way."

It took a lot to rile Pollard, but hearing the brashness of the commander's words, he decided the time had come to take matters into his own hands. Reaching over his shoulder, his hand found the reassuring grip of his sword. Pulling it free of the double baldric housing its two, individual blades, his teeth gnashed together with an ominous growl. "*This* gives me jurisdiction. Have your people stand down until I sort this out."

Pollard

The insolent commander balked. "I most certainly will not. You forget yourself, son of Thoril. With Danth Emerald and the baron dead, I command the Watch *and* the city."

Two measured breaths escaped Pollard. He stretched his neck and threw back his shoulders, readying himself. "It is *you* who have forgotten his role. In the absence of the baron, the Master of the council is in charge of the city."

The commander scanned the crowd. "Thoril's not here. Therefore, it's my duty to act in his place. If you insist on siding with murderers, I will be left with no choice but to condemn you as an accomplice."

A collective gasp rippled through the crowd.

Pollard gave Carnoch a subtle sign, prompting the Songsbirthian Guard to unsheathe swords and string bows; their open display of resistance reverberating off the high temple walls.

"If you're man enough, commander, why don't you come down here and arrest me yourself?" Pollard held his chin high. Not dropping the commander's stare, he said under his breath to Carnoch, "Protect Lozen."

The commander's face turned a darker hue of purple but held his tongue.

"I didn't think you had it in you." Pollard searched the crowd, taking note of the vast number of Watch who were descending on the commons. If it came to blows, his troops would be hard put to save themselves. Undeterred, he indicated the arriving Watch. "Typical of those trained under Danth Emerald. Have someone else do your dirty work."

The commander appeared ready to spit. "This doesn't concern you." He gestured to his swelling ranks. "You're surrounded and outnumbered. We're not afraid to engage, if that's your choice. Now, do the sensible thing and have your people stand down and let us go about our duty. I'm willing to forget this minor disagreement ever happened."

Pollard scoffed and raised his voice to ensure he was heard by everyone present. "I don't wish to be responsible for spilling the blood of the citizens of Storms End. But neither can I stand by and allow a grave injustice to be perpetrated here today. The people who stand condemned before the commander of the Watch are residents of Storms End, just like you and me. Perhaps their actions were harsh, but given the history of the present Watch commanders and the baron, I can only imagine they were left with no choice. People are dying in the streets. *Our* people. Many by the hands of those sworn to protect them. In the spirit of benevolent King Malcolm, I beseech you to disperse and not get caught up in what's about to transpire."

An eerie silence settled over the commons. A cold breeze blew in off the bay, ruffling hair and playing with the hems of tunics and cloaks. The odd cough sounded from different quarters, but no one spoke—their rapt gazes bouncing from the Watch, to Pollard's troops, to the three people at the centre of the stand-off.

A strange sound drifted over the commons, catching everyone's attention. A murmur rippled through the crowd again as everyone looked around for the source of the new commotion.

The commander pointed his sword at Pollard. "What devilry is this?"

Pollard frowned. He had nothing to do with it. He followed Lozen's hand to the street that was visible above the temple rooftop. It was lined with people marching toward the commons.

Pollard

Men, women, and children descended upon the civic square bearing crude weapons—hammering them against makeshift shields.

A man in black robes hobbled at the front of the first line of people that marched into the commons. Though his face was face hidden within a cowl, Pollard knew at once who had organized the mob.

"What's the meaning of this?" The commander glared at Pollard. "On whose order have you arranged this uprising, Master Banebridge?"

Pollard's heated retort was interrupted as a collective gasp gripped the crowd—their attention on the figure in black approaching the gallows' steps. Members of the Watch made to intercept him.

Pollard pushed his way through the crowd; people shoving each other to get out of his way lest they get trampled. To his relief, the Watch disengaged when they realized who was ascending the platform to confront the commander. Whispers of, "Old man Banebridge," "Council Master," "Half-Hand," and many other names swept across the crowd.

As he rounded the front of the gallows, Pollard heard the distinct sound of his father's voice.

"On my order, commander."

"M-Master Banebridge? To what do we owe the honour?" The commander's incredulous voice sounded above the noise of the crowd.

"Save it, commander. You've done enough damage. Have your men stand down at once."

Pollard's concern sloughed away. His father suffered fools with less enthusiasm than he did.

"Now commander, or should I allow the true citizens of Storms End to have their way?" Thoril Half-Hand ordered.

Pollard

Pollard took the steps four at a time—the attending City Watch anxiously jostling each other to get out of the way. Approaching his father's back, he crossed his arms, his mighty sword tips protruding above Thoril's shoulder.

The commander had more sense than Pollard gave him credit. Purple-faced, the leader of the Watch held his stare for but a moment before storming away.

Pollard

To Catch a Tiger

After a glorious respite at Banebridge Manor that had allowed Pollard time to catch up with people he hadn't seen in a long while, he was glad to climb aboard the *Crusher* and watch as his loyal crew turned the brig west, toward Thunderhead. Though he had thoroughly enjoyed seeing his best friend, Gom, Pollard wasn't one for small talk. He had too many concerns pressing on him. If his father and Master Pul had the right of it, there was little time left to them to bolster the ranks of the Songsbirthian Guard before the predicted storm hit Zephyr. If they weren't prepared, the elders' prophecy may well spell the end of days for King Malcolm and the realm.

Happy to be reunited with Lozen, he was grateful she hadn't suffered harm at the hands of the Watch. He wasn't sure what he would have done, had they acted against her, but he knew for certain his reaction would have been catastrophic for the city guard.

In an effort to push his troubled thoughts aside, his gaze found the young woman known by many as the Storms End Lightning Bolt. His father had spoken highly of her, though he had cautioned Pollard to watch his step.

Pollard wondered what he was getting himself into. Thoril claimed that although Larina possessed the character and fortitude suited to the Songsbirthian Guard, she likely wasn't one that adhered to the norm. As strange as that sounded,

Pollard

Thoril had insisted that her high moral pedigree may cause havoc in a crew governed by a chain of command.

To offset her challenges, Thoril had been implicit when he stated that she was a person of unwavering values. She had proven time and again her lack of hesitation to literally kill in an effort to adhere to those deep-rooted tenets.

A cold breeze laden with the heavy scent of brine swept across the deck as the fjord's familiar walls told those in the know that the *Crusher* would soon be preparing to berth in Thunderhead. Standing on the bow, Lozen and Larina studied the sleek form of Lozen's falcon. Pollard smiled. If the Lightning Bolt was half as tenacious as his father foretold, the coming months were going to prove challenging.

The *Crusher* slipped up to the pier with nary a bump—Captain Crow and the surly helmsman, masters of their craft. Pollard absently noted the three warships flying Madrigail Bay's pennants tied off around the *Crusher*. He likely knew many of the men and women aboard the formidable vessels but he had no time for pleasantries. He needed to find someone to compliment Larina and then get the group back to the Splendoor Catacombs.

Though he didn't know the recruits very well, he was certain there wasn't one amongst them that would be able to work effectively with Larina. In order for her to attain the position his father and Master Pul had in mind, she would require a partner. Someone as bold and off the wall as her Storms End Lightning Bolt's reputation.

Not waiting for the lines to be secured, Pollard flew down the steep staircase fronting the quarterdeck. Hitting the main deck hard, he put two fingers to his lips and emitted a shrill whistle.

Pollard

The gangplank had barely touched down when Pollard's heavy footsteps bowed the length of weathered wood—Carnoch and several members of the Songsbirthian Guard on his heels.

Thunderhead was notorious for its brazen citizens. The ship building port was every bit as rough as Storms End but it was four times the size. If there was anyone in Zephyr who might remotely fit the bill to match Larina for grit and attitude, Thunderhead would be the place to find them.

He hadn't ventured more than several strides beyond the heavily guarded gate at the end of the naval dock than he became aware of a commotion in the marketplace ahead. Looking over the heads of a gathering crowd, he spotted a woman being attacked by at least four nasty looking thugs.

Pollard's trained eye surveyed the situation, ascertaining the potential outcome by virtue of the combatants' interaction. Arms folded; he nodded. The incident should prove most interesting. Aware of Lozen and Larina coming up behind him, he settled in to enjoy the spectacle.

Larina forced her way past him to get a better view. At once, she spun and beseeched him, "We've got to help her. They'll rip her apart."

Pollard snorted, his attention rivetted on the auburn-haired woman thrashing in the grip of two burly sailors. "Nay, lass. This is not our fight. I have a feeling those poor men are about to find out what happens to people who try to catch a tiger."

He had no sooner spoken, than the captive woman kicked out at a man threatening her with a broken piece of wood. Before anyone in the crowd appreciated how fast it had happened, the woman bit one of her captors and spun to face the other.

Pollard winced at the pain the second man surely experienced as the woman's boot caught him between the legs. Not once, but twice!

The man doubled over in agony, only to receive a third kick in the face; laying him out flat on his back.

The bitten man ran at her. He tried to avert his charge—his eyes growing wide at the curved knife in the woman's hand.

Without hesitation, she jabbed it into his stomach, driving her thrust up and under his ribs.

Bloody knife in hand, the woman spun to face the man brandishing the length of wood.

The man observed the scene, disbelief written on his face, and wisely let the wood fall to the ground.

"Hah, hah, hah!" Pollard's throaty laugh attracted the attention of those around him. Had he not witnessed the sight with his own eyes, he would never have believed his good fortune. Pointing to the berserk woman in the middle of the circle of spectators, he declared, "She's the one!"

He slapped a meaty hand on Larina's shoulder, a huge grin lighting up his face. "You two are going to make a mighty fine fighting pair."

The incredulous look Larina shot him, made him laugh that much harder.

He nodded toward the auburn-haired woman as she threatened the mesmerized crowd with her bloody knife, daring anyone to take her on, and forced his way through the people in front of him. Approaching the young woman, he held his hands out in a placating gesture. "Easy, lass."

To his surprise, Larina grabbed onto his elbow and tried to pull him back. "Easy yourself, big fella." She stepped between him and the woman. "You're big enough to scare a troll from a corpse. Look at you. Eighteen feet and bursting with muscle."

Pollard

Not missing a beat, Larina smiled for the young woman's benefit. "Not the brightest, these giant types."

Pollard was sure the woman was about to stick Larina with what appeared to be a filleting knife.

"Don't come any closer. If you're part of Ivar the Blade's crew, I'll gut you," the woman snarled.

Faced with the potential threat, Larina didn't back down. Instead, she drew her own dagger. "I don't take kindly to people threatening me. I don't know who this Igor is but—"

"Ivar."

"Whoever. We don't know him. We've just got in from Storms End and…" Larina paused and shrugged as if at a loss for words. She stepped aside. "I'll let Pollard tell you."

The woman's wild eyes met Pollard's.

Larina winked. "Don't worry. The big oaf is a pussy cat." She waggled her dagger. "But remember. *I'm* watching you."

Larina's response made Pollard hesitate. Considering the blood-smeared blade pointed at them, he said, "I am Pollard Banebridge; son of Thoril Half-Hand, the Master of the Storms End Council."

It was obvious his words meant nothing. The woman's panicked gaze fell on Lozen.

Lozen's warm smile held her stare. "You don't need to fear us. We're here to find a warrior. You're a warrior, no?"

The woman frowned. "You have me mistaken with someone else."

"No." Pollard shook his head. "I'm pretty sure you're the one I've been looking for."

"You don't even know me. I'm not from around here." The woman searched the crowd as if looking for someone. "If you don't mind, I'd like to be away from here before more of these people show up." She pointed her knife at the burly man who had threatened her with the length of wood.

Pollard followed her gaze. "You needn't worry about him. *Or* anyone else he may be associated with. If you agree to listen to what I have to say, I'll make sure you never have to worry about them again."

As the woman contemplated his words, Lozen held out a hand, but the woman backed away. "Where are we going?"

"To the ship to talk." Lozen wiggled her fingers for the woman to grab onto.

The woman accepted Lozen's hand, allowing herself to be led across the marketplace toward two officious looking buildings. They stopped at the entrance to a broad laneway warded by eight guards. Upon seeing Pollard, the guardsmen retracted their polearms, permitting them access to the naval docks.

Back aboard the *Crusher*, Pollard gave the order to make ready to cast off, but insisted they weren't to set sail until he said so. Once the crew were busy preparing for the journey south to Madrigail Bay, he found the young woman surrounded by a few of the new recruits; some of his contingent from Songsbirth standing watch to ensure that no one came aboard unannounced.

He strode up behind the woman and cleared his voice. "So, young lady. Before we go any further, what do we call you?"

The woman jumped. In a soft voice, she stammered, "You...you can call me Sadyra."

"Just Sadyra?"

"Um...yes. *Just* Sadyra."

"See?" Pollard playfully punched Larina in the shoulder. "You two are more alike than you know."

Larina staggered sideways, scowling.

Pollard

"Ha! Take more than a closed fist to hurt the Lightning Bolt." Pollard laughed and turned his attention back to Sadyra. "Care to tell us what happened in the marketplace?"

"No. Not really."

"Do your parents know where you are?"

Sadyra snorted. "Who cares?"

Lozen stepped close. "Is Sadyra in trouble?"

"Ya, you could say that."

"You want Lozen to find Sadyra's parents?"

Sadyra frowned "If you mean, do I want you to get my parents for me, the answer is no."

Lozen bowed her head to Sadyra and looked up at Pollard. "She needs you."

Sadyra's frown deepened. "Look. I don't know who you people are. I appreciate that you mean well, but I really must be going." She looked to the gangplank.

Pollard could sense that something much deeper troubled Sadyra. "You're running from something. Something isn't right between you and your parents."

"That's an understatement. But yes, you could say that."

"Can I be of assistance to smooth things over?" Pollard asked.

Sadyra stared at the deck planks between them and muttered, "Not unless you know how to exorcise a dragon witch."

Pollard couldn't make out her words. "What's that?"

"Nothing." Sadyra lifted sad eyes to meet his. "I should leave. I don't want to cause trouble."

Lozen grabbed Sadyra's hands. "Sadyra is no trouble. Lozen will watch over you."

"If I remain here, trouble will find me," Sadyra said. "If not from the friends of the man I stabbed, then I suspect from the city Watch."

"Pfft." Larina scoffed. "I'll deal with the Watch."

Pollard could tell that Sadyra was doubtful they could protect her from whoever assailed her. He pulled his sword over his shoulders—two separate sword blades fused into one guard.

Sadyra gaped.

"No one will bother you in my presence, aboard *my* ship. As third in command of the Songsbirthian Guard, and son of Thoril Half-Hand, you can rest assured, you are safe aboard the *Crusher*."

Sadyra stared long and hard at those around her. Finally, she sighed. "Where did you say you were going?"

"Songsbirth," Pollard said.

"And that's a long way from here?"

Pollard shrugged. "A good tenday if conditions are favourable."

"Ten days?" Sadyra thought out loud. "Are there other places along the way?"

"Aye. There's Madrigail Bay. The Forke. Millsford."

"And what would it cost me to travel with you to one of those places?"

"Cost?" Pollard frowned. "Why, nothing. You will be my guest."

"But what if I don't wish to go all the way to Songsbirth?"

Pollard could tell he was losing her. He knew in his heart she was the match Larina needed.

Lozen squeezed Sadyra's hands. "It's okay. You go where you go. We'll not stop you." She looked over her shoulder at Pollard. "Right, Master?"

Pollard felt the urge to protest, but trusted Lozen's discretion. "Well, um, I guess. But—"

Lozen interrupted. "There. You see? Pollard is a man of honour."

Pollard

Spirit Companion

Lozen approached Pollard on the quarterdeck as the sun crested the mountain peaks dominating the eastern horizon; her falcon resting on the leather vambrace she wore on her forearm whenever she trained the bird of prey.

She nodded toward the bow. "What did you say?"

Pollard followed her gaze to where Sadyra and Larina sat huddled together in the crook of the port and starboard railings. "Nothing, really. Apparently, they've been there all night."

"They okay?"

"Beats me. I'm afraid to intervene." He reached out a hand to gently stroke the falcon. "How's Naiche? Did I pronounce that right?"

"You'd make a big heap warrior." Lozen laughed and said the falcon's name properly, "*Naiche* is good. The boat rats are not good."

Pollard laughed. "That *is* good. We've dealt with enough vermin lately."

"Naiche is a hunter. Lozen trained her well."

"Lozen is an excellent trainer, for sure. The best I have." He indicated the two women on the bow. "That's why I'm trusting you to personally train those two."

Lozen nodded. "They'll make fine warriors. Lozen will train them in the ways of the Elk tribe."

"I'm counting on it."

"Madrigail Bay!" A sailor announced from his perch within the crow's nest high atop the main mast.

𝕻𝔬𝔩𝔩𝔞𝔯𝔡

Pollard ducked to look beneath the yardarms at the distant peaks. Not yet visible from the quarterdeck, he knew the sailor in the crow's nest had identified the volcanic peak south of a long inlet that led into Madrigail Bay.

Though it would take the better part of the afternoon to reach the port city, it was time to prepare for his contingent's imminent departure. If the captain of the river going vessel, *S'gull*, was true to his word, the launch would be waiting to ferry them up the mighty Madrigail River.

Sadyra listened to the bustle and commotion that had taken over the *Crusher*, but she only had eyes for the city of Madrigail Bay as it revealed itself beyond a gentle bend at the end of a seemingly interminable inlet cutting between mountains on either side. She expected another Thunderhead, but the sight that unfolded before her eyes left her breathless.

The north shore was littered with countless, odd shaped buildings varying in size—some built of mud and brick, others of wood. The more spectacular edifices rose predominantly upon the hills rising up from the south shore, beyond an endless line of grey warehouses lining the wharfs. Large structures sculpted of granite and polished marble built into the side of the mountain, shone in the late afternoon sunshine.

Sadyra became aware of Pollard taking up a spot behind her. She spared him the slightest of glances and continued her study of the grand city; considering the possibilities of disappearing amongst those buildings and never being heard from again.

"Quite a place, Madrigail Bay. In all of Zephyr, only Carillon is grander in scale and appearance."

"Will your travels take you close to there?"

Pollard

"The capital? I'm afraid not. The Madrigail River meanders many days south of Castle Svelte—right to the base of Splendoor Falls and that's our destination."

Sadyra nodded to herself. If she didn't feel safe in Madrigail Bay, she could always go to the capital. "Is Carillon by the ocean?"

"Hardly. It lies hundreds of leagues inland, surrounded on three sides by desolate plains. It's built on the shores of a large, inland lake, but it can't be reached by boat from here. Why do you ask?"

She shrugged. "No reason."

Returning her gaze to the myriad of docks and ships of all sizes, she reconsidered her plans. A landlocked city would prove a much better place to lose herself. Her father would never find her there.

"Have you made up your mind about my invitation to join the Songsbirthian Guard?"

She pondered her options; her gaze falling on the docks they approached on the north shore. "Our journey inland...Will it take us closer to Carillon?"

"Oh, aye. Considerably. We'll pass through Millsford. From there, the capital is four or five days by foot."

"And how far is it from here?"

Pollard raised his eyebrows. "Not sure. Never done it before. I'd estimate it's twice the distance, but there's the mountains to consider, so I'd hazard a tenday or longer."

Sadyra nodded but said nothing more. She didn't owe these people anything other than the voyage south, and that, Pollard had freely offered.

The captain piloted the craft north of an enormous, iron-latticed portcullis suspended between tall towers on either side of the mouth of a wide river. A high bridge spanned the space between the towers—its roadbed busy with people and horse drawn wagons.

The helmsman gave a hulking, four-masted ship anchored in the middle of the bay a wide berth and brought the

Crusher alongside a large pier projecting beyond a tangle of busy docks.

Sadyra absently noted the name engraved behind the impressive bowsprit of the large ship anchored in the bay. *Gerrymander.*

"Quite a ship, that one. Too big to moor." Pollard slapped his hands together. "Well? Shall I inform the *S'gull's* captain of your presence?"

Sadyra nodded. "Sure. Why not?"

"I see you've decided to join us," Larina said to Sadyra as she followed her across the thin gangplank leading to the deck of the riverboat Pollard had commandeered to take the company upriver. The wooden plank bowed precariously beneath their feet but Larina wasn't concerned. Pollard had crossed it moments before.

"Got nothing better to do."

Larina critically eyed Sadyra's auburn hair as it bounced above her hips. Sadyra's hair was longer than her own. For some reason, that bothered her. She shook her head. She had formed a strange bond with the village girl last night, but watching Sadyra's spritely movements, she couldn't decide whether to despise her or get to know her better.

"I know how you feel. Anyplace is a better place to be." Larina ignored the proffered hand of one of the *S'gull's* crew, and jumped to the deck on her own. She followed Sadyra to the far rail to allow room for those coming aboard behind them—young men and women appearing as wonderstruck as she felt. "I'm looking forward to seeing Splendoor Falls. Lozen claims there isn't another place like it in the world."

"Seen the *whole* world, has she?"

Pollard

Larina could tell Sadyra's smile was forced. "What? Aren't you excited?"

"Couldn't care less, really. I don't plan on going that far."

Larina nodded and settled against the railing. If the girl didn't want to join the Guard, it didn't make much difference to her. Though, according to Pollard, that would mean she'd have to get used to someone else.

Fully loaded with passengers and provisions, the *S'gull* rowed away from the pier. Larina and many of the newcomers craned their necks as the sloop's tall masts slid beneath the raised roadway of the Rivergate Bridge.

The oarsmen fought to make progress through the swirling current, propelling the *S'gull* into the wide mouth of the Madrigail River.

Larina wondered how long it would take them to reach their destination at that rate, but rounding the first bend, they entered a long canyon and the captain ordered the sails unfurled. In no time, the oars were shipped and the sloop slid easily upriver on a westerly breeze.

Pollard joined them. "That's better. Now we can relax. The cross currents and whirling winds around the river mouth make for a harrowing few moments."

Larina and Sadyra waited for him to elaborate, but he merely smiled and nodded.

"I'm happy to see you're becoming fast friends." With that said, he walked away to speak to another group of recruits.

'I wouldn't go that far,' Larina thought, watching him go. Her eyes lingered on his wide shoulders—the corded muscles shooting sleekly up his thick neck. He was an impressive looking man.

She sighed and joined Sadyra on the railing—looking way up to see the top of the canyon walls on either side of the boat. "You think he has someone in his life?"

Sadyra frowned, catching her gaze.

Larina's cheeks flushed.

Pollard

"He's a long way from home," Sadyra muttered, raising her eyebrows.

Sadyra's response shocked Larina as she caught Sadyra's mischievous look.

Sadyra laughed and stared upriver. "I'm just kidding."

Larina blinked and followed the young woman's gaze. A slow smile curled her lips. Studying Sadyra's profile and her long hair blowing in the canyon wind, an odd sensation filled her heart with warmth. A feeling she thought was lost to her forever after Allard's passing.

"The Forke. A fun town. Populated by nice people," Pollard said casually as the *S'gull* drifted between the busy banks of a city full of women tending chores and children splashing about.

Not nearly as impressive as Madrigail Bay or Thunderhead, the wooden buildings of The Forke were still much grander than anything Fishmonger Bay had to offer.

As the sloop slowed to navigate the confluence of the Frothe River and the Madrigail, Sadyra entertained the idea of jumping ship to begin the next step in her life—free from everything that reminded her of her past.

A series of cow bells clattered onshore. Upriver a stone and wooden bridge blocked their path. Without thinking, Sadyra dug her fingers into Pollard's forearm—her eyes flicking between the bridge and the *S'gull's* masts.

Pollard gently extricated his arm from her grip and laughed.

Before she could question him, the strangest thing happened. The middle of the bridge split apart. Equal halves of the span rose into the air long before the *S'gull* slid between the stone bridgework.

Sadyra nodded, impressed.

"The joys of modern engineering." Pollard beamed. "Much like the drawbridges at Castle Svelte."

Mesmerized, Sadyra turned toward the stern to watch the bridge lower again; its two halves joining in the centre with no apparent break.

"If you think that's impressive, wait until you see the marvels of the Splendoor Catacombs."

Free of the constriction of the drawbridge, the *S'gull* crew raised her mainsail, and the sloop picked up speed.

"How far until the next city?" Sadyra asked.

Pollard shrugged. "Depends on the wind. If it holds, we'll be there in a couple days. If not, I would hazard three or four."

Her chance to get off safely had passed. She almost asked Pollard if he would have the captain stop the boat near the bank, but let it go. "Will that be closer to the king's city?"

"Carillon? Oh, aye. By a good day's walk."

"Still thinking of ditching us, huh?" Larina asked.

Sadyra didn't know how to respond, especially in front of Pollard.

Pollard tilted his head. "You're not staying with us?"

"No…" She sighed, her bleary mind leaving her feeling lost. "I don't know. I'm not much of a people person."

"Oh." Pollard seemed surprised. "That's a shame."

Sadyra couldn't hold his gaze. The man had been nothing but kind to her. He had helped her escape a situation that had the potential of becoming much worse if the Blade's crew had tracked her down in the Thunderhead marketplace.

"Well…At least think about it. If you change your mind, we'd be happy to have you." Pollard's gaze lingered on Larina before he walked away.

Sadyra followed his slumped-shouldered progress across the deck. Her response to his question echoed in her head. It had been a knee-jerk answer in the hopes of changing the subject. Thinking on it, nothing could be further from the truth. Sadyra loved company. If not for her father's meddling, she would have been happy spending her days in Fishmonger Bay amongst her mates.

"I hear Carillon is an amazing city. You'll like it there." Larina's voice snapped her attention to the woman in black.

"If it's anything like Madrigail Bay, I'm sure it is." She held Larina's stare and assumed her usual place on the railing. Part of her wanted the woman to leave her alone, and yet, something deep inside secretly hoped that Larina would remain by her side, if only to keep her company. It was all she could do not to smile as Larina settled in beside her.

Neither woman said anything, but to Sadyra, Larina's company was more than enough to lift the malaise that had taken hold of her heart. The betrayal of Captain Gitch and Scruff had rocked her world. A deep bitterness toward people had festered in her as she had rowed her floundering skiff into Thunderhead the other morning.

She struggled to identify the reason preventing her from accepting Pollard's offer to join the Songsbirthian garrison, but the thought of trusting someone again so soon left her numb. Relying on strangers to watch her back was too much to comprehend.

She snuck a glance at Larina's pretty face, admiring the freckles around her eyes. As cute as Larina was, there was something startling in her stare. Something missing. Larina had been reluctant to make Sadyra's company at first. Getting to know her a little, she found Larina's straight forward attitude refreshing. If she wasn't mistaken, the hard-nosed woman from Storms End had taken a shine to her.

Reports overheard from the *S'gull* crew that they would be in Millsford before high noon filled Sadyra with apprehension. It was time to decide. Her broken heart wanted nothing else but to be rid of anyone that remotely reminded her of her past. Though she had only met Pollard and Larina in Thunderhead, she associated her escape from her previous life with their presence. Fairly or not, it did little to exonerate their role in her freedom and thus her dark memories.

She shook her head. As silly as that seemed, even in her own mind, she was helpless to rid herself of the awful feeling. Every time she looked at either one of them, she instantly thought of her fight in the marketplace and the people involved.

Her dour gaze settled on Lozen. The strange woman had kept her distance over the last couple of days. It shouldn't have mattered to Sadyra—the warrior woman was little more than a stranger, but something about Lozen piqued her interest; she wanted to know more about Lozen's ancestry.

Lozen had spent most of the trip up the Madrigail sitting beyond the bow railing, training her falcon. The impressive bird would fly so high in the sky that if Sadyra took her eyes off it, she couldn't find it again. And then, out of nowhere, it would shoot out of the sky like a crossbow bolt and slam into an unsuspecting bird; an explosion of feathers marking their impact. More often than not, the falcon's victim would recover and fly away to live another day, but every so often, the falcon's prey plummeted to the ground beyond the riverbank, never to rise again.

Swallowing her apprehension, Sadyra strolled to the bow railing to admire the sleek bird sitting calmly on Lozen's upraised forearm—its keen eyes not missing a thing.

Lozen followed her bird's focus. "Ah. Sadyra. You're still here?"

Sadyra stopped herself from responding with a sarcastic remark. Keeping her lips firmly together, she nodded.

"That's good, no?"

Sadyra didn't know what to say. "I guess."

"You've decided to train with Lozen and Naiche?"

Sadyra didn't know who Naiche was but didn't care enough to ask. She shrugged. "Hadn't planned on it."

Lozen tilted her head; intelligent eyes boring into Sadyra. "That's a shame. Pollard and I think you would make a fine warrior. Make Lozen proud."

Sadyra tried to pretend she couldn't care less what Lozen thought, but standing before the warrior and her bird of prey, it seemed as if her soul had been stripped bare. She regretted her decision to walk over to see the falcon.

Lozen spoke a few words to the bird in a language unfamiliar to Sadyra.

The falcon blinked, bent its legs, and took to the sky.

Sadyra marvelled at how fast it flew. "Aren't you afraid it won't come back?"

"No," Lozen answered, the denial long and drawn out. "Naiche sees everything. He won't get lost."

"Ah. Naiche." Sadyra struggled to pronounce its name. "That's the name of your bird."

Lozen's round cheeks lifted in delight. "See? You learn Indian. Naiche." She nodded to the quickly disappearing falcon. "It means, mischief maker."

Sadyra offered her a nervous chuckle. "Aye. Sadyra is a master of your language."

Lozen frowned.

"I'm kidding. I have no idea what you're saying."

"Sadyra is a strange woman, no? Different from the others."

This time Sadyra's laugh was genuine. "Ya. You may be right about that."

Lozen nodded. "Sadyra is frightened."

The warrior's words startled her. "What do you mean?"

"Sadyra is running."

Sadyra frowned and shook her head. "Not anymore."

"Are you coming to Songsbirth?"

"No…Well…I don't know. I doubt it."

"Then, you're running. Lozen sees this."

"Whatever. You can think what you want. I'm just looking for a new place to call home."

"So, you have no idea where you're going."

Sadyra had to think about that. It wasn't a question. In order to sound like she was in control of her life, she said, "I'm going to Carillon."

"Carillon is a big place. Anywhere in particular?"

Sadyra's cheeks reddened. She had no idea. Being grilled by Lozen made her feel like a child. She hung her head and whispered, "No."

Lozen stared long and hard.

She waited for Lozen to berate her for her foolishness— about her irresponsible and immature rash decision to flee her troubles, but the lecture never came.

The warrior grabbed the railing, and with seemingly no effort, went from a sitting position to springing over the waist high barrier; landing beside Sadyra. She stared out over the river to where Naiche had disappeared. "Naiche is a free spirit. He answers to no one. And yet, he returns each day without fail."

Sadyra followed Lozen's gaze, trying to see the falcon in the distance. If Lozen could see him, it was a wonder, as she could not.

"I have often considered why. He's not dependent upon me for food. Nor does he require assistance to find shelter. It took many years of soul searching to discover the answer to that question." Lozen looked Sadyra in the eye. An underlying warmth radiated behind her gaze. "Do you know why Naiche, the mischief maker, returns to me?"

The warrior's stare intimidated Sadyra. She swallowed and shook her head.

"Because he found a kindred spirit in me." Her smile transformed into a serious look. "No. I am not a bird. And no, I cannot talk to him—well, aside from a few commands. Our relationship runs deeper than that. We are individual spirits who have formed a bond that in many ways is stronger than our family ties. We share an underlying trust that transcends the usual spoken promises and expectations people place upon one another." She broke Sadyra's gaze and leaned on the railing, staring at the horizon.

Sadyra joined her on the rail; the warrior's words lost on her. Distant rooftops and what appeared to be a high wall came into view. The fortified city of Millsford was almost upon them. If she meant to continue on to Carillon, the time to leave was drawing nigh.

"Weighty decisions must not be made lightly. I shall leave you to your thoughts." Lozen pushed away but stopped and put a hand on Sadyra's shoulder; her long hair ruffling around her muscular frame as the eagle feather, held fast by a leather headband, bent in the breeze. She looked across the busy deck of the *S'gull*. "I hope that someday soon, you too, will find your spirit companion."

Sadyra followed her stare. At first, all she saw were the crew and new recruits preparing to disembark for the afternoon as the ship readied itself to take on new provisions for the last leg of the trip.

Goosebumps riddled Sadyra's skin. The crowd parted, seemingly on command, clearly exposing Larina who stood against the starboard rail amidships.

Though no further words were spoken, Larina lifted her head—a faint smile lighting up her face as she caught Sadyra's gaze.

Lozen patted Sadyra on the shoulder and walked away.

Millsford provided a pleasant distraction to break up the monotony of being crammed onto the *S'gull's* deck with little to do but watch the terrain slip past the boat—nondescript for the most part since leaving The Forke. The Zephyr midlands consisted of flat, farmlands stretching away to the horizon in all directions. The dark smear of the lofty heights of The Spine were occasionally seen beyond the trees along the riverbank—the mountain range days away by foot.

South of Millsford, a few stray peaks dominated the skyline. Pollard claimed they were a spur of The Spine that reached out to encompass Lake Refrain—a place Larina had never heard of before.

Breaking free of everyone's company, Larina preferred to be alone to wander the streets of Millsford. Pollard had invited her to join him for a midday meal at the baron's manor, but she refused. An unusual melancholy had taken hold of her as they sailed up to the docks outside the city walls. She wanted to be left alone with the sadness she couldn't name.

Side streets and narrow alleyways reminded her of Storms End, although most of Millsford was built on the delta flatland between the confluence of the Madrigail River and the Canorous River—another large waterway that fed the Madrigail from the north.

Thoughts of Allard and Rock left her mind numb for the better part of the afternoon. Putting their memories aside, she reflected on her old friend Cassie, and that led her thoughts to Bear. Her best friend. Her only friend since Cassie's death. The idea of Bear joining the Storms End council lifted her dark mood as she made her way back to the Millsford piers.

Not looking forward to returning to the cramped quarters of the *S'gull*, she found comfort in Pollard's assertion that with favourable winds, they would reach the end of their journey by sundown tomorrow.

Passing beyond the manned gatehouse breaching the south wall, Larina scuffed her boots along the dirt roadway, approaching the docks and kicking up dust. The *S'gull* was by far the biggest launch berthed there.

Pollard

She stopped to take a last look at the walled city. Exhaling a heavy sigh, she had the strangest sensation she had left a part of herself within its walls. Sadyra would be well on her way to Carillon.

She forced herself to look away. It was time to resign herself to the uncertain future awaiting her. Pollard and Lozen appeared nice and all, but they were busy with their own responsibilities. She doubted they had time for her, other than to train.

She looked up to gather her bearings and her heart skipped a beat. Standing beside the gangplank, Sadyra watched her with a beaming smile that dimpled her freckled cheeks. "I thought you'd left me to fend for myself with the Songsbirthian Guard."

Larina gaped. "Why you cheeky little imp."

Her pace picked up. As hard as she tried to keep the huge smile from her face, she failed miserably. The reason for her deep despair had disappeared, and her heart swelled. Sadyra had changed her mind about leaving them.

Reaching the auburn-haired girl, she wrapped Sadyra in a tight embrace—unwilling to release her in case Sadyra saw the tears streaming down her cheeks.

She had found her spirit companion.

Pollard

Labyrinth

Breathtaking. Visible above the treetops, dominating the horizon, Splendoor Falls cascaded thousands of feet from a break in a ring of mountains known as the Muse; its base lost to view in a shroud of mist that permeated the lush forest covering the rocky foothills they sailed amongst. Snow-capped peaks stretched north and south of the colossal waterfall as the line of mountains disappeared to the east.

The *S'gull* crew plied her oars to augment the sails in a continual fight against an ever increasing current.

Sadyra's awestruck expression matched Larina's; the two of them stood captivated between Pollard and Lozen at the bow.

Lozen held her leather-wrapped arm to the side, bearing Naiche's weight—the falcon calmly sitting beneath a leather hood.

"There it is, ladies." Pollard beamed; his chest swollen with pride as if he were the fall's creator. "Splendoor Falls. You'll never see anything more beautiful if you were to live as long as the elves of South March."

Sadyra frowned at the reference. Sheltered in Fishmonger Bay her whole life, she had been denied the wonders of the wider world. To her, elves and dwarfs were races of old—claimed by the myths of centuries past. The revelation that Scruff was part giant had unsettled her, but here she was, with Pollard Banebridge, a self-professed half-giant. Even though he stood beside her, she found it hard to appreciate.

"Where are the catacombs you spoke of?" Larina raised her voice to be heard over the growing roar of the distant falls.

"You're looking at them."

Sadyra and Larina stared at Pollard.

Lozen laughed. "The catacombs lie within the mountains behind Splendoor Falls."

A lone dock protruded into the fast-running river. Judging by the sloop's progress, Sadyra wasn't sure the *S'gull* would make it that far.

"And here's our stop. I'd best get everyone ready." Pollard stepped back and left them.

Sadyra searched the shoreline. Other than a small hut close to the dock, there was nothing to see beside endless forest and white water crashing down a tumble of rock beyond the dock. "I don't understand. I thought we were going to Songsbirth?"

"We are." Lozen pulled Naiche's hood free and spoke a few words in her alien tongue. Naiche leapt from her arm and rose into the air, his form quickly enshrouded by the encroaching mist as he flew up the height of the falls. "Naiche is going there now to alert Master Pul of our arrival."

Sadyra frowned deeper and pointed. "Up there?"

"Aye. We've a long climb ahead of us." Lozen followed Pollard into the throng of people milling about the deck.

Sadyra glanced at Larina.

Larina shrugged. "Don't look at me. I don't know any more than you."

Together, they stared at the magnificent splendor of the cascade resplendent in the setting sun. The mist rising above the treetops captured the sun's orangey-yellow rays—all beneath the most glorious rainbow either woman had ever seen.

Most of the people aboard the *S'gull* slept onboard overnight. As dawn broke over the basin region at the base of Splendoor Falls, Pollard and Lozen organized everyone heading to Songsbirth; outfitting them with large rucksacks stuffed with supplies, and marched them up a rough trail for the better part of the morning. The trail climbed over foothills littered with rock ledges they had to clamber onto to reach the base of a cliff several hundred yards south of Splendoor Falls. Even this far away, the roar of the falls was daunting.

Sweat streaming off his face, Pollard shrugged an overstuffed rucksack from his back and dropped it to the ground at his feet. He spread his arms and faced the inquisitive stares of the recruits. "Here we are."

Larina shrugged free of her rucksack and stretched her back, looking around for some kind of sign that indicated where the trail went from this point. Everyone gathered around and did likewise.

Pollard sat on a moss-covered log and pulled a piece of bread from the top of his sack. Washing it down with a swig from his waterskin, he scanned the trainees. "Best you get some food in you. The easy part of the trip is over."

Larina raised her eyebrows at Sadyra as they pulled pieces of bread from the top of their sacks and chewed on the tough fare. "Easy part? I thought the big oaf was trying to kill us this morning. What's he expect us to do? Climb the cliff?"

Sadyra had to cover her mouth to keep from spitting a mouthful of food onto the ground. She nodded and choked down what was in her mouth.

Pollard regarded them as if he had heard Larina.

Larina wasn't sure he hadn't. She sat on the damp earth beside Sadyra and ate the rest of her meal in silence—her eyes scanning the woods. A side path headed toward the base of the falls. Studying the main trail, it was as if it ended at the foot of the unscalable cliff towering hundreds, if not thousands of feet, above the lofty treetops.

"Okay. Break's over."

Sadyra still held half of her bread in her hand. She cast a puzzled gaze at the giant. They had only just sat down. She glanced at Larina. "That's it?"

Larina shrugged, cramming bread into her mouth and trying to chew it. The rest of the recruits didn't appear to be faring much better.

"If we wish to reach Songsbirth before the trolls, we daren't tarry." Pollard shouldered his sack and approached the wall of rock. Curiously, he ran his palms along the cliff's surface until it appeared like he had found something. Most people were busy closing their sacks and trying to shoulder them and didn't notice what he was doing.

The ground rumbled underfoot. A tooth-rattling scrape of grating rock made everyone stop to watch as a round-topped doorway appeared in the base of the cliff—a stone slab receding into the wall of granite.

Pollard gestured with an outstretched arm for everyone to follow Lozen into the mountain. "Welcome to the Splendoor Catacombs."

The darkness beyond the doorway flashed a couple of times and burst into light as Lozen lit a torch. Using it, she lit several others; handing them out sporadically as the recruits filed in one at a time.

Larina and Sadyra waited until everyone else had entered before following. Pollard nodded to each person in turn, as if counting them.

Larina stopped on the threshold, scanning the rock face for something she couldn't see. "Some security that is. Any fool could find that switch."

Pollard

Pollard smiled. "They may try." He nodded at a cluster of trees growing along the base of the cliff several steps away. "But they'd be taken down long before they did."

Searching the trees, Larina couldn't be sure but she thought she could just make out the grey forms of people against the cliff wall, sitting amongst the tree limbs. She shrugged. "Wouldn't be hard to get rid of your guards once they give away their position."

Pollard's arrogant smile threw her. "Perhaps." He searched the face of the cliff. "And then again, perhaps not."

Larina searched the indistinct wall of rock, not seeing anything unnatural.

Pollard nodded. "Aye. If you two are successful, this will be one of your duties." He motioned for them to enter the catacombs. "Come."

Larina let Sadyra go ahead. She smiled at Pollard and entered the tunnel that had obviously been carved into the mountain; wide enough for two people to walk abreast. A few steps inside, a metal basket held a few unlit torches.

Pollard touched an unremarkable spot on the wall and moved aside. The ground rumbled beneath their feet. The slab of rock grated along a hidden track and sealed itself in place.

Larina examined the end wall, unable to discern where the door ended and the tunnel began.

Sadyra joined her, running long fingers over the rock. She made a fist and knocked; pulling her hand away to cup her knuckles.

Larina kicked the dead-end and then the wall to either side. Every thump of her boot sounded the same. Nothing she or Sadyra did gave evidence to the fact there was a door hidden in plain sight.

"You see?" Pollard beamed. "I told you back in The Forke that the drawbridge you saw was nothing compared to the Splendoor Catacombs."

Pollard

He grabbed a burning torch Lozen had left hanging from a ring hammered into the wall and started after the receding light of the others. "You ain't seen nothin' yet."

Larina exchanged looks with Sadyra.

Sadyra shrugged. "Come on, before the big oaf leaves us in the dark."

Sound in the close confines of the tunnel was muted. The passage of so many boots on stony ground should have raised a clatter, but Larina found it hard to hear Sadyra a few steps in front of her.

The passageway continued straight into the mountain for a long time, its surfaces changing little as they went.

Pollard walked hunched over—his well-kempt, red hair brushing the smooth ceiling.

Before long, the light ahead increased. Sadyra and Pollard stepped to the side to allow Larina access to a small cavern. Visible in the light of many torches, stalactites hung from the cavern's roof high overhead. From where Larina stood, there didn't appear to be an exit.

Everyone's eyes fell on Pollard. He placed his torch in an iron wall loop and strode into the middle of the group to stand beside Lozen—his light blue eyes taking in the cavern walls. "Seems like we've come to a dead end."

"Looks like it." Lozen nodded. She searched the curious eyes of everyone as they scanned their surroundings. "If we were an enemy raiding party," her gaze fell on Larina, "and we managed to find the mechanism to operate the entrance door, how do you think we would proceed from here?"

A smaller man put up a tentative hand. "Go back the way we came and search for a hidden doorway like the one we entered through?"

$\mathfrak{Pollard}$

Lozen held the young man's gaze. "How do you know such a doorway doesn't exist within this cavern?"

"I don't. I guess we would check here as well."

Pollard's voice filled the cavern. "And how do you know we haven't stumbled into a trap?"

The young man shook his head.

"Because," Sadyra mumbled, "you wouldn't have led us in here if it was."

Pollard spun on her. "I'm sorry? Did you say something."

Larina could tell Sadyra hadn't meant for anyone to hear her—the young woman's cheeks reddening noticeably in the torch light.

"Nothing important."

Pollard's eyes held her defiant stare for a few moments. Breaking eye contact, he returned his attention to the group. "Anyone else?"

A blonde-haired woman, directly across the makeshift circle from the young man who had spoken, pointed at the ceiling. "We should try those hanging rock formations."

Pollard nodded, his chin in hand as he followed her gaze. "Not a bad idea. Those are called stalactites." He stretched his arms overhead. "How do you propose we do that? They're even out of my reach."

She shrugged. "I could stand on your shoulders."

"Aye. That might work." He turned to the short young man. "But, in the interest of time, you sir, were correct. We passed the exit a ways back. Come." He grabbed the torch from the ring and started back up the tunnel.

Larina fell in behind him and whispered over her shoulder to Sadyra, "I liked your answer best."

"I heard that!"

Pollard's muted voice startled her. She rolled her eyes for Sadyra's benefit and hurried in the wake of the giant's long strides.

A short while later, they were confronted by the opposite end of the tunnel.

Pollard

Pollard spun; the feigned look of surprise on his face made Larina shake her head. Weary from the morning hike, she wanted nothing more than to be rid of her heavy rucksack. Pollard's lesson in finding a way through the tunnel felt like an exercise for five-year olds. She glared at him. "Really?"

Pollard ignored her and waited until the line of people had crowded into the tight confines behind her and Sadyra.

"Hmm? Did anyone notice a side tunnel?"

The recruits shook their heads.

"So now what?"

Sadyra leaned her back against the wall. "*Obviously* there's a trap door in here somewhere."

Other than the first time she had met Pollard in the city centre of Storms End, Larina had never seen the man anything but happy. The glare he shot Sadyra bespoke of his patience wearing thin.

Sadyra returned his glare. "What? There's a trap door in here. Somewhere. We all know it. Once you make us feel stupid because we can't find it, you'll show us where it is."

Larina shot Sadyra an incredulous look.

Sadyra sensed Larina's attention. "What? Am I wrong?" She looked at Pollard. "Well?"

The atmosphere in the packed tunnel became uncomfortably silent.

Pollard appeared on the verge of exploding, but to his credit, he folded his arms across his chest and said nothing.

Lozen pushed her way through the crowd to stand beside Pollard. "Very well, Sadyra. If you're as good as we think you are, how about you find the door for us?"

Sadyra frowned, looking to Larina for help.

Larina shrugged. "Don't look at me. You're the cocky one."

Pollard and Lozen shrugged out of their rucksacks and sat down with their backs against the wall where the hidden door to the outside world should be. Without another word, they opened their packs and rummaged for something to eat.

Sadyra and Larina rolled their eyes at the same time and shrugged free of their packs.

"What're you doing?" Pollard asked. "We're waiting for you to show us the way."

Lozen and the dozen Songsbirthian Guards that had travelled with Pollard trained expectant eyes on Sadyra.

Sadyra sighed. Throwing her pack over her shoulders, she adjusted it and shook her head; pushing through the crowded tunnel to start back toward the cavern. The darkness beyond the last trainee's torch swallowed her receding form.

Larina and the others watched her go. Dropping her bag to the ground, Larina went to undo its thong.

"I'm sorry. I don't recall saying it was time to eat," Pollard growled. "That goes for all of you."

Larina swallowed a snide remark. She glanced at the recruits around her and rolled her eyes—hefting her sack into place.

"From this point forward, you will act as a unit." Lozen's voice drew the recruits' attention. "What happens to one, happens to all. In the Splendoor Catacombs, we fight together or we die together. The choice is yours."

Larina sighed. Snatching up an unlit torch from the basket, she ignited it with the flame of the closest recruit bearing one, and pushed past confused faces. "Come on. We'd better help little miss cheeky before we find ourselves in further difficulty."

The trainees muttered amongst themselves, but she could tell by their muted footfalls that they followed her into the tunnel.

"Now what?" the blonde-haired girl who had suggested trying to reach the stalactites in the cavern asked—her weary features mirroring how Larina felt.

Larina waited for the angular-faced, young woman to stand beside her. "Klara, right?"

The woman nodded; straight, shoulder blade-length hair bouncing around thin shoulders. "Yes. From Ember Breath."

"Right." Larina faked a smile. She raised her voice to include everyone around her. "I guess we should split up and start searching the walls. I'm not sure if anyone noticed how Master Banebridge tripped the entryway?"

No one answered.

Larina patted the wall in front of her with her palms. "He ran his hands along the cliff face until the door revealed itself."

"Magic?" The short man who had originally suggested that they needed to search the tunnels for a secret door, wondered.

"Magic? I hope not, Mikter, or we're all screwed." Larina hoped that was the name she heard someone call the man.

She started up the tunnel; her movement causing those before her to start walking again. "There must be a trip lever hidden amongst the rock. Likely camouflaged within an imperfection in the wall's surface. You two start looking here." Larina indicated Klara and Mikter. "The rest of you, spread out and work in pairs."

A few people milled about, not sure what to do.

"Nyler. Onynx." Larina walked back and grabbed the former by his thick elbow and pulled him toward a tall, gangly, redheaded, young woman—her skin as pale as snow.

Nyler's dark skin contrasted sharply with Onynx's—the two appearing as polar opposites. They regarded each other shyly.

Larina recalled hearing their names spoken during a hushed conversation Pollard and Lozen had while travelling up the Madrigail. She hadn't meant to overhear them, but she couldn't help it. Though most of what they spoke of made little sense, the way they mentioned Nyler and Onynx bespoke of something mysterious. She'd have to keep an eye on those two.

Larina released Nyler's arm; indicating with her eyes that they should start right where they stood. "The door isn't going to reveal itself."

Pollard

She left them staring after her and pushed through the rest of the group until she caught up to Sadyra halfway to the cavern, standing by herself in the total darkness. As her torchlight lit up Sadyra's freckled face, she gave the auburn-haired woman a '*really*' look.

Sadyra snorted. "Guess I'm not everyone's favourite, huh?"

Larina raised her eyebrows and shook her head. "Come on. Drop your bag and let's show mister giant pants how you and I are above his silly lessons."

"Mister giant pants!" Sadyra spit out a laugh and dropped her rucksack to the ground.

Larina dropped her pack beside Sadyra's. Chin in hand, she muttered, surveying the walls. "Now, if I were a door latch, where would I hide?"

They searched the walls for what seemed like forever—running their hands along its rough surface, picking and prodding at anything that remotely protruded from the wall.

Larina extended her half-burnt torch up the tunnel—the opening to the cavern lay barely visible ahead. She yawned and shook her head. "This is stupid. We could be here all day."

Sadyra slumped against the wall. "The big oaf and his crew are probably laughing at us."

"Us? You're the one with the big mouth."

"Like you weren't thinking the same thing."

Larina had to admit, Sadyra wasn't far from the truth. "Ya, well, I had the sense not to speak up."

Sadyra looked dejectedly at the opposite wall, absently studying the nuances in the rock. Face twisted, she gazed at Larina with a haunted look in her eyes.

"What? You see something?"

Sadyra shook her head, holding her hand up for Larina to be quiet.

Pollard

Sound in the tunnel didn't carry far, but as Larina listened, she couldn't hear anything besides her exasperated breaths. It was as if they were the only ones in the tunnel.

"No…" Larina echoed the fear in Sadyra's expression. "They better not have left us alone in here."

Sadyra's throat moved up and down with an obvious swallow.

Larina and Sadyra screamed as a figure rushed at them, appearing out of the dark without a sound.

Lozen stopped and held up her hands to ward off the two daggers waggling between her and the shocked girls. "Whoa. It's just me."

Larina lowered her blade, willing her heart to settle down. If she wasn't mistaken, Lozen's smirk said the warrior enjoyed the fright she caused.

"Master Banebridge is wondering if you two are going to stay down here all day, or would you care to explore the catacombs by yourself?"

Larina frowned. "What?"

"Onynx found the hidden door a while ago. We've gone up to the next level. We've been waiting for you two to catch up."

Larina exchanged glances with Sadyra. "Nice."

As one, they rolled their eyes and pushed by Lozen. They grabbed their rucksacks and stomped toward the beginning of the tunnel.

Several paces before the dead-end, the flames from Larina's torch exposed a hole in the tunnel's roof.

Pollard popped his head through the opening. "Ah. There you are. We were beginning to wonder if something had happened to you."

Larina glared at him.

Pollard reached down. "Hand me your packs."

Larina gave Sadyra the torch and shrugged free of her burden; struggling to hoist the heavy sack over her head.

Pollard

Pollard grabbed the bulky pack and hoisted it through the hole as if it weighed nothing. "Give me your hand."

Larina thought her arm was being yanked out of its socket as he lifted her out of the entrance tunnel and stood to deposit her in a similar tunnel running perpendicular to the one she had just left.

Amused faces of Songsbirthian Guards and trainees alike met her gaze as she took in her surroundings.

Sadyra's sack thumped against her legs, and then Sadyra appeared—the expression on her face as Pollard pulled her effortlessly through the hole was one of wonder mixed with embarrassment as she laid eyes on the smiling faces in the crowded tunnel.

Pollard pulled Larina's torch through the hole and handed it to Sadyra so he could hoist Lozen up.

Lozen had no sooner set foot in the new tunnel than a grating sound rumbled the floor beneath Larina's boots. Though she hadn't seen who, someone in the tunnel had tripped the mechanism to close the hatch. A thick slab of rock ground into place, closing off the tunnel below, leaving no trace of its existence.

Pollard beamed at his audience, slapping his hands together. "That wasn't so bad, was it?" He motioned for the group to start moving. "One down, fourteen to go."

"Great." Sadyra moaned.

Larina shot her a dark look, cutting off anything else Sadyra might have added.

"That's if you find the proper doors. There are many more that lead to dead ends and traps. If you're not careful, you'll find yourself lost in the heart of the mountain." He smiled and nodded for Larina and Sadyra to follow their mates. "Welcome to the labyrinth."

Pollard

Well of Despair

The second tunnel's floor sloped upward and curved deeper into the mountain. Arriving at a junction, Lozen took charge of the procession and led them along the left fork, pointing out where she claimed two different trapdoors were set into the left wall—neither one of them visible. "They empty onto the edge of the cliff, providing our archers hidden nooks in which to guard the path that leads to the base of the falls.

"What's at the base of the falls?" Mikter asked.

Lozen pegged him to be the inquisitive one of the bunch. "Other than a spectacular view? Nothing."

Mikter nodded, running his hands along the second hidden door Lozen had indicated, his face showing how impressed he was at the masterfully worked stonework.

The tunnel they followed veered right and rose steeply for a few paces toward a second junction.

Lozen led them down the left passageway.

"What's down there?" Mikter asked, squinting in the torchlight in an effort to see into the darkness of the right tunnel.

"Why don't you go find out?"

Larina's sarcastic whisper reached Lozen's ears. She smiled. The Lightning Bolt was going to be as much trouble as the wildcat from Fishmonger Bay. Considering herself an excellent judge of character, Larina and Sadyra showed great promise. They had the potential to become important members of the Songsbirthian Guard if they didn't allow their off-the-wall personalities to interfere with what the Guard stood for.

Lozen started up the left tunnel filled with an inner warmth. There was also the possibility that Pollard's patience might wear thin enough to kill them first.

Traversing a long bend to the left, they were met by a welcome breeze wafting into the tunnel. Lozen led the group toward a light in the distance. As they approached the edge of the mountainside, the passage reverted into a natural channel cut through the stone; wide enough to allow several people to stand side by side.

The tunnel ended abruptly, high above the multi-coloured forest canopy. The roar of Splendoor Falls made talking without raising their voices impossible. A damp mist coated the exposed ledge and the tunnel walls and floor for several feet.

Lozen stepped back to allow the recruits a chance to look out.

Once everyone had had their fill of the wondrous view, she led them back to the second junction they had passed and stopped—the space large enough for the recruits to gather around. "There are countless places where tunnels end at the edge of the drop-off. Some are strategic points for the Catacombs Guard. While other dead ends are just scenic places to visit if you desire a moment of solitude."

"I'm sorry, Miss Lozen," Mikter interrupted. "I keep hearing Songsbirthian Guard and Catacombs Guard. What's the difference?"

"Good question Mikter. In the grand scheme of things, they are one and the same, though the members of either garrison will strongly refute that. The Catacombs Guard is a division of the Songsbirthian Guard whose primary directive is to keep the only route to Songsbirth safe. The *Songsbirthian Guard* is the group dedicated to the safety of the Songsbirth Chamber of the Wise." She smiled at various guardsmen and guardswomen standing beyond the recruits.

"There's a friendly rivalry between the two groups. It'll depend on where you're stationed as to which garrison you think is better."

Her gaze fell on Pollard—his huge frame dominating the tunnel they had just come down. "Master Banebridge would tell you the Splendoor Catacombs Guard is the most highly trained group of fighters in all of Zephyr. Being one, I won't disagree."

She smiled and nodded at a no-nonsense woman with thick shoulders blocking the original tunnel. "Quincette, a member of the Songsbirthian Guard, would take issue with that statement."

The stocky female in question nodded her huge head—no trace of levity on her hard features.

"Does that answer your question?"

"Yes. Kind of."

Lozen started down the new tunnel. "Good. Now, if you'll follow me, we've a long way to go."

The roundabout route had Sadyra's head spinning by the time Lozen called a halt to their trek. The tunnel curved back and forth, as if they walked within a giant snake. They passed two more tunnels before entering the next level through a trapdoor in the tunnel's roof.

The third level tunnel ran in a complete circle. By the time Onynx pointed it out, they had travelled the circular route twice.

Pollard commended the gangly woman. "Very astute. Most of you would have walked around in circles until you dropped." He walked several paces and inspected two places at the base of the wall on opposite sides of the tunnel.

Pollard

Touching something, the tell-tale rumbling exposed a trapdoor in the floor. Pollard stepped over the hole and faced them from its far side. "After you, warrior friend."

Lozen disappeared into the floor.

Puzzled faces regarded Pollard as the recruits dropped to their backsides and handed their bags through the hole before dropping to the tunnel below. Aside from Pollard and Quincette, Sadyra and Larina were the last ones through.

Shrugging into her pack, Sadyra watched Pollard slip into his own with Quincette's help. She muttered to Larina, "Look at the big oaf. He's loving this."

Larina gave her a dark look. "He can probably hear you."

Sadyra did a double take. Bowing her head, she handed Larina the torch and ducked behind her.

Trapdoor after trapdoor were located by the trainees as they continued through the intricate tunnel system comprising the Splendoor Catacombs—most of the concealed egresses found with the help of the accompanying guard. Hidden doorways in walls, hatches on the floor and roof—even a couple in the natural caverns they traversed were revealed to the recruits.

A long time passed before Pollard brought them to a halt on the threshold of the largest cavern they had seen yet. "Beyond this threshold lies the height of our engineering achievements. Not even magic could create a more effective fortification. Built by master dwarves centuries ago as a gift to King Hammaspaul for Zephyr's part in pushing back the Kraidic horde, the Well of Despair is a last-ditch defensive battleground with which to stop an invading army from reaching the higher levels."

Pollard stepped aside to allow the group to file into the cavern. Even with the dozen torches amongst them, the light wasn't sufficient to illuminate the cavern's opposite wall nor shine beyond the brooding stalactite tips hanging in the shadows of an unseen roof.

Pollard

Sadyra pushed her way through the lollygagging recruits to see what all the fuss was about. Other than a circular dais rising up from the sloped floor at the centre of the round cavern, nothing struck her as awe-inspiring. Her eyes lingered on a smaller cylindrical object atop the platform.

Larina bumped her forward. "Hmm. Real impressive."

Larina's sarcastic words made Sadyra laugh out loud. Horrified, she tried to stifle her outburst.

A few of the Guard looked their way.

"You're going to get us kicked out before we reach the top of the labyrinth," Larina whispered. "They'll probably leave us in one of the tunnels and we'll never be heard from again."

Sadyra covered her mouth with her wrist and snorted.

It became apparent that all sound at the mouth of the cavern had ceased. Looking over her shoulder, Sadyra swallowed. Everyone was looking at her. She faked a large smile.

Pollard glared. "Is everything okay?"

Sadyra nodded, not trusting herself to speak.

Pollard kept his stare on her. His thick chest, protected by the brass cuirass he wore so proudly, lifted with what she assumed was an exasperated sigh.

Larina's warning was close to becoming a reality.

"What you're about to witness is something you never want to fall victim to." Pollard took his gaze from her and stretched his arms out wide to usher everyone onto the downward sloping cavern floor. He put his fingers to his lips, emitting a high-pitched whistle.

The ground shook beneath their feet. A slab of rock rapidly descended behind them. Everyone jumped and turned to face the tunnel they had recently come down. It was gone—the wall behind Pollard sealed shut.

The distinct sound of water slapping the cylindrical object on top of the platform in the centre of the cavern drew everyone's attention. Awestruck recruits migrated toward a trickle of water that fell from somewhere above and disappeared into the well-like structure on top of the cavern's centrepiece.

Larina elbowed Sadyra's ribs, her lips close to Sadyra's ear. "The gods help us. I'd hate to be the victim of a shower."

The deadpan way Larina spoke made Sadyra look away to keep from laughing out loud.

"How dare they threaten to cleanse us."

Conscious of how much trouble they would likely get into if she and Larina kept making a mockery of Pollard's tour made it that much harder for Sadyra to hold back. She covered her mouth but couldn't contain a high-pitched snicker. She didn't dare look at Larina.

A finger tapped her on the shoulder. She spurted another short laugh. Larina was crazy if she thought she was going to risk looking at her.

"Um, Sadyra." Larina's voice sounded from farther away than it should have.

Ever so slowly, Sadyra turned to meet Lozen's hard stare. Wide-eyed, her need to laugh abandoned her. She raised her gaze over Lozen's head. Towering behind the warrior woman, Pollard glared.

"Care to share with everyone what's so funny?" Pollard's deep voice resonated in the cavern above the noise of falling water.

Sadyra looked at the ground between her and Lozen, shaking her head.

"I believe we have a volunteer," Lozen announced. "Sadyra, how would you like to run to the centre column and demonstrate how you would scale such an obstacle?"

"Me?" Sadyra pointed at Larina. "She made me laugh."

Lozen nodded. "Very well. We have two volunteers."

Larina gaped.

Sadyra regarded the dais as she walked up beside Larina. A steady stream of water poured into the well-like structure. She smiled for Larina's benefit. "Shouldn't be too difficult. With a running start, it won't be hard to reach the platform."

Larina raised skeptical eyebrows and muttered, "I'll get you for this."

Sadyra chuckled, not sure if Larina was serious or not. "Come on. Let's show them how easy it is to get past their defenses."

Larina stretched her shoulders and adjusted her belt, checking the hilt of her dagger. With a subtle nod, she ran toward the stone dais; the flames of her torch whipping behind her.

Sadyra kept pace, feeling the cavern floor pass beneath her soft-souled boots—the stone darkening as the angle of the slope steepened. One of her feet slipped—her other following in its wake. She cast a startled look at Larina as the two of them tried to halt their headlong slide.

They fell hard to the damp floor, flailing their hands and legs. Larina lost her grip on the torch—neither woman able to prevent their bodies from slamming into the unforgiving wall of the central platform.

The torch slid to a halt in the thin layer of dark green muck that coated the cave's floor, hissing and sputtering.

Laughter reached them over the increasing noise of the water cascading from above.

Stunned by the impact with the curving wall of rock, Sadyra got to her knees and considered the slime covering her hands. The look of disgust on Larina's face matched her own.

She got to her feet, wiped her hands on her leggings and helped Larina up. Glaring at their companions, they were shocked as a wave of ice-cold water washed over them, drenching them to the skin.

Sadyra put her arms over her head and bent sideways in an effort to see what was happening but the deluge of bone-chilling water increased in volume—its force driving her to her knees, fighting for breath. Scrabbling for purchase on the slick rock, she attempted to climb the sloped cavern floor to get away from the rushing water. Her feet shot out from underneath her and she slid back to the base of the platform, half submerged in a growing pond of water.

Afraid she might drown, her mind drifted back to the day Bano had pulled her out of the surf back home. Just the thought of the traitorous man made her mad enough to fight harder. She forced herself to take a shaky step against the incessant torrent. And then another.

Getting out from beneath the cascading water that had risen to just below her knees, she glared past Larina at their new companions. The men and women, guardsmen and trainees alike, were bent over and howling with laughter.

Larina squealed, fighting to remain on her feet but was unsuccessful. She went down with a splash and slid into Sadyra, her momentum taking Sadyra's legs out from under her. Together they floundered in the frigid water.

The thunderous clamour of falling water dissipated as fast as it had hit.

"Reveal!" Pollard's voice echoed throughout the cavern.

High above, interspersed amongst the myriad of thick stalactites comprising the roof's surface, torches flared to life.

Pollard spread his arms wide and proclaimed, "Welcome to the Well of Despair."

Sadyra stood up and stumbled in thigh deep water. Catching herself, she swung her head around and up, snapping most of her long hair from her face. Blinking past the water dripping off her pale skin, she observed a dazzling display overhead. Dozens of archers sat or stood on small, wooden platforms built into the sides of thick stalactites; bows strung and trained on her and Larina.

Ringing the water from the ends of her hair, she glared at Larina who was fit to be tied. Their chagrinned cleansing had been their first lesson in humility with the Songsbirthian Guard.

Pollard

Beyond the Mere Bonds

Pollard put his pointer finger and thumb in his mouth and emitted a shrill whistle.

The archers suspended from the rooftop lowered their bows, slid their arrows into their quivers, and disappeared into crevices within the stalactites.

The water surrounding the platform and the sodden forms of Larina and Sadyra, shimmered; its surface covered with countless ripples as the cavern floor shook and light flooded into the huge chamber. Dozens of torches appeared beyond the central platform; illuminating a large section of wall on the far side of the cave as it rumbled aside to reveal men and women clad in slate grey uniforms.

"Captain. I'd like you to meet the newest selection of recruits." Pollard's voice echoed in the cavern.

A middle-aged man separated himself from the guardsmen fanning out along the far wall. A shorter, younger man with bouncing sandy-blonde hair accompanied him.

The older man laughed as they skirted the edge of the newly formed lake; his eyes on Sadyra and Larina, soaked to the skin. "I see this group doesn't lack its share of mischief makers."

Pollard smiled. "Aye, captain. There's always one. Two this time."

The captain gripped Pollard's beefy hand; patting his corded forearm. "Glad to have you back. The tunnels aren't the same without you."

Pollard

The younger man accepted Pollard's hand as the captain moved to greet Lozen. "By that, he means, they aren't blocked by your presence." He pulled Pollard into an embrace, the disparity in their size almost comical.

"Ah, Guardell. I wish you could've come with us. The kingdom is beautiful this time of the year." Pollard turned to indicate the two women dragging themselves from the water. Neither one looked happy. "It would have made your heart swell to witness the one there called Sadyra, single-handedly take out three men in Thunderhead."

Guardell stepped back and nodded, his gaze on the miserable-looking women; expanding puddles forming around their feet as they dripped on the stone floor. "By the looks of them, I pity anyone who crosses them."

Pollard's laugh echoed throughout the cavern.

Guardell waited for the captain to finish speaking with Lozen before embracing her. "Welcome back. I hope the lummox wasn't too hard on you guys."

"Nothing I couldn't handle." Lozen's eyes smiled. She seemed reluctant to release Guardell from her arms.

Pollard raised his voice to include the rest of the recruits. "People. Before you stand the leaders of the Splendoor Catacombs." He dipped his head toward the captain and Guardell. Placing his hand on Guardell's thick shoulder, he proclaimed, "Guardell Caulder is second in command. If my attempts to maintain order and discipline fail, you'll answer to him. Don't let his size fool you. I fear the day I ever fall on his bad side."

The recruits frowned, obviously finding it hard to believe that Pollard was afraid of the little man.

Pollard released Guardell's shoulder and directed the trainees' attention to the captain. "Captain Johnnes Holmann's word is your law. When he says jump, you don't hit the ground again until he tells you. Anyone stepping out of line from this point forward will find their sorry arse making a hasty exit from the catacombs." He purposely caught Larina and Sadyra's chagrinned stares. "Is that clear?"

A few recruits mumbled an unintelligible affirmative.

"I can't hear you?" Pollard's voice boomed, reverberating off the walls like residual thunder.

"Yes, Master Banebridge!"

Pollard raised his eyebrows at Sadyra and Larina—their dark expressions clearly stating it was all they could do not to say something that would get them into further trouble.

Both women's chests heaved; their response anything but enthusiastic. "Yes, Master Banebridge."

Pollard's stare lingered, daring them to transgress. Finally, he nodded. "Very well. Thank you, captain. We'll sleep here tonight."

Captain Holmann raised his eyebrows. "You sure you don't want to house them in the spare quarters? There's room."

"No, captain. Here's fine."

A few of the recruits frowned.

"Very well." The captain started back toward the large breach in the far wall. "I'll have food brought out. I'm sure everyone can use a decent meal after floundering about the labyrinth."

"That won't be necessary. They have their rations."

Larina and Sadyra gaped.

"Unless they've eaten more than they should have. In that case, it'll be a valuable lesson."

"Suit yourself," the captain laughed and strode away. "I've already sent word to the Birth that you've arrived."

Guardell slapped Pollard's bicep on his way by. "Always the hard ass, eh?"

Pollard winked. "Only way to break them."

Pollard

Larina struggled to find a comfortable position on the unforgiving cavern floor. The darkness in the natural chamber was absolute. She couldn't see the tip of her nose. Judging by the continued restless noise beside her, Sadyra wasn't having any luck either.

She reached out and poked Sadyra, whispering, "Sadyra."

Sadyra grunted.

"Sadyra!"

"Mmph."

"You awake?"

"Mmph."

"You know what I think?"

Sadyra didn't respond.

"Sadyra!" Larina grabbed onto a part of Sadyra's body. She wasn't sure what part it was, but it was soft in her hand. Embarrassed she let go.

"Ow! What the…?"

"Shh! You want to wake everyone?"

"Like who? Me? I just got to sleep," Sadyra growled. "What is it?"

"I think the big oaf has it in for us."

"Pollard?"

"Who else?"

When Sadyra didn't answer, Larina wondered if she'd gone back to sleep. How, on the uneven floor, she couldn't imagine. Larina was used to sleeping in alleyways and hardwood floors, but something about the cavern floor kept her awake. Staring into the darkness, she surmised that perhaps it had something to do with the million thoughts roiling through her mind. Images of Bear trying to sound diplomatic on the Storms End Council. The accusations of Bear's parents about her role in Cassie's death. Allard and Rock. All of the helpless people she had left behind. The remainder of her gold—likely seized when the Watch arrested Bear. She couldn't believe she hadn't asked him about it afterward.

Pollard

So many unanswered questions and here she was, hundreds of leagues from home, lying in a dank hole in a mountain, not sure where life was leading her. Though she had no delusions about obtaining honest employment in Storms End—not with her reputation proceeding her—at least there, she had a purpose. Out here, in the heart of nowhere and bereft of friends, a darkness seeped into her soul and wouldn't let go.

"He's testing us," Sadyra whispered.

Sadyra's voice startled her. She fought to steady her breathing. "What good are we going to be if he kills us first?"

Again, a long silence.

"Lozen won't let that happen." Sadyra's voice sounded closer. "There's something different about her."

"Lozen? I'd say. Scares the evil from me."

"She means well. You can tell."

This time Larina chose to be silent.

"I mean, yes, she's loyal to the big oaf, but I believe she has our best interests at heart."

"Ya. She's okay, I guess. Took me a while to get used to her." Larina recalled her last few days in Storms End. "Especially after the way she hunted me."

"Huh? She hunted you?"

"Aye. I never told you that? The first couple of times I met her, she tried to fill me with arrows."

"Really? How come?"

"Um…" Larina pondered how best to phrase what she wanted to say. "Let's just say I bent the rules in Storms End and ran afoul of the Watch. In the end, they used Lozen to track me."

"Wow. What happened? How come she isn't working for them now?"

"It's a long story. According to Pollard, he had her planted in the Watch as one of his father's spies."

"Planted for what?"

"To make sure I didn't come to harm?"

"I thought you said she tried to fill you with arrows?"

"She did."

"That makes no sense."

"Tell me about it. Apparently, she intentionally missed me."

"Do you believe that?"

"I didn't at first. The more I get to know her, though, I'm thinking that if she had wanted to shoot me, I wouldn't be here."

A long silence followed before Sadyra said, "Do you like the big oaf?"

The question shocked Larina. "I'm not sure what you mean. He's overbearing and takes great pride in demonstrating he's superior to the rest of us, so, I guess if I think about it, I'd have to say he can be insufferable at times."

"No. I mean, do you *like* him?"

Thankful for the cover of darkness, Larina felt her cheeks redden. "What? You mean as a mate?"

"Ya. Something like that."

"No!" Larina said so adamantly, she knew at once her lie was obvious. "Well…He is handsome."

"And strong."

"That too." Larina smiled, not quite believing she was having this conversation. She had never spoken this openly with anyone except for Bear, Rock, and dear Cassie many years ago. If she didn't know better, she would have sworn that her heart was swelling—bursting with happiness. Shivering in the absolute darkness, lying upon the cold, unforgiving cavern floor, she felt as if she was building a bond with Sadyra that felt as if it had the potential to go beyond the mere bonds of friendship.

Pollard

Brilliant Minds

Pollard's booming voice grated in Sadyra's skull. She had barely gone to sleep when the rumbling of the large wall on the opposite side of the cavern shook the ground beneath her. Torch light flooded the chamber.

Shielding her squinted eyes, she made out the lumbering form of Pollard with Lozen at his side; both carrying burning torches in one hand and unlit brands beneath their opposite arm.

"Time's a wasting. First ones up get a torch. The rest can try to keep up. Anyone falling behind will be escorted from the catacombs and left at the base of the falls to fend for themselves."

Larina sat up, red-eyed and bleary.

Sadyra grumbled, "Remember what we were talking about last night? I'm not liking him at all at the moment."

Larina smiled through a wide yawn. Getting to her feet, she held a hand out. "Come on, before the big oaf throws us off the mountain."

Sadyra and Larina fell in line ahead of Quincette as they exited the cavern the way they had entered. The thick shouldered woman bore a torch and brought up the rear of the procession.

Sadyra regarded the stocky Songsbirthian Guard. "Good morning. Or whatever time of day it is."

Quincette's hard features stared coldly back.

Sadyra caught Larina's gaze and rolled her eyes; making sure Quincette didn't see her reaction.

Pollard

They followed the group down a gently sloping corridor, the pitch bizarre if they meant to climb the height of the waterfall.

Sadyra couldn't tell how high inside the mountain they had ascended, but she doubted they were near the top.

The procession came to a standstill in front of them.

Sadyra looked at Larina. "What's going on?"

Larina rose to her toes and shrugged. "Beats me. Everyone's stopped."

Sadyra raised her eyebrows at Quincette.

"They're at the next transition," was all the Songsbirthian Guard offered.

Sadyra looked back at Larina and raised her eyebrows. "So there."

Larina struggled to keep from laughing.

In front of them, Mikter, and another young man Sadyra only knew by the arrogant way he conducted himself, started forward. It wasn't long before they reached the next hidden doorway—a circular hole exposed in the centre of the corridor's floor.

Lozen stood beside the gaping hole, helping recruits steady themselves on the brink of the drop, while Pollard waited in the tunnel below to ensure no one fell too hard.

Lozen dropped through last, barely ahead of the slab of granite rumbling across the opening to seal the gap. A small stalactite hung from the hatch's centre—the tell-tale indicator of the portal's presence. She landed without a sound; momentarily dropping into a crouch before stepping in beside Quincette to follow Larina and Sadyra up the next nondescript tunnel.

"This place is incredible," Larina said; large brown eyes taking in the man-made tunnel hewn through solid granite. "How could anyone possibly dig through so much stone?"

"Dwarfs," Lozen answered as if that was sufficient.

Sadyra slowed and glanced over her shoulder. "Dwarfs? Like, little people?"

Lozen's exotic complexion lit up behind her warm smile. "Yes. Though they don't take kindly to being lumped in with mankind."

"Are there dwarfs here?" Larina asked, wonder in her voice.

Lozen chuckled. "Nay. I haven't heard tell of a dwarf in Zephyr for decades. Once in a while you might see them attend the Royal Tournament, but other than that, they tend to avoid the realm of man."

Being from Fishmonger Bay, secluded from the day-to-day life of the greater kingdom, most everything beyond Thunderhead was alien to Sadyra. The thought of seeing a full-grown man no higher than her waist didn't seem real to her.

Time passed slowly as they trudged along. So enrapt in her own thoughts, she nearly ran into the back of Mikter. The procession had stopped.

"Oh goodie. Another doorway." Larina's words dripped with sarcasm.

Up ahead, a secret gap breached the right wall. The closer they got to the egress, the louder a peculiar roar became.

Waiting their turn to go through the breach, Sadyra asked Lozen, "What's that noise? Are we at the top?"

"Hardly. We're over halfway, though."

Sadyra almost choked on her words. "Halfway? Master Banebridge hurried us along yesterday saying we needed to reach Songsbirth before the trolls."

Lozen said through a patient smile, "Aye. Tonight."

Though Sadyra had no idea how long they had been walking, if they had indeed set out in the early morning like she thought, they still had a long way to go. "So, what's the noise then?"

Lozen nodded for her to follow Larina. "You'll see."

Stepping through the gap, Sadyra trailed Mikter and the arrogant male down the tunnel to the left. The floor continued to descend rather than slope upward.

"No wonder it takes so long to get through the tunnels," Sadyra mumbled to Larina. "The dwarfs must have hit the ale hard while digging this tunnel."

Larina chuckled.

Rounding a bend, the roar grew into a thunderous din. Natural light flooded the tunnel causing everyone to squint. The floor underfoot darkened with dampness.

The procession thinned out to single file as the recruits slipped past a large break in the tunnel wall, exposing cascading water so thick that only muted sunlight penetrated it.

"We're behind Splendoor Falls!" Lozen's voice was barely distinguishable above the roar. "Rumour has it the dwarfs miscalculated their route."

Sadyra leaned in to Larina, "Ya think?"

The ground underfoot was slick with moisture. Passing beyond the gap, her clothes damp, Sadyra noted the tunnel floor sloped upward.

The ever-present darkness of the tunnel lightened beyond the heads and shoulders of the recruits as the men and women shuffled to a halt.

Sadyra elbowed Larina. "Great. Another door."

Lozen leaned her head between them. "Aye. But, whatever you do, don't step through this one."

Sadyra and Larina frowned, but Lozen didn't elaborate.

Soon, the ranks ahead pressed against the wall to allow first Pollard, and then the head of the procession, to squeeze by.

Larina's frown deepened.

Sadyra shrugged and followed Mikter toward the brightness.

The recruits filing past them on their way back toward the gap behind the waterfall spoke in awe of what they had just witnessed.

Mikter stopped, as if refusing to go any farther. Squeezing past him, Sadyra's heart caught in her throat. Not out of fear, but out of wonder. The tunnel had come to an end—opening onto a brilliant blue sky and the varying hues of green at the bottom of a thousand-foot drop.

Unphased by heights, Sadyra leaned out over the brink. A great cloud of mist clung to the base of the cliff where the plummeting torrents of Splendoor Falls crashed into the land far below.

The Madrigail River appeared out of the far edge of the roiling mist, meandering westward to be swallowed by a large body of water Pollard had referred to as Lake Refrain. Barely visible north of the lake, the Madrigail continued its course, flowing out of the low mountains and winding its way inevitably northwestward to where it disappeared amongst the foothills of the iron-grey monoliths of the Spine.

"Watch you don't fall," Mikter said, eyes wide. He and his partner had stopped well short of the drop.

Larina pretended like she was going to shove Mikter forward.

He braced himself against the far wall, shaking his head. "That's not funny."

The mischief on Larina's face transformed into amazement as she stepped in beside Sadyra. "You can see the whole world from here." She pointed northwest. "Look. Isn't that Millsford?"

Sadyra shrugged. "Probably."

"Aye," Lozen stepped in behind them. "If you know where to look, far to the west, you can just make out The Forke nestled amongst the foothills of the Spine."

Sadyra squinted but couldn't see what Lozen pointed at.

"Follow the Spine north of the Madrigail. Another large river flows south along the base of the mountains. That's the Frothe River. Just follow it back to the Madrigail. They meet at The Forke."

"I see it!" Larina announced.

Sadyra leaned out farther, as if that little bit would help her to better see clear across the realm. She glanced at Larina, disgusted, and stormed back into the tunnel, mocking Larina's words, "I see it."

The tunnel sloped upward, sometimes at a steep angle. As they trudged along, Sadyra speculated what kind of incredible city must be awaiting them to justify such an elaborate approach. Songsbirth must be a city of wonder.

Tendrils of an idea swirled through her thoughts. What better place in all the world to start a new life in? Tural and Gitch's crew would never find her here. She didn't need to waste time trying to impress Pollard or Lozen. She could find employment in Songsbirth and start a new life.

She nodded to herself. That's exactly what she would do. Stumbling on the uneven floor, she caught Larina's gaze. Her only friend in the world smiled back at her for no apparent reason. Sadyra swallowed. She would miss Larina.

Since the tunnel never widened to allow more than two people to walk abreast, Pollard insisted that if anyone wanted to eat their rations, they do it while they walked. There was no time to stop.

The light bearers had lit their third torch by the time the procession reached its destination.

Sunlight filled the tunnel ahead, accompanied by the sound of rushing water. Waiting their turn, Sadyra and Larina impatiently shuffled up the last stretch of tunnel—the passageway ending at a wooden-rung ladder that led to an open hatchway—a welcoming azure sky visible beyond.

A large, metal basket sat beside the bottom of the ladder, full of unspent torches. The acrid smell of recently extinguished brands turned up Sadyra's nose. She bounded up the ladder and was dumbfounded by the view awaiting her.

Pollard

She stood upon a small rock platform at the base of an unscalable cliff, the ledge barely large enough to hold the recruits crowding onto it. A large lake lay at the edge of the platform, its vast perimeter hemmed in by a ring of mountains stretching to the eastern horizon.

Tethered to iron eyelets, three large dories pulled at their ropes, threatening to be swept around a low promontory into the violent current at the brink of Splendoor Falls. Three men dressed in livery matching Quincette stood patiently in front of the boats, conversing with Pollard.

The people packed on the ledge shifted back and forth as curious recruits made their way to its northern edge, taking their turn to gape at the thundering water plunging over the brink of Splendoor Falls, two thousand feet to the mainland below.

Sadyra jostled her way to the narrow spot between an outcropping of rock and the cliff rising up from the fall's edge. Onynx and Nyler were on hands and knees, tentatively stretching their bodies forward to get a better view. They didn't remain on the edge for long. Ashen-faced, they crept back from the precipice, wide eyes following Sadyra and Larina to the brink.

Sadyra placed one hand on the cliff's edge rising straight up beside her and leaned out over the gap. "Wow!" she gasped, the word long and drawn out.

Larina leaned in beside her. "Incredible."

The view they had experienced earlier in the day hadn't prepared them for this one.

Sadyra followed the Madrigail to the foothills of the Spine and smiled, contented—The Forke clearly visible on the edge of the shadows creeping across the land as the sun dropped beyond the distant Spine. She swore she could see the entire world.

Pollard's shout for attention drew them away from the brink. "Gather 'round. Songsbirth lies directly northeast of our current position. Take care when loading the boats. One slip and you'll make a hasty descent. Your body will never be seen again."

Pale skinned Onynx and dark skinned Nyler helped each other shakily to their feet; neither recovered from their brief glimpse of the drop-off.

Onynx gaped at Sadyra and Larina as they cued up to board the boats. "Weren't you afraid of falling?"

Larina paused. "Please. I could scale that cliff."

Larina craned her neck to take in the spectacular vista of the mountains—the setting sun sparkling off jagged, snow-capped peaks. Pulling her tunic tight around her thin frame, she shivered uncontrollably; thankful for the scant protection from the wind provided by those crammed in the dory around her. The size of the mountain lake was incredible.

Twilight had entrenched itself into the mountains by the time an excited chatter rippled through the recruits. If she looked hard, Larina could see buildings on the north shore. Songsbirth sat nestled at the base of a cliff, its flowing designs of stone and wooden buildings fronted a sliver of shoreline.

As the boat scraped the bottom, Pollard jumped knee-deep into the water and pulled the heavy boat halfway onto a stony beach—his strength unbelievable considering the amount of people the dory carried.

Tired of being in wet clothes lately, Larina was happy she had been included in the boat with Pollard as the other two boats were not faring as well. Their occupants were forced to jump into the waist-deep water to assist with the beaching. Judging by their gasps, the water was every bit as cold as it looked.

Pollard

Sadyra jumped out of the boat beside Larina and crunched across the gravel beach toward the city—the look of disappointment on her face plain to see. "That's it?"

"What's the matter?" Pollard asked as he steadied the boat to help the unloading of passengers—his breeks soaked to the knees.

Larina watched on as Sadyra scowled; taking in the eclectic buildings that were painted in a kaleidoscope of colour; their façades dotted with countless birds' nests—the singsong of avian wildlife drawing their attention to hidden aeries in the cliffs above the quaint little village.

Sadyra turned on Pollard. "Where's the rest of the city?"

"The rest? This is it."

"Then why the elaborate catacombs?"

"I don't understand." Pollard strained on the bow rope after the last person disembarked, pulling the dory completely out of the water.

"Why would anyone go to so much trouble to protect a collection of..." She scanned the hamlet, looking for the right word. Flustered, she said, "This! A few wooden buildings painted in garish colours. Who would possibly want to bother with a place like this?"

Pollard appeared taken aback. "I'm not sure what you're asking?"

"The catacombs. Leagues of tunnels, painstakingly dug into the mountain. Each one hidden from the next. And the cavern with the well." Sadyra swallowed, exasperated. "Why go to all that trouble to protect," she spun around, her arms wide, "this?"

"Ah." A sly smile crept across Pollard's face, splitting his reddish beard. "The Splendoor Catacombs wasn't built to protect Songsbirth."

Larina's surprise matched that of Sadyra. They stared open-mouthed at Pollard.

Pollard

"The Splendoor Catacombs were built to protect something far more important than buildings." Pollard paused, nodding smugly.

Sadyra and Larina glared at him to continue.

"The Songsbirthian Guard is entrusted to protect the very things that will save the kingdom should the day ever come that our existence is threatened." He nodded. "Aye. Brilliant minds. Don't you ever forget that."

Pollard

Pul

Larina, Sadyra, and the rest of the recruits were led through an iron studded door set into the face of the cliff that formed the backdrop of Songsbirth, following Pollard, Lozen, and Quincette into a well-lit passageway beyond.

Pollard ducked, even though the arched ceiling comfortably cleared the top of his head.

The short corridor beyond housed several doors on either wall. Arriving at the last door on the left, Pollard knocked and slid inside, leaving the others in the cool passageway.

The door opened again. A stooped, old man shuffled into the corridor, his forearm in Pollard's tender grasp.

Watching the old man assist himself with a gnarled cane startled Larina's senses. A pang of grief gripped her, tightening her throat. He reminded her of Allard. She had tried to keep the dear memories of her friend from the forefront of her mind over the last few weeks; not to forget him, but to allow her to function without being collared by the ever-present guilt his death had shackled her with. His life had been taken from him as a direct result of her actions.

"Master Pul," Pollard released Pul's arm and rose to his full height. "Allow me to introduce to you the candidates hoping to become the newest members of the Guard. Many of Zephyr's finest talents, located from as far away as Apexceal."

Master Pul squinted, leaning his head forward on a thin, baggy-skinned neck. His wrinkled face lit up with a toothless smile. "Very good, Pollard. You have done well."

Pollard

"Thank you, Master Pul. I couldn't have found them without the aid of the rest of our quest." Pollard nodded to Lozen and Quincette, the only two members of Pollard's expedition to have followed them into the building.

Quincette, thick arms folded below her breasts, nodded to the master.

Lozen stepped up to Pul and embraced him, her movements careful.

Pul wrapped a shaky arm around the small of Lozen's back. "Ah, my dear friend. Your presence is a delight—enough to keep at bay the dark clouds on the horizon, if only for a short while. The Songsbirthian Guard is blessed to share your expertise. I fear the day will soon be at hand when you must answer the call of your people. You will be dearly missed."

Not letting Pul see her as she held him, Lozen frowned up at Pollard, clearly baffled by Pul's proclamation.

Pollard raised his eyebrows and shrugged.

Lozen gently unwrapped her arms and held Pul at arm's length. "You honour me and my tribe with the opportunity to return a semblance of gratitude for what your people did for mine all those years ago. I, too, shall be saddened when that time comes."

Pul's comical grin lifted his sagging wrinkles. He turned a serious eye on Quincette—a subtle nod barely perceptible—and shuffled toward the last door on the opposite side of the hallway.

Without a word, Quincette strode smartly down the hall and exited the complex.

Pollard stepped aside to allow Lozen room to escort Pul through the doorway. Turning on the recruits, he said in no uncertain terms, "You're about to enter the hallowed hall of the Songsbirthian Chamber of the Wise. Treat it with the reverence it deserves. As much as King Malcolm depends on the counsel of the Gritian Chamber of the Wise, the kingdom would never have become as great as it is without the wise counsel it receives from the Songsbirthian Chamber."

Pollard's declaration left Larina with no illusion that any transgression would be severely dealt with. Following the awestruck recruits through the oaken door, she hoped Sadyra understood the sentiment. If anyone was going to cause Larina difficulty, it was Sadyra's deadpan way of commenting on things. Although she had grown to love her for it, Sadyra's silver tongue had proven a sure-fire way to land them in trouble.

The doorway opened onto a surprisingly wide tunnel. Polished granite walls were adorned with colourful tapestries portraying larger than life faces of men and women Larina had never seen before. Beautiful statues, some carved from the same stone as the walls, while others consisted of chiselled white marble, were spaced uniformly along the corridor. The stone effigies depicted rearing horses bearing men and women in armour, people of different sizes robed in flowing cloaks, and even a dragon with a female rider carrying a staff in one hand and a small book in her other. The procession slowed to appreciate the artistry within the descending tunnel.

Sadyra paused and ran her hand across the dragon's head, her fingertips coming to rest on the end of one of its temple horns.

"These are amazing," Larina said, more to the air than anyone in particular.

"Don't touch!" Pollard's voice boomed as he brought up the rear.

Sadyra withdrew her hand.

Larina waited for him to chastise Sadyra, but instead he took a moment to appreciate the carving.

"To think there used to be a time when people actually flew dragons," Pollard said, his voice full of wonder.

Sadyra never took her eyes from the statue. "That would be incredible."

Pollard

The noise of boot falls in the hallway died away.

Larina cleared her throat to get Sadyra and Pollard's attention. "Whenever you two are done gawking, perhaps we should join the others."

Pollard snapped out of the spell the statue had induced. He stretched his neck, clearly embarrassed. "Yes. Quite right. It wouldn't do to keep Master Pul waiting."

He gestured for Sadyra and Larina to continue along the sconce lit passageway that ended at an open set of bronze-strapped, iron doors.

Passing over the threshold, the Songsbirthian Chamber of the Wise lacked the awe-inspired vision Pollard's speech had instilled in Larina. She wasn't sure what she had expected, but the non-descript, roughly hewn cavern left her senses lacking.

Rows of rickety, ancient benches lined the immediate area beyond the doors, filling a small area between the entrance and a stone table that dominated the cave's far end.

Master Pul sat at the head of the table, his meek form hunched between Lozen and an empty chair. The Chambermaster and the warrior woman spoke quietly as they waited for the recruits to occupy the other nine chairs around the table and the first row of benches.

Pollard left Sadyra and Larina in the narrow aisle and assumed the empty chair on Master Pul's right.

An expectant hush settled over the chamber, only interrupted by the creaking, second-row bench Sadyra settled on.

Larina attempted to lower herself onto the empty bench across the aisle from Sadyra without making a noise, but the ancient wood groaned just the same. Looking up and swallowing, she noted Master Pul staring at Sadyra—the intensity in his aged eyes, frightening.

Not taking his gaze from Sadyra, Master Pul said, "Welcome to the Chamber of the Wise. Within these hallowed walls, grave decisions are made. Ones that affect a great many people. The fate of the masses hinge on the deliberations of the few."

Pul's gaze slid from Sadyra to scan the rapt audience. "Entertain no misconception. The true power of the land lies not with the king's army or his resident wizard, but on the stooped shoulders of old men and women who are thankful they can get out of bed in the morning." He nodded, his toothless grin anything but amused. "Aye. Your elders are the key to the kingdom's salvation. The knowledge they possess, passed down from generation to generation, is priceless to those who deal with the drudgery of everyday rule."

Larina wasn't sure anyone in the chamber had drawn a breath since Master Pul began speaking. Against her better judgement, she dared to observe Sadyra—the usual mischief absent from Sadyra's freckled cheeks and storm-grey eyes. Looking around, even the smug arrogance of the recruit that had accompanied Mikter in the tunnels was not in evidence beneath his long, black hair.

"I'm sure Pollard has informed you of the danger Zephyr faces in the not too distant future. For those of us in the know, the signs point to a catastrophic event that will happen in *your* lifetime. A malign force stirs. The enemy in the north is restless. In the face of the prevalent evil, our heroes have faded from existence—their absence undoubtedly rendering King Malcolm, the Learned, unable to field an army formidable enough to deal with our perceived doom."

Larina was sure no one breathed.

"I charge you, the young men and women of Zephyr, to help us bear that burden of knowledge. Each and every one of you have been personally selected by Pollard Banebridge and his advisors as candidates to safeguard the ancient lore in the hope that it may yet save our realm." Master Pul's voice dropped to an eerie timbre. "Be warned. Your task will be fraught with grave danger. In order to become one of the

Pollard

elite Guardians of Zephyr, you must be prepared to defend these walls with your life."

Pollard

Home

"**Well,** that was…different." Sadyra walked up the passage leading from the Chamber of the Wise with Larina beside her. "Uplifting, even."

Larina caught her smirk and shook her head. "Scary is more like it. His words echo the speech Thoril Banebridge gave me."

"Pollard's father?"

"The one and only."

"The guy you stole from, right? The one with the mangled hand."

Larina raised her eyebrows and nodded, passing through the doorway at the end of the rising corridor. Turning left, Quincette awaited them at the end of the entrance tunnel, holding the exit door open.

Quincette didn't as much as acknowledge them with a nod or a smile. She simply said, "Follow me," and stepped into the night.

Crisp, cold, mountain air caught in Sadyra's lungs. Pulling her tunic tight, she kept pace a couple of steps behind Quincette; the curt Songsbirthian Guard leading them through the sleepy hamlet. Breath vapour escaped Sadyra's lips as she admired the clear sky. Billions of pinpricks of light illuminated the firmament, reflecting off the glassy surface of Madrigail Lake in magical splendor—the water so still, it appeared as if it were polished stone.

The haunting trill of a loon somewhere on the lake reached them; as if protesting the clomping of their boots across the hamlet's wooden walkways. Scattered windows in the multi-coloured tenements abutting the base of the cliff flickered in soft candle glow; their blinds edged aside by occupants sneaking a peek at the strange young men and women who had fallen upon their remote village.

Built into the cliff, a four-story building dominated the centre of town. Quincette stopped at the base of a grand set of rounded stairs fronting the structure's granite façade. At the head of the stairs, multi-paned double doors opened on the night as if on command, and a man and woman dressed in grey serge, laced up the front, and piped in black, bowed their heads as the curious recruits made their way up the steps and between them.

A great foyer greeted the newcomer's weary faces; lushly appointed in thick broadloom and adorned by a polished, mahogany counter on its far side. A curving stairwell swept up the right wall, disappearing into the exposed cliff face, while a short hallway on the left of the counter terminated at a wide, single door.

Three more men, and three women, dressed similarly to those atop the steps, bowed their heads; deferring to a man clad in black serge piped in grey as he stepped between them.

"Greetings weary travellers. Welcome to the *Lullaby Inn*," the man in black said, a great smile cleaving his thin face. "We've been expecting you. Master Banebridge sends his regards. You're to be housed here tonight. I invite you to take full advantage of our amenities. Hot water to lave, good food to sate, and downy pallets to provide you the best sleep you've had in a long while, hmmm?"

Without further ado, he nodded to the servants. "If you would be so kind."

The doors closed behind them, shutting out the cold. The man and woman who had greeted them on the front steps, started up the curving stairwell. The woman stopped on the first step. "Follow, please."

Pollard

Sadyra nudged Larina ahead and the two of them were the first up the stairs. As they climbed, the man in black's voice followed them. "You're advised to retire early. It'll be a long time before you enjoy the comforts of a good bed again. Rest assured, Master Banebridge will come calling at the crack of dawn."

The portly woman leading them up the stairwell paused at the top—raw granite exposed above her head and a masterfully carved tunnel hewn from the mountain behind her, lined with tapestries that were separated by slender doors standing open. "Welcome. Mister Glenco," she nodded at her cohort, "and I will be your host and hostess this evening. My name is Miss Lanny. Ladies will be housed on the second floor. Gentlemen on the third. If the men would kindly follow Mister Glenco through the archway and up to the third floor, that would be greatly appreciated."

The archway she spoke of branched off to the right, exposing an upward sloping tunnel that spiralled out of sight.

Miss Lanny proceeded to the first door. With a congenial smile, she nodded at Larina and Sadyra. "You two will share this room." Not a question but a statement of fact.

Not waiting for a response, she stepped across the hall and indicated Onynx and Klara. "You two will share this room."

The hostess turned and led the rest of the young women deeper into the mountain passageway.

Sadyra raised her eyebrows at Larina. "Alright then. I guess it's you and me."

The room was surprisingly large. A wide bed butted up against the stone wall at its far end, beyond a couple of knee-high chests that sat open against its footboard. Two, highbacked armchairs boasted thick cushions beneath a tiny window overlooking Madrigail Lake on the left side of the room. A stone washbasin and a peculiar wooden stand with a cushioned shelf at its base stood between the chairs and the end of the room.

Pollard

Sadyra slumped into the chair beside the wooden stand and sighed with satisfaction. "Ahh. That's better." She adjusted her position and closed her eyes. "I could sleep right here."

Larina tested the bed with her palms and nodded, clearly impressed. "Wow. This is amazing." She turned and sat on its edge, bouncing twice. She laid back, a mischievous grin creeping across her face. "What do you think the big oaf would do if we didn't show up in the morning?"

Sadyra's eyes were closed. She considered the possibility. "He'd probably be thankful."

"Hah! You may be right. I doubt he's as enamoured with his twin tigers as he thought he would be."

Sadyra frowned and opened her eyes, catching Larina's smirk. "Twin tigers? He called us that?"

"Aye. Well, maybe not in so many words. He called you that, though. When we were watching you in the Thunderhead market dealing with those thugs. He claimed you and I would make quite the fighting pair."

Sadyra's smile grew wider. She closed her eyes, enjoying the comfort of a soft place to rest her body. "Can't say I disagree with him. If you did half of the stuff you claim you did in Storms End, you must be a fierce person to cross."

Larina sat up. "*If?*" She grabbed one of the pillows and threw it at Sadyra.

The pillow hit Sadyra's upraised hands. "Okay. Okay. You're a tiger too." She laughed and threw the pillow back.

Larina caught it. Lying down, she put her arms behind her head.

Before long, soft, regular breathing told Sadyra that Larina had drifted off fully clothed—boots and all.

Unable to sleep, the room door barely made a sound as Sadyra eased it closed behind her. Sconces lining the wall had been turned down to save fuel, casting the top of the stairwell and the gaping archway in deep shadow. Listening, she heard the muted voices of Onynx and Klara from beyond their closed door but couldn't make out their conversation.

Carpeted steps passed quietly beneath her soft-soled boots as she descended to the foyer.

Lanny's pleasant face looked up from where she sat behind the counter. "Can I help you?"

Unsure whether she should bolt back up the stairs, Sadyra said, "Um, no. I was just, uh…?" She glanced at the exit. "I thought I'd go for a walk."

Lanny surprised her. "It's cold out tonight. Autumn temperatures in the mountains can be unforgiving."

"So…It's okay if I go out?"

Lanny shrugged. "Ain't no one stopping you. The door's always open. Just remember, Master Banebridge will be by early in the morning. I advise you not to keep him waiting."

"No, ma'am. I won't forget." Feeling uncomfortable talking with Lanny, Sadyra smiled for the hostess' benefit and slipped out the front door of the *Lullaby Inn*.

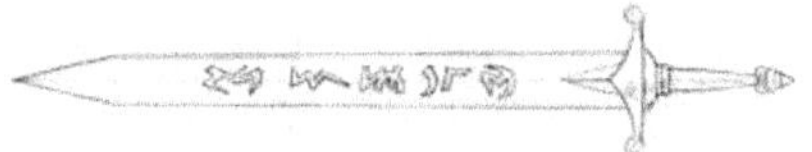

Lanny's warning haunted Sadyra as she crunched across the gravel beach and stopped on the edge of Madrigail Lake. If she didn't get to bed soon, she would be useless when Pollard came to round them up.

Hugging her arms around her did little to stave off the cold, but it served to heighten her awareness of everything around her. Silhouettes of cragged, snow-capped sentinels rose out of the dark waters—stark against a cloudless sky. The full moon reflected far out in the lake, so clearly that Sadyra mused she could jump into one of the beached skiffs and visit its surface.

Pollard

Though Songsbirth was built high on the shoulders of the Muse, her mind lay hundreds of leagues to the west, lamenting her sisters' safety. She vividly recalled telling Sable, "I could never leave you." And yet, here she was.

The moon's reflection blurred through her moistening eyes. What had she done? She had left Sable and Sleena to the mercy of her parents. Without her there to shield them, who knew what Tural or Areeza Ors were capable of?

The realization that she referred to her parents by their given names struck her. She had emotionally distanced herself from them years ago, but it had taken her forced separation to make her fully understand how wide that gulf had become.

A large skiff lay on its side close to where she stood. If she thought she could have manhandled it by herself, she may have set it in the lake and rowed back to the ledge beside Splendoor Falls. Contemplating doing just that, she chastised herself for being silly. Even if she found the ledge at the far end of the lake without being sucked over the brink of the waterfall, there was no way she could navigate the intricate tunnel system. Other than at the artificial lake in the great cavern, they hadn't encountered another living soul during the two full days they travelled through the tunnels. There was the very real chance she would die long before anyone found her wandering the maze.

She sighed. She was trapped. As much as she feared returning home, the passage of time had dulled the raw emotion of the betrayal by the people she had considered her friends. Her sisters were more important to her than her own life. She had abandoned them and now she had no way to get back.

Travelling with Larina and the rest of Pollard's contingent had given her an excuse not to dwell on what really mattered, but her time in the catacombs had allowed her to think back to a time not long ago. A time when she had run in the face of danger—away from the people that mattered most.

She knelt on the edge of the placid lake, wiping her cheeks on her shoulders, her body visibly shaking as she released her pent-up frustration at her inability to deal with her father.

Her brief time with the Songsbirthian Guard and the recruits had been a welcome distraction. Befriending Larina had filled her with the hope that perhaps there was a better life awaiting her. That she didn't have to answer for something that she wasn't sure was her fault. Out here, in the Zephyr wilds, she was free to be Sadyra. No expectations. No one to walk delicately around. No one to fear.

She fought to still her shaking, but the more she dwelled on her sisters' predicament, the harder her shoulders shook. It was her fault. All of it. Tural claimed *she* was the root of their family's misery. She wished she had never been born.

So enrapt in her misery, she didn't hear the approach of the warrior woman. Lozen's abrupt appearance almost made her fall over in shock. If Lozen *had* made a sound, which she doubted, it had been lost to her tortured mind.

Lozen knelt in beside her, a comforting arm coming to rest across her shoulder.

Sadyra tried to pull away, but Lozen held her against her side. The darker-skinned woman didn't say anything; she just knelt with Sadyra and watched her with concern.

Sadyra swallowed, not wanting to meet Lozen's gaze. She sniffed loudly, imagining what a mess her face must look like. "I should go. Master Banebridge will be calling early."

Lozen lovingly removed a long strand of Sadyra's hair from her face and draped it behind her ear. "You have lovely hair."

Sadyra swallowed. Before she could stop herself, she looked questioningly into Lozen's intelligent eyes. The moon glinted off the sheen of Lozen's shiny black hair, its length matching her own.

Sadyra spit out a gruff reply, "This coming from the woman with the most amazing hair I've ever seen."

A warm smile lifted Lozen's cheeks. "Different. Not better."

Sadyra didn't have a response for that. A shudder of sorrow shook her and she looked away.

"Much like you are different."

The proclamation made Sadyra stiffen. Of that, she knew all too well. Her father had been quick to tell her as much whenever he had the chance.

"Much like Larina is different. And Pollard." Lozen gave her a quick squeeze and released her. Standing up, she held out her hand.

Sadyra accepted it and straightened, trying to release the woman's grip, but Lozen's was strong. The warrior woman gazed out over the lake, leaving Sadyra to her thoughts.

Intimidated by the confident woman, Sadyra didn't know what to say. She followed Lozen's stare and found herself wondering what had happened to Naiche. She thought about asking but Lozen's words startled her.

"You of all people should take Master Pul's wisdom to heart: 'The fate of the masses hinge on the deliberations of the few.'" Lozen let that sink in before adding, "Master Pul believes you possess the ability to make a difference one day."

Sadyra's head whipped around. "What are you talking about? He doesn't even know me."

Lozen remained quiet for a while before meeting her gaze. "Master Pul is more than the frail husk of a man your eyes permit you to see. So much more. When he says something, only the foolish ignore his words."

Sadyra contemplated Lozen's words. She shook her head. "I've never met the man before. Still haven't, actually, other than when we listened to him in the Chamber. He doesn't even know my name."

"Names are nothing but identifying labels. Unless you're famous, they're nothing more than a series of letters. When spoken aloud, they allow someone to get your attention."

Lozen released her hand and cupped Sadyra's cheeks with callused palms. "It's what's inside here that determines the measure of a person. Your tenacity. Your heart. Your soul. Your spirit." She nodded and squeezed Sadyra's cheeks, pulling on her skin. "Master Pul possesses the ability to see beyond these trappings. He sees things that no one else can. A sixth sense, if you will."

Sadyra stepped back to break Lozen's hold and glared. "That hurts."

Before Sadyra could react, Lozen placed the palm of her hand above Sadyra's left breast. "Not as much as the ache that has gripped your heart."

Sadyra looked at the woman's hand, shocked.

Lozen dropped her hand to her side. "You come from a troubled past. That is plain to see for those who wish to look. I sense you struggle to do the right thing. You profess a desire to run away. To flee from your troubles, and yet, here you are."

There was no denying Lozen spoke the truth. Sadyra thought about their trip up the Madrigail River. "I haven't found a place to go. *Yet*." She looked back at the sleepy hamlet. "Before I realized how small Songsbirth was, I thought I might start a new life here." She shrugged. "I guess I'll have to look elsewhere."

Lozen nodded, respectfully allowing her to express her feelings. When she said no more, Lozen continued, "You're looking in the wrong places. You'll never find the refuge you seek in Songsbirth. Or Carillon. Or Millsford. What you seek cannot be found in any of these places." She paused, compassion in her eyes. "There's only one place in all the world that the answers you desperately seek can be found."

Sadyra considered Lozen's statement. Her face transformed into wonder. She nodded. Lozen knew it too. "Of course. Fishmonger Bay..." She trailed off. Lozen was shaking her head.

Pollard

Lozen replaced her hand above Sadyra's left breast. "The place you seek lies here. Only your heart can determine your course. If you refuse to acknowledge what it's telling you, you'll be forever lost."

Before Sadyra could respond, they turned at the sound of gravel crunching underfoot.

Larina strode toward them, squinting in the darkness as if to see them better framed against the moon's reflection. "Sadie? Is that you." She walked up to them, a genuine look of relief softening her face as her gaze flicked between Sadyra and Lozen and back again. "Thank the gods. I was so worried about you."

Goosebumps riddled Sadyra's skin. She placed her hand on the spot Lozen's had vacated. Her heart was swelling; trying to push through the fabric of her tunic.

Tears of happiness ran down her cheeks. She didn't care. Holding out her arms, she accepted their embrace; burying her head on their shoulders and holding them tight.

Surrounded by the genuine love of two people she hadn't met until recently, a random thought sent tingles along her skin. Home wasn't a place at all. It was wherever her heart longed to be.

Pollard

Commencement Day

True to his word, Pollard's bellow created pandemonium within the *Lullaby Inn*. A loud rap shook the room door.

Larina had no idea what time it was, but judging by the chill in the room and lack of discernable light, dawn hadn't broken over the hamlet.

Sadyra grunted between her and the wall—her long hair splayed across the top of the bed they shared. She had had a rough night, but in the end, Larina thought her new friend had exorcised the burden that had been weighing her down for as long as she had known her.

On the way back to the *Lullaby Inn* last night, Sadyra had informed Lozen that neither she nor Pollard need worry any longer where her focus lay—promising Lozen that the Songsbirthian Guard had better brace themselves for the dervish they had allowed into the midst.

A warm smile crept across Larina's face; recalling her last words to Lozen before they had parted ways for the night. "The big oaf better prepare himself for the tempest that is about to take over his training regimen. I doubt he's equipped to handle the Storms End Lightning Bolt *and* the Fishmonger Bay tiger. He'd be well advised to watch his step."

As soon as she had spoken the words to Lozen, she feared she had overstepped her boundaries with Pollard's confidant, but the sparkle in Lozen's eyes and subtle nod as she turned to leave them at the base of the steps fronting the inn had filled Larina with the confidence that she and Sadyra were ready for the challenge ahead.

"Sadie." Larina shook Sadyra's shoulder. Lightly at first and then harder. "Hey. Sadyra. Wake up. It's time to go."

Sadyra opened her eyes, squinting in the flickering candlelight; freckled cheeks twisted in a frown. She searched the gloom, her gaze coming to rest on the outside window. "It's not even daylight."

Larina put the candle holder on the edge of the kneeler and splashed cold water over her face—wiping her wet skin on her sleeves. "Ya, well, blow hard is in the hallway demanding our presence. I say we surprise him and be the first to answer his summons."

Sadyra shot her an, 'are you crazy,' look, and rolled over to face the wall.

"Suit yourself." Sitting on the end of the bed, Larina slipped her boots over her bare feet and laced them up. She patted Sadyra's feet. "Remember your resolve last night? Today's the first day of the rest of your life. Let's make it memorable."

By the time Larina had buckled her utility belt beneath her black tunic, Sadyra sat on the edge of the bed rubbing at her eyes and mumbling. "If he thinks we're getting up this early everyday, he's in for a rude awakening."

Larina waited with her hand on the door lever.

Sadyra didn't take long to get ready. Sleeping in her clothes, she hadn't bothered to remove her boots. She took great pains to delay getting to her feet—stretching vocally through a drawn-out yawn.

Cold air assaulted them from the dimly lit corridor. The weary face of Onynx regarded them from across the hall. They weren't the first to answer Master Banebridge's call to action.

Larina nodded at the gangly woman—Onynx's pale skin making her appear as an apparition.

Pollard

Movement at the far end of the hallway caught Larina's attention. Pollard's unmistakable bulk loomed over several women; along with Lozen's black hair shimmering in the sconce light. Where the female warrior had spent the night was a mystery. Larina absently mused that perhaps she shared a bed with Pollard. She raised her eyebrows. She could hardly blame her if she did.

Sadyra pushed into the hallway, not bothering to greet Onynx or her roommate, Klara, her heavy-lidded eyes barely open.

Larina nudged Sadyra with her elbow. "Look smart. Here he comes."

If not for the granite floor, Larina was certain the hallway would have shaken under Pollard's feet as the goliath stomped past them and ducked beneath the archway to ascend the ramp to the third floor.

Lozen stopped at the top of the stairwell leading to the lobby. She smiled at the bleary faces confronting her as the female recruits stumbled into the hall and shuffled toward the steps. Her gaze lingered on Sadyra and Larina. "You two get any sleep?"

"Some," Larina mumbled and indicated Sadyra with a flick of her eyes. "I think she's still asleep."

The unmistakable roar of Pollard's voice could be heard coming from the floor above.

"Not to worry. By the time Master Banebridge has his way with you, you'll be wide awake." Lozen started down the steps. "Follow me. We'll wait outside."

Sadyra blinked at Lozen. "What about food?"

"You haven't eaten yet?" Lozen shrugged. Without another word, she descended the stairwell.

Larina rolled her eyes and fell in beside Onynx. "Gonna be one of those days."

If the pale-skinned woman knew the comment was directed her way, she never let on.

Pollard

Her boots scraping along behind them, Sadyra said, "Great."

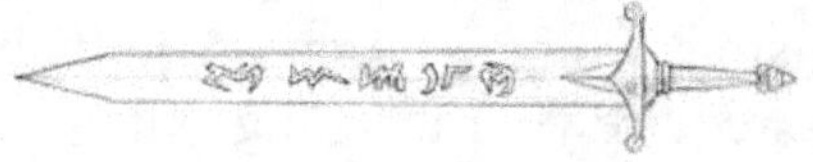

Pollard shoved the lead boat into the lake. With practiced ease, he grabbed the outwale and jumped into the craft as it slipped away from the shore—the resulting spray from his boots not endearing him to those in his boat. Nobody dared complain.

He squeezed between Sadyra and Larina; his bulk squishing them against Klara and Mikter into the sides of the dory. A nod to Quincette at the oars and they were away—lurching with each oar stroke into the first vestiges of light that filtered through the pervasive shadows clinging to Madrigail Lake.

The occupants of three other boats struggled to drag their craft into the water and keep pace—all four boats heading to the Splendoor Catacombs laden with sacks stuffed with supplies.

"What a bonnie day," Pollard said to no one in particular. "A shame we'll be running the maze."

Quincette caught his eye, a slight smirk giving life to her usual dour expression.

It wasn't until the boats had been secured to the platform at the brink of Splendoor Falls that sunshine shone through a break between two mountain peaks on the eastern horizon—brilliant rays providing the shivering company some appreciated warmth.

Lozen opened the hatchway in the middle of the platform and assisted the recruits onto the ladder with their burden. Each of them was required to carry one of the unwieldy sacks—provisions for the men and women living within the catacombs.

Pollard

Pollard didn't bother descending the ladder to help them in case they slipped. Instead, he spoke with Quincette. Grasping her by the wrist in a modified handshake, he addressed the stoic woman. "Thank you, Quince. I'll send word when we require your teaching skills. Oh, by the way, I asked Master Pul to have you along on the final trial. You know. In case things don't go well."

Quincette merely nodded, turned, and motioned for the rowers who had propelled Pollard's crew across the lake to shove off. She settled into the last boat and accepted the rope from Pollard. Her green eyes met his as she positioned the bow to the east. Thick shoulders undulating with the precise cut of her oars, her dory resisted the pull of the falls.

He smiled for her benefit and turned away, rueful about how life might had been if only…

He shook it from his mind. He was responsible for molding two dozen fresh recruits into shape. If they were to be even remotely ready to march south for their final test, he had a lot of work ahead of him before the first snow flew. Once winter gripped the Muse, they would find themselves stranded until spring.

One thing he knew for sure. Commencement day would be long remembered by everyone taking part. Training to become a contributing member of Zephyr's elite garrison didn't allow for slackers.

Pollard

Attrition

The great cavern containing the Well of Despair was both a welcome sight for Sadyra's beleaguered body and one of raw remembrance. Not allowing herself to give in to the aching fatigue in her arms, shoulders, and lower back, she waited for the remainder of the recruits to enter the cavern; her sack clutched firmly in her arms. She feared that if she put her burden down, she'd never be able to pick it up again.

A tunnel lay exposed beyond the breach in the far wall. Whoever was down here had expected them. Sadyra looked to the roof, but the stalactites were lost in shadow. If there were archers stationed in the heights, she couldn't tell.

Larina slumped against the wall beside her, abandoned sack at her feet—her freckled complexion a sheen of perspiration, dripping continuously from the tip of her nose to a growing stain on the floor between her boots.

Pollard bustled into the cavern, his daunting presence urging those entering before him to pick up their pace. He carried two of the larger sacks in his arms and a third hung from a tether draped over the hilt of the sword protruding over his shoulder. If the extra burden bothered him, it didn't show on his face.

He cast a quick glance around, his attention finding Lozen. "How many did we lose?"

"Three."

His eyebrows lifted. "See them out."

Lozen nodded, leaned her sack against the cave wall, and disappeared back up the tunnel.

Pollard

Four men attired in the slate-grey uniforms of the Songsbirthian Guard strode across the cavern from the breach in the wall. They relieved Pollard of his burden and grabbed Lozen's, each man nodding as they met Pollard's gaze. "Master Banebridge."

"The rest of you…" Pollard scanned the faces of his trainees. "Congratulations. You survived the first test. If you'll kindly follow last year's successful recruits, they'll direct you to the storeroom. Meet me back here when you're done."

Larina groaned as she hoisted her sack off the ground and staggered along with everyone else across the cavern floor, muttering, "Oh sure. He has someone carry his the rest of the way."

Sadyra shot her a disapproving look—her eyes flicking to Pollard. Thankfully, he didn't appear to be listening.

"Are you crazy?" Sadyra whispered harshly as they made their way around the darker section of floor surrounding the central well, making sure to avoid the damp algae clinging to the rock.

She searched the faces of the remaining recruits, trying to figure out who hadn't made it to the cavern. As far as she could tell, it was no one that she had really met yet. To reinforce her shock at Larina's words, she added, "He just kicked three people out."

Larina glared but said nothing more.

By the time they reached a large chamber chiselled into the tunnel wall, Sadyra swore her arms had stretched to her knees. Stepping inside the room, she immediately noticed a difference in air temperature. The tunnels were cool, but the storage room was cold. She scanned for blocks of ice, absently wondering which poor soul was charged with climbing the mountain heights to harvest it. Rubbing at the goosebumps on her arms, she exited the room and moved out of the way.

The short, pleasant looking man Pollard had introduced to them to when they had first entered the water trap cavern oversaw the provisioning from the passageway. He smiled at Sadyra. "Cold in there, huh?"

Sadyra swallowed, trying hard to recall his name. Pollard had said he was second in command of the Songsbirthian Guard. A man Pollard had pointedly claimed that he wouldn't want to cross. Looking at the blonde-haired man, she would never have thought he was anything but kind. "Yes, sir."

Larina joined her, rubbing at her arms and stretching her back. "I'm glad that's over with."

Sadyra nodded and leaned in to whisper, "What's his name again?"

Larina leaned out and met Guardell's gaze. "You mean him?"

Sadyra scowled, keeping her head turned away from Guardell to hide her flushed cheeks.

"That's Master Guardell Caulder," Larina said and nodded to the man.

Guardell's face lit up. "Aren't you the two who were caught in the water trap?"

Sadyra rolled her eyes at Larina and met Guardell's smirk with a forced smile.

"That part of the tour never fails to amuse me," Guardell said. "I must say, I was surprised when I saw you two. It's usually a headstrong male who Pollard makes an example of."

An example of, huh? Sadyra stewed but kept her thoughts to herself.

Guardell changed the subject, his attention on the recruits filing out of the storage room—each one noticeably feeling the effects of the cold. "Quite ingenious, that chamber. One of the many masterful engineering feats the dwarfs of Sarsen Rest incorporated when they built this place."

"How's it work?" Larina asked, stepping around Sadyra to stand before Guardell, flicking her hair from her face.

Guardell shrugged. "Beats me. Someone tried to explain it once. Something about convection vents or some tripe like that."

Convection vents meant nothing to Sadyra, but standing there, she wondered about Larina's intentions with regard to Guardell. An odd emotion gripped her. Jealousy? She shook her head to rid herself of the ridiculous notion. Watching Larina carry on, smiling and batting her eyelashes, intensified the foreign emotion. Straightening to her full height, conscious she was shorter than her friend, Sadyra pulled back her shoulders and rounded on Guardell. "Master Banebridge said the four guardsmen who led us here were recruits from last year? How many do you keep on every year?"

Guardell raised his eyebrows and pursed his lips in thought. "It varies. They're the only ones who made the grade last year." He shrugged. "Sometimes half a dozen. Sometimes none."

Sadyra imagined she mirrored Larina's stare. "None? Out of how many?"

"Usually a couple dozen. That seems to be the number Pollard and his crew like to start with."

Sadyra exchanged glances with Larina before frowning at Guardell. "And who makes the final decision?"

Guardell held his palms up. "Why, Pollard, of course. Though I'm sure that he's listened to Lozen over the past couple of years. In the end, however, he's the one who decides your fate."

The last of the trainees exited the storage room. One of last year's recruits did something to the tunnel wall and a granite slab rumbled into the recess to seal off the room.

Pollard

Sadyra inspected the wall where the doorway had just been. No matter how hard she looked, she couldn't determine its edges.

Guardell stepped into the middle of the corridor, poised to address the faces watching him. He leaned toward Sadyra. "The dwarfs sure know their craft."

Sadyra nodded, impressed.

"We'll leave you now. Master Banebridge will be waiting by the Well of Despair." Seeing the confusion on the faces regarding him, he tipped his head the way they had just come. "I don't suggest you keep him waiting."

Arriving back at the Well of Despair, Sadyra was surprised to see Lozen speaking with Pollard. She must have handed off the three ousted recruits to someone else.

Pollard waited until the twenty-one people vying for a position with the Guard stood around him. "Again, congratulations. That first trek has been known to weed out far more than it did today." Pollard put a meaty hand on Lozen's shoulder. "From this point forward, we will be splitting you into two groups. Half will go with Lozen, and the other half will come with me."

Sadyra subconsciously stepped closer to Larina.

"Though I shouldn't have to, I will only warn you once. You've been hand-picked from a larger number of prospects that were recommended to us to earn the right to safeguard one of Zephyr's most precious commodities. Do *not* let this opportunity go to waste. You won't get a second chance. At least, not as long as I draw breath. The gods willing, being half-giant, I'll outlive everyone in this cavern.

"Lozen, here, is the best archer I've ever had the pleasure of knowing, *and*, her tracking skills are second to none. Not even King Malcolm is privy to anyone of her skillset, so please listen when she speaks. I daresay she knows more about nature than anyone in the kingdom."

Lozen folded her arms and gave him a dubious look.

"Well, anyone outside of the Altirius Mountain tribes."

According to the stories Larina had told Sadyra over the last few days about her dealings with Lozen, Pollard's estimation of Lozen's abilities were accurate. Sadyra's own archery skills had improved tenfold under the tutelage of Gitch's crew back in Fishmonger Bay. She couldn't wait to pit them against Lozen.

Pollard stepped away from the wall. "Remember your number." Starting with Sadyra, and then Larina, he pointed to each recruit in turn. "One, two. One, two. One, two…"

As the significance dawned on her, Sadyra wanted to protest but Pollard's tone left no room for negotiation.

"Twos with Lozen. Ones, follow me." He strode across the cavern without looking back. "Don't become the next victim of attrition."

Sadyra didn't move. She searched Larina's face. Larina indicated with a nod for her to follow the other ten trainees scrambling to keep pace with Pollard's long strides.

Two layers below the Well of Despair, the tunnel Lozen led them down opened to the brilliance of the outside world. A ledge, just wide enough for everyone to stand side-by-side, jutted out from the cliff face several hundred feet above the forest floor. Judging by the faint mist clinging to the treetops, Larina estimated them to be halfway between the ground entrance and the base of Splendoor Falls.

Mikter squeezed in next to her, his cold hands gripping Larina's elbow.

Larina glanced at his hands and then at his face. She was about to let him know how she felt about anyone touching her, but the terror in his eyes stopped her. His whole body trembled as he craned his neck to see out.

"Afraid of heights?"

He caught her stare and nodded.

She bit back the words that came to mind. *Why are you here then? How do you expect to become a Songsbirthian Guard if you're afraid of the very essence of your prospective workplace?* Instead, for some inexplicable reason, empathy filled her. Nearly as strong as the compassion she had expressed for Allard and the oppressed citizens of Storms End. Here was a young man, presumably following his dreams, only to realize that everything he desired was about to be dashed by an inherent fear of something he had no control over.

Looking to make sure Lozen wasn't watching, she turned sideways and gripped his upper arm with both hands and whispered, "It's okay. I got you."

He stared into her eyes, his head shaking quickly, but to his credit, one of his feet scraped forward half a length.

He gripped her arm so tightly, it was all she could do not to cry out. Gritting her teeth, she encouraged him, "See? You can do it."

He swallowed, almost hanging from her arm. His wide, brown eyes darted to the wondrous vista, and bulged with fright. Burying his face against her arm, he shook his head profusely and tugged, urging her to step back.

Mortified, Larina realized everyone on the rock shelf was looking their way. Even Lozen. With the greatest of care, she eased Mikter into the tunnel and prized his fingers from her arm; deferring to Lozen who had come up beside them.

"Mikter Wainwright, correct?"

Mikter nodded, barely meeting Lozen's hard gaze.

"Come with me."

The fear in Mikter's eyes returned, but this time, Larina knew it wasn't his fear of heights.

$\mathfrak{Pollard}$

"The rest of you remain here until I come back," Lozen said. Motioning for Mikter to precede her into the tunnel, they were soon lost to sight.

The sun had discernably moved across the sky by the time Lozen returned; a leather vambrace on her right forearm, a torch in her left hand. Though nobody said anything, the shock was clear on everyone's face. Lozen was alone.

For no reason that made sense, Larina felt like she'd been kicked in the stomach. She didn't know Mikter any more than the other recruits, but her brief interaction with him had left its mark. She started to doubt her own merits at her inclusion in the selection process. An old man, whom she had stolen from, had recommended her to Pollard. Perhaps as a penance for almost spiralling Zephyr into a maelstrom Thoril Half-Hand had claimed Zephyr would never survive.

She shook her head to clear the negative thoughts. According to Pollard, Thoril had had his eye on her for a long time; long before she ever met the man with the black warhammer. She was sure Allard must have had something to do with that.

Another thought took root as Lozen suspended her burning torch in an iron bracket and walked to the edge of the ledge and emitted a shrill whistle. If what Thoril and Pul intimated had any basis in fact, the theft of the Crusher Scroll wouldn't have made a difference. The scroll had been returned to Banebridge Manor and yet both men were still adamant about the imminent threat Zephyr faced in the not too distant future.

A flutter of wings snapped her attention to the ledge. Naiche dropped out of the sky, wings wide as he gracefully glided into view and landed on Lozen's upraised forearm. A leather hood appeared in Lozen's left hand. She deftly placed it over Naiche's head. "For those of you who haven't met him, this is Naiche. He's my friend, but more importantly, he's my eyes and ears when I venture into the world."

Klara stepped closer and held out her hand. "May I pat him?"

Larina had only ever seen darkness cross Lozen's face once—when she had feigned her assistance with the female captain of the Storms End Watch to help keep Larina under control after the assassination of the baron and that scumbag, Captain Danth Emerald. Until now.

Klara pulled her hand back.

"Naiche is not a pet. He's my spirit companion. I respect him more than any other. I trust Naiche with my life."

Klara swallowed and dropped an embarrassed gaze to the ground.

Larina expected Lozen's demeanour to soften but the warrior woman's icy glare spoke otherwise.

"As I mentioned to a few of you on our journey here, if you wish to survive in the circles you desire to enter, you must find your spirit companion. They come in many shapes and sizes. Some can carry a conversation." Her hard features softened as she regarded Naiche. "Some, not so much. But, whoever, or whatever, is destined to be your spirit companion, only you will know."

Lozen turned on the ledge and removed Naiche's hood. She spoke something no one could hear, and held up her arm. Naiche regarded her for a moment. Blinking twice, he launched into the air and was soon lost to sight.

"Unfortunately, most of you will never know such a bond. Of those that are given the opportunity, few possess the presence of mind to embrace it." Lozen's gaze sought out Larina. "For those lucky enough to find your spirit companion, don't ever forsake that bond. Even separated, your fates are bound together. It's incumbent upon you to be each other's light in the darkness."

Pollard

Lozen dropped Larina's gaze and strode boldly up the tunnel; snatching her torch from the iron ring hammered into the wall.

Without needing to be told, the gaping recruits hustled after her.

Pollard

Inner Strength

Onynx made a point of keeping Sadyra close. Other than Klara and Nyler, the pale-skinned woman didn't seem like she had formed a relationship with any of the recruits. The awkward way she carried herself and her shy demeanour certainly prevented her from making inroads with the others.

Their group traversed leagues of tunnels; dropping through hidden hatchways and stepping through breaches exposed in the tunnel walls. The going had been slow at first. Pollard insisted the trainees find the concealed doorways themselves.

After a short break to eat what Sadyra assumed was a midday meal, a few of the more astute recruits found it increasingly easier to locate the latches used to spring the secret doorways.

Onynx proved she was the most capable of the group. Unfortunately, the praise Pollard heaped upon her further distanced her from her peers.

Sadyra, on the other hand, was glad *someone* was able to locate them—fearing their trainer's disposition might have soured as the day went on if no one showed that they had been paying attention. She made a point to remind herself later to get Onynx to show her.

Though Pollard claimed they had traversed through the cave system up to the top level, they had done so by following a totally different route than before. Whenever they found a doorway, he allowed them to choose whether or not to go through it. If they chose to, which they almost always did, he would point them in the direction he wished them to travel.

Sadyra knew there was no way the path they followed was the most efficient means to reach the large, sconce lit, rectangular cavern they stood within. Its scraped roof and smooth walls left no illusion that it was a natural cave.

The torch bearers snuffed their brands and deposited them in the appropriate basket; fanning out to gawk at what the chamber contained. Weapons of all descriptions stood in racks or sat upon stone ledges carved into the walls. The roughly hewn, wide floor was discoloured in many places—the dark stains looking very much like…

"Put your rucksacks against the wall and familiarize yourself with the gear in this room. This is the weapons training arena. Here you'll not only learn how to defend yourself, but also how to attack your opponent. You'll work with many different instructors. Some adept at parrying, ducking, and the art of the feint." Pollard reached over his shoulder and slid his double sword blade clear of its baldric—his corded muscles flexing as he brought the savage-looking blade to bear. "I, on the other hand, am all about finishing. A dead man won't fight back."

"Or woman," Sadyra mumbled unable to stop herself. As soon as the words escaped her, she regretted them.

"I'm sorry, Sadyra?" Pollard asked, plainly irked. "You have something you wish to say?"

She was tired of him ragging on her. Ever since they had left the decks of the *S'gull*, his attitude toward her had taken a turn. She wasn't sure what she had done to deserve his scrutiny, but her long temper had its limits.

That's what scared her. She tended to approach life with a lackadaisical attitude; a trait she had learned at an early age to help offset the hurt of her parent's demeanour toward her. She preferred to make light of the things happening around her rather than get bent out of shape over things she couldn't control. Even so, when pushed, the resulting aftermath of her reactions usually left few bridges unscathed. Pollard's persistence to question everything she did threatened to thrust her past that point of no return.

It took everything she had to say calmly, "You said a dead man won't fight back. I just wanted to add, neither will a dead woman."

Pollard held her stare, his expression unreadable. Finally, he looked away to address the group. "Weapons come in many different sizes and weights. In the proper hands, a mace is as good as a warhammer; a dagger as effective as a halberd. Only you can decide which weapon suits your fighting style. Personally, I can crush stone with a hammer and disarm experienced fighters with my bare hands. Yet, my weapon of choice is this sword. I've learned to utilize its unique double blade to trap opponent's weapons and disarm them. Once disarmed, the fight's usually over."

His words resonated with arrogance, but he spoke them matter-of-factly. Never having seen him engage in combat, Sadyra was fairly certain he was capable of backing up his boasts.

"I'm a half-giant by birth. That has endowed me with a large body. Even so, I pride myself in the fact that my real strength comes from within. Without total dedication to improving my agility and muscle mass, I'd be nothing but a large man."

He deftly sheathed his sword, demonstrating in that simple act more flexibility than Sadyra thought possible for a person with arms as big as his.

Reaching behind his back, Pollard undid the clasps holding the baldric to a shoulder strap that was hidden beneath his brass cuirass. He held the black leather baldric in front of him, nodding for Onynx to take it.

She regarded him with wide eyes. At his nod, she reached out to take it from him. As soon as it was in her hands, she promptly fell to the ground in a heap of gangly arms and legs; desperately trying to keep the massive weapon from hitting the ground. Miserably unsuccessful, the tang clanged off the ground and reverberated throughout the chamber.

With horror in her eyes, she looked up at Pollard. "I-I'm s-sorry, Master Banebridge."

Pollard's reaction shocked everyone. A bellowing laugh escaped his throat. He looked at each recruit in turn. "Anyone man enough," his gaze fell on Sadyra, "or woman enough to pick it up may do so."

He held out a hand for Onynx and hoisted her to her feet.

As everyone took a turn lifting the beast of a sword, Pollard strolled between them. "That's precisely why not every weapon is meant for you. Onynx, for example, would only hurt herself if she tried to wield a weapon of that size. Its weight gives the bearer a definite advantage over a lighter sword should the two engage, but if the weapon's weight deprives the bearer of the agility to use it quickly, a smaller adversary who is trained properly can dance around the larger weapon and attack with a faster, more effective strike."

He walked to a series of weapon racks and pulled a narrow-bladed scimitar and a rapier from their respective stands. The blades appeared as child's toys in his hands. "If swords are Onynx's weapon of choice, her thin body and lean muscles would likely suit blades of this type. Though light in weight, they're deadly in the right hands.

"And that," he raised his heavy brow, "is a good point to learn here and now, rather than after it's too late. Do *not* judge your opponent by the size of their weapon. I mentioned before how I'd hate to cross Guardell Caulder. I didn't say that to kiss his arse. I meant it. If you ever have the opportunity to lock weapons with the man, you'll know what I'm talking about. His mastery of using a dagger and short sword in combination is a wonder to behold. Unless you're his opponent, that is."

Sadyra inwardly chuckled at Pollard's broad smile—his attempt at humour falling on deaf ears. She suspected no one was brave enough to openly react for fear of offending him if they had misjudged his intent.

Pollard cleared his throat. "Whatever you decide is your weapon of choice, don't be put off if you fail miserably when we train with the ones that aren't in your comfort zone. For the record, I'm horrible with bows and crossbows. I'd be lucky to hit the ground." He paused to allow for a reaction.

Sadyra and two others snickered, but that was it.

"Anyway. Lozen's skill with ranged weapons is unrivalled. If that happens to be your preferred weapon, you'll have ample opportunity to learn from her.

"For today, I want you to check out the wide assortment of weapons we have at our disposal. You'll be hard-pressed not to find a weapon that suits you. Previous Splendoor Catacombs weapons masters prided themselves in obtaining every available weapon known so you'll likely find some that are unique."

He paused to allow the recruits to gape at the wondrous armaments. "Songsbirth and this complex were built by dwarfs. At one time in history this area was renowned for the elves and dragons that frequented it on their journeys between South March and the Kraidic Empire." He nodded at Onynx. "Aye. Better known as the Great Kingdom back then."

"Actually," Onynx said with a haughty tone, "the Great Kingdom wasn't formed until after the end of the Windwalker reign."

Pollard's beaming smile dropped. "What's that?"

Onynx swallowed, but her voice rose in volume as she asserted her knowledge. "The formation of the Great Kingdom came about as a direct result of the banishment of the last of the Windwalker line. A period known as the Great Upheaval. The dwindling line of Windwalkers and their dragons were exiled from the realm of man."

Pollard's smile appeared forced. "Yes. Of course." He dropped Onynx's gaze and cleared his throat. "Anyway. The weapon styles contained in this room date back centuries. Most of them reconstructed by the master smiths of Songsbirth, but if you look hard, you might find the odd, original weapon that has withstood the annals of time."

Pollard's roaming gaze fell on Sadyra. "Since we have an odd number, I'll be one of your sparring partners today. Choose a weapon, and pair off. Don't worry about with who. By the time you're begging me to stop for the day, you'll have been everyone's partner at least once."

Everyone looked at each other, not sure what to do. Sadyra raised her eyebrows at Onynx and started across the chamber to a shelf carved into the far wall—the surface of the ledge draped in a dun-coloured cloth and bearing a wide assortment of daggers. Long ones, curved ones, serrated ones, thick bladed ones, and spike-like ones. Some were heavy in Sadyra's hand while others were fused on thick handles. Many bore wide cross guards while others had virtually no guards at all. There was even a set of six blades; each one not much thicker than a couple of sheets of parchment—their composition one continuous cast of shining steel.

Sadyra picked one up, cognizant of its razor-sharp edges. Holding it by its opposite end, she held it out to Onynx. "Be tough to defend yourself with these."

Onynx's eyes grew wide as a shadow fell over them.

"Throwing knives. Nasty." Pollard's deep voice noticeably made Sadyra jump. "Deadly in the right hands. Cut you down before you know you've been attacked. Assassins blades if you ask me."

Sadyra hadn't noticed the brute come up behind them, so engrossed with her inspection of the astounding variety of daggers in front of her. She spun with the throwing knife in her hand.

"Easy. Those edges are honed to cut through tough leather. So sharp that you won't know you're cut until you see your blood pooling on the ground." He nodded at the blade. "Is that something that interests you?"

"This? No." Sadyra carefully put the knife back and withdrew her own from a worn sheath on her belt—a filleting knife; its hooked end thinned unevenly from years of being sharpened by a hand millstone. "I'm not much of a sword woman, though I'm not afraid to use my knife."

Pollard's smile surprised her.

"Aye. I saw."

Sadyra grinned at his reference to the time she had dispatched one of Ivar the Blade's crew in the Thunderhead market. She looked over her shoulder at the unstrung bow poking above her shoulder. "I prefer the bow."

Pollard held out his hand.

She spun her knife around and handed it to him, worn, wooden handle first.

He closed thick fingers around it and inspected the thin blade. "Hmmm. Can't say I'd want to be shanked by this. Looks as sharp as the throwing knives." He nodded at the assassin blades. "Probably cut through small bone."

"Ya. Pretty much," she said as a bittersweet memory made her shiver. Her father had always insisted that she take care of her equipment. It was the only good thing he had ever done for her.

She accepted her knife back and slid it into its sheath. Feeling uncomfortable in Pollard's presence, she looked at Onynx. "Anything interest you here?"

Onynx shook her head.

Together, they left Pollard at the knife display and moved on to inspect an assortment of maces.

Though the afternoon hadn't turned out as bad as Pollard had made it sound, by the time he called a halt to the recruits'

initial sparring session, Sadyra doubted anyone in the chamber had much energy left. Without air flow, the training room stank of perspiration.

Pollard stood at the entrance. "Remember to care for the weapons as if your life depends on them." He raised his heavy brow twice in quick succession. "Someday, it just might." With that said, he turned and disappeared into the tunnel.

Wiping their weapons with rags found by each rack, Rync, the burly young man Sadyra had last sparred with, urged her to look up from what she was doing and pay attention to the pale-skinned woman.

Onynx stood at the entrance, her face more ashen than usual. "He's gone."

Sadyra frowned at Rync.

He shrugged.

It didn't take long for Onynx's statement to register with everyone in the chamber. Pollard had left them.

The recruits abandoned what they were doing and crammed into the tunnel; staring dumbfounded at each other.

Sadyra shook her head, not surprised by the turn of events. "I guess the big oaf expects us to find our own way back. Anyone remember the way?"

Blank stares met her query.

She sighed. "Well, it's going to be a long night then."

Onynx's meek voice silenced the disbelieving chatter. "I think I do."

A smirk lifted the side of Sadyra's mouth. She had expected as much. If the gangly woman proved true to her word, it would go a long way to elevating her standing with her peers. "Lead on."

Though it took them a good deal of time to find their way back to the Well of Despair and the rooms beyond, Onynx had proven she was by far the most adept at navigating the elaborate tunnel system. The way she picked out the nuances in the rock that told her where to search for hidden door trips was uncanny.

Four days of wandering the intricate byways had done little to enlighten Sadyra about the secrets of locating the doorways. Even with Onynx's guidance, Sadyra didn't think she could find her way if left to her own devices.

Pollard's trainees seated themselves around several stone tables in the catacombs mess hall—a natural cavern whose non-existent roof disappeared into the darkness of a cleft that continuously dripped water into troughs chiselled into the floor. Runnels of water channelled through a crevice at the back of the chamber. The four recruits from last year's class entered the mess hall through a gap in the side wall, their arms laden with food trays.

Sadyra couldn't help thinking, *Great. If I'm successful in becoming a member of the Guard, I get to look forward to being someone's servant next year.*

She accepted the chipped, wooden platter proffered by the most muscular male in the room, and waited as the young man slopped a steaming ladle of chunky stew onto it.

The dark-skinned man moved to serve Onynx, beside her.

"What? No utensils?" Sadyra searched the table and the tray the man held deftly in one hand.

The man shook his head. "Sorry. You should be carrying your own." He scooped a hearty portion onto Onynx's plate and said as he moved to the next person down the table, "You're lucky we're providing you with a platter."

Sadyra stared after him. "Ya. Real lucky."

"There you are." A whirlwind of black clothing and long, black hair rushed up behind Sadyra. "You just getting back now?"

Sadyra forced a smile and nodded for Larina's sake.

Larina draped an arm over Sadyra's shoulder and knelt between her and Onynx. "So. How'd it go?"

"Alright, I guess. I haven't been kicked out yet."

Larina laughed. "That reminds me. You know who did get kicked out?"

Sadyra shook her head.

"The arrogant one."

Sadyra frowned, and then it dawned her who Larina was talking about. "Really?"

"Ya. He was one of the ones who couldn't keep up yesterday morning."

"I bet that went over well."

The grin on Larina's face fell. "You know who else got kicked out?"

Sadyra shook her head, her filleting knife in hand as she tried to figure out the best way to use it on the stew. "No, who?"

"Mikter."

Sadyra's knife paused overtop of her platter. "Mikter? The shorter guy, right? What'd he do?"

"Lozen took us to the end of a tunnel overlooking the land and he seized up. Apparently, Mikter is afraid of heights. Lozen saw him cling to me for dear life. The next thing I knew, she was escorting him away."

"Wow. They don't fool around." Sadyra stabbed at a piece of meat and put it in her mouth; wondering all the while how she was going to scoop up the more liquid part of her meal. Talking around her food, she added, "Shame about Mikter. He seemed okay. I guess you'd better watch your smart comments."

Sadyra stabbed at another chunk and stuck the end of her knife in her mouth. She was surprised Larina hadn't reacted to her comment. Her gaze caught Larina's puzzled expression—her friend staring at something behind them. Turning on the bench, Sadyra located what had drawn her attention. "Isn't *that* Mikter?"

Larina nodded and rose, her eyes following Mikter's progress to an empty seat at another table.

Pollard

Lozen stepped into the doorway. She locked eyes with Larina and motioned for her to follow. Without waiting, Lozen disappeared from view.

"Uh oh," Sadyra said around a mouthful. "Perhaps she's changed her mind and decided to toss you instead."

Larina gave her a scathing glare. Jutting out her chin, she stormed across the room, not looking back.

Sadyra swallowed what was in her mouth, her eyes following Larina from the mess hall. "What? I'm kidding!"

Lozen walked to where the trigger latch in the wall of the Well of Despair was located. The wall rumbled as it parted; opening just enough to permit them to walk into the dark cavern.

"Grab a torch," Lozen ordered and stepped into the darkness.

Larina took a torch from a bucket and lit it with the help of a wall sconce.

The air in the cavern was considerably cooler than that of the living area of the Splendoor Catacombs Guard. Oppressive darkness muted the reach of the single torch and it took Larina a moment to realize Lozen had continued walking toward the centre of the cavern where the cylindrical dais supporting the well had been carved out of the natural rock.

A vision of her original foray into the cavern with Sadyra gave her pause. Not wanting her instructor to have to navigate the slippery floor in the dark, she swallowed her apprehension and scrambled after her.

The sloping floor, slick with muck, dampened the bottom of Larina's soft-soled boots, but she wasn't about to complain. Lozen's boots were similar to her own.

Pollard

The light of the torch cast Lozen in an eerie glow as the woman turned and waited for her at the dais wall. Fresh footprints around where Lozen stood told Larina others had been here recently. She looked around, expecting to see who but Lozen's soft voice snapped her attention back to the warrior.

"You continue to surprise me, Larina from Storms End."

That caught Larina off guard. She had prepared to verbally defend herself against Lozen's perceived accusations. "I'm sorry?"

"Because of your actions and your cocky nature, you have come to the attention of both Pollard and myself."

Larina swallowed at the ominous portent; unsure whether Lozen's proclamation boded well or not. Many questions came to mind but Lozen's next words stilled them.

"Many people pretend to be leaders. They boss people around and make boastful assertions. They strut about like they know everything. We removed one of these people this morning."

Larina thought of the arrogant recruit she had told Sadyra about.

"When we first entered the catacombs from the river valley, it wasn't lost upon us that you were the one who gave the order to start looking for the secret door. You organized your peers into pairs and told them where to start looking. Do you remember doing that?"

Larina thought hard; vaguely recalling saying something to that effect. She hadn't meant to be bossy. She just wanted to get everyone moving so that they could get on with whatever Pollard had in store. She didn't think she was doing anything wrong. "I think so."

"Well, you did. And then, when we first entered this very cavern, you were ordered to accompany Sadyra as she tried to ascend the well."

Larina gaped. That wasn't her fault. She wanted to explain to Lozen that she had no choice in the matter—that it was all

Sadyra's fault, but decided it best not to. Instead, she sighed and let her shoulders slump. It would be good to see Bear again. Who needed these people anyway?

"I saw what you did for Mikter today."

Larina frowned. She hadn't done anything, really.

"The young man was terrified. Not a good trait to have if you wish to become a Songsbirthian Guard," Lozen said quietly.

"I didn't know what else to do. He was in distress."

Lozen nodded, a small smile lifting her pudgy cheeks. "He was indeed, but it was the way you helped him without judgement that caught my eye. You held him up and gave him the strength to confront his fear."

Fat lot of good that did him. He almost wet himself. Larina kept that thought to herself.

"I was of two minds on how to handle the situation, and that left me reeling myself. One of the strongest ideals we try to instill within our members is to have the confidence and belief to act swiftly and concisely. To hesitate is a good way to find oneself dead." Lozen's voice rose with conviction. "My first thought was to have him escorted out, but as I led him away, your actions served to remind me of someone I knew long ago. A wise old woman in fact. High in the Altirius Mountains, she helped a little girl confront her fear of walking along a precarious ledge trail my tribe used to collect rare herbs. Herbs that for some reason would only grow on an exposed granite face that overlooked a deep gorge. Shiichoo mentioned something about earth blood."

Larina studied Lozen's face, tempted to ask a question that immediately came to mind but Lozen beat her to it.

"Yes. That little girl was me. I was about nine name days back then. My Shiichoo, known as a grandmother to you, took me by the hand and lovingly led me across the terrifying ledge. It was no wider than her bare feet, and Shiichoo was *ancient*. Bent over, and relying on an old, gnarled stick…" Lozen trailed off, a far away look on her pensive features.

She refocused on Larina and winked. "She used that stick to cane my bottom on many occasions." She winced. "I can still feel its bite."

Larina returned her smile—the impending doom hanging over her head dissipated in the quiet cavern. She glanced around, as if seeing the vaunted chamber for the first time. The amount of work that would have gone into constructing such a place as the Well of Despair boggled her mind. To think people, or dwarfs as she had learned, were responsible for something as wondrous as the Splendoor Catacombs was nothing short of miraculous. So caught up in her idle musings that were somehow inspired by Lozen's tale, she jerked sideways when Lozen spoke again.

"In that moment, as I walked a solemn Mikter away from where you had hung onto him, I was struck by the realization that had it not been for Shiichoo's patient love, I would never have become the woman I am today. That simple act of kindness moved me in more ways than I knew at the time. Though forever cognizant of the danger of heights, my brain changed how it reacted to them. Shiichoo planted the seed of confidence I lacked. Her love nurtured my mindset." Lozen gazed into Larina's eyes. "Do you understand what I'm trying to say?"

Larina nodded. "I think so."

Lozen held her stare. "Good. I can tell you're more at ease than a few moments ago. What did you think I called you in here for?"

"Honestly? I thought you were going to kick me out."

Lozen gaped. "Really? What would make you think that?"

"I don't know." Larina shrugged. "I thought you took exception to how I helped someone who might not be cut out for this role."

Lozen studied her long and hard. "You may find the decisions Pollard and I make over the next few months harsh, but know this. We do it for the good of all." She nodded. "Especially for the good of those we send away. If they were to remain, we'd be guilty of endangering something more valuable than their lives. Any lenience on our part will weaken the very essence of what makes Zephyr such a great kingdom. Not to mention, letting King Malcolm down."

Lozen stepped away from the well. "Come. It's time we joined the others." She started for the breach in the wall, turning momentarily to wink at Larina. "We don't want them thinking you have my favour."

Pollard

Maze Running

Sadyra returned the small-headed warhammer she had tried to use against the male trainee, Ulk—a beefy, blonde-haired man with tresses halfway down his back and a faint sprouting of facial hair that clung to his lower chin in a clump.

Ulk's fair looks and personality made him a favourite with both the female and male recruits. His easy-going attitude irked Sadyra for reasons unknown. He had never done or said anything wrong to her—nor anyone.

She slammed the well-used weapon down harder than she meant to and stepped out of the way for Ulk to caringly return his.

"You okay?" he asked, concern on his face. "I didn't hurt you, did I?"

Sadyra fought back the grimace attempting to twist her face—her right shoulder aching from where Ulk's warhammer had slipped past her buckler and gave her a solid whack. "Please. My father hits harder with his fists."

As soon as the words left her mouth, she wanted them back. The odd look Ulk gave her threatened to send her into a tirade she would regret. Glaring at him, she spun and stormed away.

The past three weeks had been filled with long hours of training; leaving little time for the recruits to socialize. After bolting down a breakfast of mush, the trainees were required to gather into their assigned groups and venture into the vast complex behind Splendoor Falls, learning the different access points, short cuts, history of the place, and take part in the daily maintenance of the catacombs.

Sadyra was shocked that even after three weeks of constant exploration, she could find herself in a tunnel that seemed alien to her. Sometimes it was because she had entered it from a different direction through a newly discovered door, but other times it was a new tunnel she had discovered crisscrossing the labyrinth.

Scores of tunnels started and ended with no apparent reason while others continued deeper into the heart of the mountain. Pollard *and* Lozen had both stated that many of the outlying tunnels were never-ending. She didn't quite believe their claim, but she wasn't about to test that theory.

The real difficulty in learning the catacombs' routes was that half the tunnels were comprised of natural fissures connecting many of the hand carved passageways. If somebody didn't know the layout, there was a good chance they might wander down one of the natural fissures, losing themselves in the heart of the mountain, never to be heard from again. The trainers were quick to point out that although the Splendoor Catacombs thoroughfares were safe, once in the outlying tunnels, the risk of encountering trolls was real.

Breakfast, supper, and the short time available to them before retiring for the night were the only times Sadyra had the opportunity to share with Larina how their days had gone. Some training sessions proved tougher than others. They both agreed that the sparring days under Pollard's watchful eye were the hardest.

Maze running, as Larina referred to the days they were given a destination and a crude map riddled with checkpoints, always proved taxing on everyone. Tasked with finding checkpoints, many were the times that more than a few of the recruits would become hopelessly lost and the remainder of the day was spent finding them. Once found, each checkpoint contained vague instructions on how to find the next one. Released on their own, with gaps of time between each participant, it was only a matter of time before the search and rescue part of the day commenced.

No surprise to anyone, Onynx generally won the bragging rights on the maze running days, followed closely by Rync. Sadyra's skills of locating the doors had improved to the point where she wasn't afraid of finding herself trapped in an obscure tunnel. Though she couldn't detect the nuances in the stone with Onynx's proficiency, she knew enough to find her way back to the Well of Despair at the end of the day.

Ulk caught up to Sadyra at the first transition door. "Hey, Sadyra. Wait up."

She rolled her eyes at the wall before spinning to meet him.

"Look. I didn't mean anything back there. I'm just concerned. You took a good hit." He leaned to her right to inspect the welt delivered by his hands. "Wow. That looks nasty."

Sadyra turned her bruised shoulder away and waited for Rync and Onynx to clear the gap in the wall.

The trip down to the Well of Despair level had become a matter of routine to everyone. If they hurried, their passage through the layered maze took no time at all between the sparring chamber and the mess hall. Their training had taught them the most efficient route.

Larina's group had began the first training day with Lozen, so the lessons they learned were the same ones that Sadyra's group would receive the following day. The same proved true in reverse with regard to Pollard's teachings. The talk around the supper table every night generally consisted of each group informing the other what they could expect come morning.

By the time Sadyra reached the mess hall, Larina was already seated at one of the tables, laughing at something Mikter had said. The two of them had gotten along famously since Mikter's brush with expulsion. The incident had lit a fire under his backside and he had come to terms with his fear of heights, so to speak. Fortunately for Mikter, other than the odd trip into Songsbirth to assist with the conveyance of supplies that were shipped up the Madrigail River, they never had the opportunity to appreciate how high the upper levels were.

Larina and Sadyra hadn't seen each other since yesterday. Lozen had roused Larina's group early in the morning and they were gone before Sadyra's group woke to Pollard's bellow.

"Sadie!" Larina's broad smile fell as she espied the dark purple contusion. She stood and inspected it. "Ooh, I bet that hurts."

Sadyra winced, pulling away from Larina's probing fingers. "It does if you poke it."

Last year's recruits had served a welcome spread of fruits, vegetables, and bread. Washing the fare down with diluted ale, Larina said, "You're going to enjoy tomorrow."

Sadyra grabbed a carrot from Larina's platter and crunched on it. "Oh ya? Do tell."

"Lozen has set up an archery course in the tunnels. You're given points for time *and* accuracy. You'll do well. I just know it. Other than Lozen and Nyler, there isn't anyone close to your skill with a bow."

Out of the corner of her eye, Sadyra caught Onynx settling down beside Nyler two tables over. The pale-skinned woman had proven herself decent with all ranged weapons. Her uncanny ability to find the door trips would make her difficult to beat.

Larina followed her gaze. "Don't worry about her. You're the fastest runner I know, *and* you can run forever. I thought I was fast, running around the streets of Storms End, fleeing for my life, but there's no way I could keep up with you."

Sadyra smiled at the woman who provided her with a platter of food, and set into her meal.

"Trust me. You'll be fine. The course will take you most of the day. Ox will be knackered by midday, you watch."

Sadyra smiled around a mouthful of food at Larina's pet name for Onynx. An Ox was the farthest animal away in comparison to Onynx's gangly, skin and bone frame.

Washing her food back with diluted ale, Sadyra wiped her mouth with the back of her hand. "Who won in your group?"

Larina's face fell. "Nyler."

Sadyra almost spit out her drink at the way Larina replied.

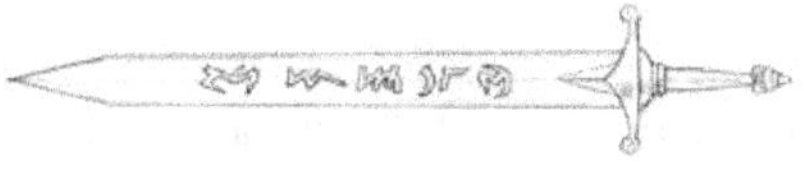

True to Larina's warning, Lozen had roused her group early. After a quick breakfast, she had led them through the complex by a route Sadyra hadn't known existed, taking them down to the small cavern on the first level. Bows and arrows lined the wall, awaiting those who didn't own them.

Onynx's lithe form slipped from the cavern and disappeared up the tunnel to where Sadyra knew the only doorway into the complex lay hidden.

"Okay. You're the last one," Lozen said, as if that fact had been lost on Sadyra.

"Here's your map." Lozen presented her with a tightly wound scroll. "Take a moment to study it. Like I said to the others, if you follow the directions correctly, you'll find the next checkpoint in a tunnel you never knew existed." She nodded at a metal basket containing the last of the new torches, freshly wrapped in oil cloth. "Grab one. Each torch should last you through at least two checkpoints, but there are fresh ones at each stop just in case."

Sadyra unrolled the scroll and tried to make sense of the route she needed to travel.

Lozen paced around the cave, collecting the unclaimed bows and quivers. Piling them beside the torch basket she asked, "You think you know where you're going?"

"Ya. Doesn't look too hard. We've been in this tunnel before." Sadyra pointed to the spot on the crude map that indicated her first destination.

Lozen didn't say anything at first.

"I'm right, aren't I?"

Lozen raised her eyebrows. "I'm not saying one way or the other. Just know this. If I were you, I would ignore whatever Larina might have told you last night."

Sadyra gaped. The woman knew them so well. Looking back at the scroll with all of its intersecting lines and a few odd symbols she didn't recognize, her confidence waned.

"Alright. Light your torch."

Sadyra tucked the scroll in her belt and did as Lozen instructed.

"Have faith in yourself. You know what to look for. You're stronger and faster than anyone in this group. I wish I had possessed your skill with a bow when I was your age. The only one holding you back is you."

Sadyra stared at Lozen, trying to understand what she was getting at. Before she could ask, Lozen nodded and pointed at the tunnel.

"Go."

Swallowing the question on the tip of her tongue, Sadyra started up the tunnel. Slowly at first, but quickly jumping into a run. She could win this day.

It wasn't hard locating the first secret door. She had passed through it many times. Stepping through the gap before the grinding door had fully opened, she checked her map to ensure she followed the next tunnel the way she envisioned the route in her mind. She had never taken this tunnel to the left, but she wasn't concerned. Given Lozen's instructions, it made sense.

Sprinting along the cool passageway, so many thoughts swirled in her mind. Not the least of which was her erratic breathing. *Slow down, Sadie, slow down. You got this. Focus.*

Pollard

The tunnel floor rose and dipped at irregular intervals, but if she had the right of it, the passageway climbed into the interior of the mountain—taking her away from the main complex.

It took longer than she thought to reach the first checkpoint but the relief that flooded through her was a welcome respite to the growing doubt nagging at her. The tunnel had long since transformed into a natural fissure—its walls closing in and spreading out as the vein of rock that water and time had carved over the millennia snaked ever downward from heights unknown.

Had she had her bow loaded, she would have impaled the stoic figure of Quincette who stood with her arms crossed behind a hanging basket bearing several spent torches and a couple of newer ones.

"Geesh. You scared me. I was beginning to think I'd gone the wrong way." Sadyra pulled up in front of the Songsbirthian Guard who stood as still as stone—arms crossed—hard features unreadable.

"Ya, ya. I get it. You're not about to tell me anything."

Quincette didn't appear like she was even aware of Sadyra's presence, but the sudden extension of her hand bearing a scroll similar to the one Sadyra's sweaty grip had mangled to the point of illegibility proved otherwise.

Sadyra accepted the scroll and tried to make sense of the scratched drawing. As she pondered her route, Quincette stepped aside to reveal one of the man-sized targets Lozen used to practise their archery skills in the woods at the base of the waterfalls. She liked to hang them from tree boughs, or prop them against a bush, and have the trainees try to hit the mark from various distances. The target beyond Quincette appeared to protrude from the cave wall.

It was second nature to Sadyra to pull her unstrung bow from her back and anchor its bottom edge against the outside of her right foot. Bending the pliable length of yew around

the inside of her muscular thigh, she strung the bow and
faced the target.

Arrow in hand she asked, "From here?"

Quincette gave her a slight nod.

Trying hard not to stare at the tough woman, Sadyra hoped
she wouldn't make a fool of herself.

She took a few relaxing breaths and drew the arrow back
with her left hand. Aiming quickly, she let loose.

The target bucked with the impact and clattered to the
tunnel floor.

Quincette led her to the target and nodded, as if in
approval, making a note on a rough piece of parchment with
a stick of lead. The arrow had taken the target in the chest.

"Not a bad shot. Grab your arrow."

Sadyra put her right hand against the rough wood, and
worried her arrow free with her left.

"You're a lefty?"

Sadyra looked up, shocked that Quincette had engaged her
in conversation. "Yes. Weird, huh?"

Quincette raised her heavy brow. "There aren't many of us
around."

It dawned on Sadyra that Quincette's weapons were
arranged on her belt to suit a left-handed draw. She stood
and smiled—experiencing what she perceived as an
unexpected bond between herself and the gruff woman.

Sadyra contained her urge to laugh out loud at the irony.
Quincette reminded her of a female version of Scruff. The
man from Fishmonger Bay who she had developed feelings
for. The man who, in the end, had betrayed her.

Pollard

Pass of Lost Souls

Running through the maze of tunnels, locating checkpoints along the way, Sadyra briefly interacted with members of the Songsbirthian Guard—many of which she had never spoken to before. Her accuracy with her bow had impressed several of the Guards—a few of them even took the time to remark on it.

The targets encountered in the catacombs varied from the usual ones Lozen employed in the woods at the base of the falls. Random ones depicted a Songsbirthian Guard being held at knifepoint by someone behind them. Sadyra had barely made the connection before loosing her arrow at the first such target—her arrow nicking the ear of the person holding the knife.

The man overseeing that checkpoint whistled his approval as he inspected the target. "You're the first person not to kill the hostage. Great reaction."

She smiled for his benefit, but her focus lay on the next map he had provided her. Before he could say any more, she was off again.

She overtook many of her counterparts in the opening stages of the course, but as she stopped to wolf down her midday meal, Onynx wasn't one of them. The much-needed break permitted her a few moments to consider the next map. Driven to catch Onynx, she set out again, a renewed determination in her step.

The solitude between checkpoints allowed her to reflect on how simple, and yet stressful, her life in Fishmonger Bay had been, and how asking her father about their family's past had turned her life on its head.

As much as she detested Bano Shell—the man her parents had betrothed her to—she now appreciated his curiosity about her heritage. The word, witch, kept echoing in her mind. She searched her inner self; afraid she might discover something she hadn't been aware of—something her father had questioned her about—but she couldn't sense anything that made her believe she was capable of conducting magic.

The regular cadence of her soft footfalls through a longer than usual stretch of natural fissure, accompanied with her methodical breathing, set the rhythm of random thoughts assailing her. An ever-pervasive fear for her sisters was never far from the forefront of her thoughts, no matter what she was doing, but for her own peace of mind, she clung to the notion that human decency would play itself out in the end. In order to function at all in the outside world she had to believe that with her out of the picture, her father's angst would be appeased. Unfortunately, every time she dared hope this might be the case, her stomach twisted and filled her with despair.

It dawned on her that she had been running along the ascending tunnel for some time. Her thigh muscles burned. Stopping to light her spare torch, she appreciated the fact that Lozen had suggested they carry at least two. Up until this point, she hadn't come close to burning out a torch before reaching the next marker. The fact that she had, screamed at her that she had gone the wrong way.

Up ahead, the tunnel ascended steeply into the darkness. An ominous sensation flitted along the periphery of her mind. She willed it away, but it wouldn't leave her alone. She hadn't seen anything in a long while that would indicate she was anywhere close to the Splendoor Catacombs complex. No hidden doorways. No sign of dwarven engineering. Nothing.

Pollard

It was as if she ventured along an ancient lava vent. Pollard had mentioned that the Muse, the ring of mountains encircling Madrigail Lake, were once a series of volcanoes. The rough stone floor didn't appear much different than the granite that comprised the complex, but something about its composition screamed at her that she had left the safety of the Splendoor Catacombs' tunnels and now ventured along uncharted cave systems deeper into the mountain.

The crudely drawn map she had received at the last checkpoint had been hard to read. Taking a moment to look at it again, a sinking feeling confirmed what her dying torch signified. The revelation that she had lost her way sapped her strength.

Onynx wouldn't have gotten lost. That was a certainty. Any chance of catching her staunchest rival had been ruined by the wrong turn she had taken. But where? It was difficult to determine that by looking at the map. She assumed it had occurred when she entered the present tunnel, but even that wasn't clear.

Doubt clouded her judgement. Had she missed the next secret door and stumbled headlong into nowhere?

The thought of retracing her steps deflated any confidence Lozen had instilled in her earlier in the day. What if the next door lay up the steep incline ahead? She stared at the map, willing its lines to reflect that notion, but knew in her heart it wouldn't.

A scream of frustration escaped her lips. She walked to the spot where the tunnel sharply rose, and looked up. Her breath caught—a faint light visible high above. It didn't flicker like a torch. It was natural light; she was sure of it.

Spirits lifted, she started up the steep incline, pushing past the fatigue that had settled into her legs. The tunnel levelled out, widening as it terminated below a gaping hole.

Fresh air filled the enclosed space, a pleasant reprieve from the usual muskiness that permeated the tunnels. The gap to the outside world proved a mixed blessing. Though it allayed her fear that she had been venturing deeper into the mountain, looking up, it was apparent that it was unscalable.

It took a while for her vision to adapt to the brightness. Staring into the clear sky, distant birdsong sounded glorious, breaking up the monotony of the deathly quiet of the tunnel. As her eyes adjusted, she inspected the walls with the aid of the natural light. If there was no way to clamber up them, there had to be a doorway somewhere. But where?

So engrossed in her search, the clicking of claws on the tunnel floor behind her didn't register at first. It sounded like it came from outside.

Comprehension of her danger stiffened her muscles. A tingle of fear slithered up her spine. The clicking became more pronounced. Whatever it was, it was advancing faster.

Spinning to face the tunnel, her strung bow leapt into her hand. Without thinking about it, she pulled an arrow free—nocking it and pulling back—all before her eyes focused on the monstrosity that lumbered toward her from out of the darkness.

As scared as she was, her arrow flew true, taking the hairy beast in the middle of the chest.

To Sadyra's horror, the arrow only stopped the troll in its tracks. It didn't fell it.

The troll emitted an ear-piercing shriek; crazed, yellow eyes locking with Sadyra's. A sickening wet noise accompanied the arrowhead as the enraged troll tore it free of its flesh. It roared—spittle spraying from behind curved fangs.

Sadyra cringed. She nocked another arrow and let fly, taking the troll in the shoulder near its neck.

It staggered sideways and bounced off the tunnel wall, shrieking in outrage. Before it took another step, a third arrow took it in the cheek—burying itself in its skull—dropping it to the ground, dead.

Pollard

The arrow clutched in her quivering hand clattered to the stone floor as she fell to her knees, shock numbing her body. Her bow shook erratically in a white-knuckled grip, its lower tip tapping the ground as her body quaked in disbelief at the abomination staring back at her with lifeless eyes.

Pollard

The distant squawk of birds, and the hiss of her neglected torch sputtering next to the hideous corpse, were the only sounds that disturbed the deathly quiet of the tunnel.

"What do you mean Sadyra hasn't come back yet? Where is she?" Larina jumped to her feet, grabbing Onynx by the front of her tunic, yanking the startled woman's face close to her own.

Onynx was tall, but not much taller than Larina. She stared wide-eyed into Larina's large, brown eyes. "I don't know. We ran the archery course like your group did yesterday. We waited for Sadyra to reach the last marker, but she never showed up." She tried to pull herself free.

Larina refused to let go. Nose to nose, she growled, "Who's we?"

"Everybody. Nobody got lost. Well, at least not for long."

Ulk walked up behind them and gave Larina a sympathetic smile. "Lozen will find her."

Larina shoved Onynx backward, releasing her. She spun and tried to step past Ulk but he grabbed her by the forearm; long fingers encompassing her wrist. She gave him a dark look.

He released her; putting his palms up as if preparing to ward off a strike.

Larina stormed out of the mess hall.

The passageway passed beneath Larina's boots in a blur. She jogged beyond the area where the secret wall opened onto the Well of Despair, and ran into the cavern's operations room.

Guardell Caulder looked up from a large map spread out across the table in the middle of the room—the chart's curling edges held down by several stone markers depicting armoured people. Before he or the other two male guardsmen with him had a chance to say anything, Larina confronted him. "How come you haven't found her yet? Who's looking for her? What can I do?"

Guardell frowned, obviously not accustomed to people demanding answers from him—especially not trainees. The smile on his face appeared forced.

"Larina, correct?"

Larina realized her blunder but knowing who she spoke with did little to alleviate the passion in her voice. "Yes, Master Caulder." She leaned over the map, the vast array of crisscross markings meaning little to her. Several flat rocks sat on one section of the map, while smaller, coloured stones were placed on lines in the same area. "Is there any word of Sadyra?"

"Not yet."

Larina fought the urge to explode into a tirade, barely able to catch her angered words in her throat.

Guardell pointed to the rocks. "These markers show where she isn't." He touched one in the centre of the cluster. "This one shows us the last checkpoint she arrived at. And this one," he moved his finger to the rock farthest from the first, "is where she was supposed to check in next. The coloured stones represent searchers who are systematically exploring the side tunnels. If she's near the complex, we'll find her."

Larina frowned. "What do you mean, *if?* Why wouldn't she be? She's not stupid."

"I never said she was. *But*, if she ventured this way," his finger directed her gaze beyond the stones to one side of the chart, "she'll be difficult to find."

Larina stared hard at the spot he indicated. She wasn't an expert map reader, but she surmised the area wasn't part of the Splendoor Catacombs. She swallowed, trying to come to terms with the implications. "So, if she made it out there?"

Guardell shrugged. "Anything could happen. The outlying tunnels aren't maintained. Nor are they patrolled." He crossed his arms and looked up at her—the disparity in their height clearly obvious as they stood next to each other. "I'll be honest with you. Trolls run rampant through the byways within the heart of the mountain. Once in their domain, all sorts of dangers await even the hardiest of travellers. Cave-ins and trolls are only a few of the dangers to expect. Even Master Banebridge is hesitant to wander the outer tunnels."

Larina stepped around Guardell and leaned over the section bearing coloured stones. "What level is that?"

"Nine, ten, and eleven."

She gaped.

He nodded. "Aye. There's a lot of ground to cover."

"I'm going to help search." She started for the door.

"No!" Guardell barked. "The last thing we need is another person lost."

She stopped, her slender frame rigid. It took everything she had not to keep walking.

"Our best trackers are looking for her. Let them do their job. The likes of Quincette and Lozen are the best hope she has of being found."

The tell-tale granite rumble emanating from the direction of the Well of Despair had everyone staring at the passageway.

Before anyone could react, Quincette's stocky frame filled the doorway. "Lozen found her, Master Caulder."

Relief flushed through Larina. "Where is she?"

Quincette glowered at Larina like someone might an insolent child. Ignoring the question, Quincette addressed Guardell. "Everyone's checked in except Master Banebridge."

Guardell held her stare. "You know which tunnel he went down, don't you?"

Quincette nodded. "Aye. I'll gather the others and go after him." She fled from the room; weapons and buckles chattering in her wake.

Pollard

"Follow me. Pollard's still out there." Quincette's muted command to people Larina couldn't see reached the control room. "Carnoch awaits us with several others."

Larina frowned at Guardell, clearly looking for an answer.

He raised his brow and directed her to a lone blue stone on the map. "Pollard took it upon himself to search the Pass of Lost Souls."

Pollard

What Have I Done?

Larina found Sadyra in the mess hall surrounded by most of the recruits. Not caring who she bumped out of the way, she forced her way to Sadyra and wrapped her in a big hug. "Scare me like that again and I'll see to it that they never find your body."

Sadyra pulled Larina's head against hers and squeezed tight; holding her best friend—her only friend—like she would never see her again.

Uncomfortable as it was being choked to death while bending over, Larina didn't try to break the hold. Nor did she care what those around them thought as tears rolled off her cheeks. The bond she had formed with the auburn-haired girl from Fishmonger Bay felt as strong as the one she shared with Bear. If she allowed herself to think on it, she might go as far as saying Sadyra meant as much to her as Cassie had, and Cassie's death had destroyed her.

Sadyra released her and stared into her eyes. "Aww. Don't cry. It'll take more than an eight-foot troll to take me down."

Larina gaped. "A troll?"

"Aye. An ugly one."

"Is there another kind?" Larina snorted and straightened, searching the mess hall. "Where's Lozen?"

Sadyra hung her head. "Gone to find Pollard."

"Alright. Break it up." Guardell stormed into the room. "Its been a long day. It's time you people thought about resting up for the morrow."

Larina raised her eyebrows at Sadyra and offered her a hand up from the bench.

Guardell approached, staying them with a downturned palm. "Not you two."

Watching the last person file out of the mess hall, Guardell indicated for Larina to grab a seat as he straddled the bench beside Sadyra. "Whenever something like this happens, we need to discuss it. Hopefully we can learn something that might help us prevent it from happening in the future."

Here it comes, Larina thought, fearing where Guardell was going with this conversation.

Getting straight to the point, he asked, "Do you know where you went wrong?"

Sadyra held his gaze, her eyes searching somewhere overhead for the answer. She shook her head.

Guardell nodded. "Fair enough. I'm sure Lozen will go over it with you."

Larina's anxiety melted away. She had feared Sadyra's mishap may have cost her friend a spot in the Guard.

"Rumour has it you faced a real-life target. Is that true?"

Sadyra swallowed and dipped her chin.

"Interesting. A troll, correct?"

Larina frowned. *What else would it have been?*

"Yes, Master Caulder." Sadyra's voice was so soft, Larina barely heard her.

"And you killed it."

"Yes, Master Caulder."

He raised his eyebrows. "Impressive."

"I don't know about that. It took three arrows."

"Three?" Guardell nodded, pursing his lips. "I'm not sure what you know about trolls, but three arrows to take one down isn't bad. From what I hear, it was a big one. Most people don't live long enough to get three arrows off. You must have seen it coming."

Sadyra shook her head. "No, sir. It snuck up on me."

Pollard

"Snuck up on you? How far away was it when you first saw it?"

Sadyra shrugged. Her gaze took in the room, coming to rest on the doorway not several steps away. "About from here to there."

Guardell followed her gaze. "From here to the door?"

"More or less. Less probably."

"And you had time to hit it with three arrows?" His face was full of wonder.

"Yes, sir."

Guardell kept nodding, deep in thought. Finally, he looked her in the eye. "Interesting. If I'm to believe the stories Pollard and Lozen tell me about you, that makes sense." He slapped her thigh and stood. "It's probably time you and Larina got some rest."

The second in command of the elite garrison stopped on the threshold and turned to look them both in the eye. "I don't often say this to recruits…Actually, I've never said it. Short of killing one of us, or dying yourself, neither of you need to worry about your future with the Guard."

Larina wondered if her face resembled the gaping awe reflected on Sadyra's.

"Don't tell anyone I said that. Besides, in the end, it's not my decision. Goodnight." He disappeared from view.

Larina looked wide-eyed at Sadyra, a great smile lifting her freckled cheeks. "You hear that?"

Sadyra jumped to her feet and squealed, embracing her friend and jumping up and down.

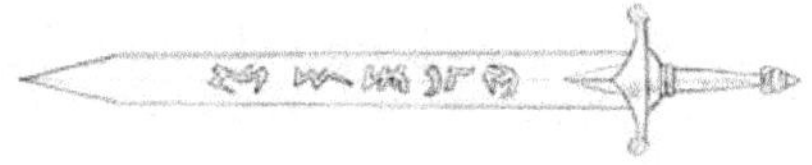

Rumour reached the recruits the next morning that training had been postponed for the day. Though living within the mountain left them ignorant of the time of day, Larina knew she had slept longer than her body was accustomed to.

Pollard

Sitting around the mess hall, choking back a second bowl of tasteless gruel, she picked up on the conversation one of last year's recruits was having with Ulk.

"Didn't come back until a little while ago," the young Songsbirthian Guard, Vector, said—his tone serious.

"And Master Banebridge was okay?"

Vector dipped his head. "More or less. He will be."

Larina whipped her head around. She poked Sadyra in the shoulder. "You hear that?"

Sadyra turned heavy eyes on Larina, shaking her head. Her run-in with the troll hadn't allowed her to get much sleep.

"Pollard was found a little while ago."

Sadyra sat up. "Pollard? Why? What happened?"

Vector turned to include them in the discussion. "You happened."

Larina wanted to take exception to his remark, but he was just answering the question.

"Master Banebridge set out to look for you like everyone else."

Sadyra exchanged looks with Larina. "Why'd it take so long for him to find out I was back?"

"Because…" Vector paused, as if not sure he wanted to answer the question. He sighed. "Master Banebridge took it upon himself to search for you in the Pass of Lost Souls."

Larina stood, hoping to avert Vector's scrutiny of Sadyra. "Master Caulder mentioned that place last night. What's so special about it?"

Vector's voice rose in pitch. "The Pass of Lost Souls? Obviously you've never heard of it."

Everyone in the mess hall stopped what they were doing and edged closer.

"Well then. Let me educate you." Vector puffed out his chest. "Of all of the tunnels you do *not* want to travel down, the Pass of Lost Souls is the worst, by far. Unless you're looking for a quick death, that is."

"Why was Master Banebridge in there?" Sadyra stood and approached Vector, her eyes intense.

Vector backed off. "Hey, easy. I'm just answering your question. You're the one who got lost."

Larina grabbed Sadyra by the back of the arms.

Sadyra shrugged her off but didn't advance any farther, her look intimating that Vector better explain himself.

"That tunnel is off limits to parties of less than ten. There's access to the Pass of Lost Souls on level nine and ten. When you went missing, we had to assume you may have taken that route."

Larina moved beside Sadyra. "Who was with Master Banebridge?"

"No one."

"You said only parties of ten or more are allowed in there. Why was Master Banebridge on his own?" Larina asked.

"Because, when they discovered Sadyra had gone missing," he looked pointedly at Sadyra, "Master Banebridge knew that if you *had* entered that tunnel, finding you quickly was paramount."

Larina recalled Vectors words to Ulk. "And he got hurt?"

Vector nodded. "Nothing he won't recover from."

"I still don't understand. If that tunnel is so dangerous, why would anyone risk going alone?"

"Not anyone. Master Banebridge. He felt there wasn't time to wait. We needed the manpower to search the other tunnels as well. Some of those are dangerous too. Since he wouldn't hear of endangering anyone else, he shouldered the burden himself."

Sadyra's face lost the bit of colour it had. She stumbled back to the bench and sat down heavily. Looking up, her concerned eyes found Larina. "What have I done?"

Pollard

Tinker, Tailor, Spy

Larina screwed the stained cap from Allard's clay inkpot shut. She smiled sadly at the old king's sigil stamped on the lid—an eagle with wings poised for landing, clutching a sword in its talons. Her dear friend had been proud of that inkpot—a talisman from a different time. The old inkpot and tattered quill were the only things he had to remind him of his days in King Peter's service.

She checked to make sure the note he had written to her on his deathbed was safely tucked away in a fold of soft leather she kept in a pouch on her belt. In the end, it had been Allard's note that had convinced her to throw in her lot with Pollard. That, and the fact that she needed an escape from the brutal memories that haunted her in Storms End. She would have never known peace if she had remained in the secluded seaport.

She folded the note she had written for Sadyra and carefully slid it between her sleeping friend's folded hands. Straightening up, Larina appreciated Vector's private room, thankful to the man for offering it to Sadyra. She envied the second-year guardsman his sparsely furnished, *private* room. She and the rest of the female recruits had to share a room not much bigger than this one. The only consolation that accompanied the attrition of trainees was that their departure provided those still in the process more room to spread out in the cramped confines allotted them.

Pollard

Using 'good ol' stick 'em,' the nickname she had given her dagger during a conversation with Allard, she scraped the end of the quill and carefully tucked it away.

She smiled sadly at her friend. It would do Sadyra the world of good to get some more sleep.

Slipping from the room, and closing the door with care, Larina set out to travel the catacombs up to the waterfall level. Vector had promised to have a boat waiting to take her to Songsbirth for the day.

She examined her breeks and winced at the fraying hems. It was about time she had them looked at.

Vector and Ulk greeted Larina on the platform abutting Madrigail Lake; the roar of Splendoor Falls deafening in comparison to the tomblike silence of the catacombs. Trying in vain to keep her hair from whipping around her face, she considered Ulk. "What are you doing here?"

Ulk shrugged, his long hair restrained in a thick braid. "I overheard Vector say he was going to Songsbirth so I asked to come along."

"I'm always looking for an oarsman." Vector winked and knelt to hold the dory steady. "Get in. With the shortened daylight, we better get moving."

Larina jumped into the bow.

Ulk assumed the oars. Though the air was cool, he opted to remove his shirt. As Vector pushed them away from the platform, Ulk set the boat into motion, bringing the bow around in a wide arc to avoid the pull of the falls.

Larina faced the rear of the boat, leaning her head back and enjoying the sunshine on her face. Of late, it wasn't often that she got to see the outside world.

Her thoughts drifted from Sadyra to Pollard to Lozen and the weeks of intense training she and the remaining recruits had endured. At last count, nine people had been sent north to continue their training with the King's Guard. To anyone not in the know, vying for a place amongst the King's Guard would be an honour, but to the people selected as potential Songsbirthian Guards, it was deemed a humiliating insult.

She sighed contentedly. She had done well enough so far to keep her place. Guardell Caulder's assurances that she and Sadyra were safe did little to curb her desire to be better than everyone else at what she loved most. Fighting with her dagger. And yet, during the training sessions with Lozen, she had discovered how much she enjoyed using a bow. When the opportunity to discharge a crossbow came around, she had fallen in love with the tenacity of the deadly weapon.

She smiled, thinking of the gruff woman, Quincette. Though the woman would never win a personality contest, Larina had to admit, when it came to fighting with short blades, no one in the Songsbirthian Guard matched Quincette's prowess. Not even Pollard. *And,* the speed and accuracy with which Quincette delivered a rapid volley of throwing knives was a joy to behold.

To Larina's delight, after working up the nerve to ask, Quincette had agreed to give her personal lessons after the regular days' lessons were over. Rumours circulating amongst the recruits as to Quincette's past weren't lost on Larina—hints of Quincette deserting her role as an assassin in the employ of the Kraidic Emperor. Larina wanted to ask Quincette about it, but every time the opportunity presented itself, she found she was reluctant to do so.

A slight chop rocked the craft as snow-covered mountain crags slipped by on either side of the lake. Larina pulled her tunic tight to quell the bite of the wind; marvelling at how Ulk withstood the cold—especially with a sheen of sweat glistening on his corded muscles.

She caught herself staring at his wide shoulder blades as they bunched together amongst the muscles rippling his back—his blonde braid swaying back and forth with the steady cadence of the oars. Lost in thoughts that instilled in her an odd euphoria, she was surprised when Vector's voice startled her back to the present.

"Good job, Ulk. That's got to be the fastest trip across the lake I can recall," Vector said from the stern.

She realized Vector was watching her with a curious look. Blinking to allow her mind to refocus, she absently noted that the sun hadn't reached its highest point in the late autumn sky.

"You okay, Larina? You seem a thousand leagues away. What were you daydreaming about?"

Ulk's angular face turned to see what Vector was talking about—his soft blue eyes holding her gaze.

Her cheeks reddened. Dropping Ulk's stare, she said, "Um…nothing, really. Just thinking about…things."

Vector nodded with a knowing smile.

She turned from his smirk and grabbed at the rope coiled in the bow. Before she could jump overboard to assist the dory up the gravelly beachhead, Vector splashed into the frigid waters and gripped the outwale, adding to Ulk's momentum to propel the boat ashore.

Ulk shipped the oars and kept the boat steady for Larina to leap overboard with the bow rope in hand, crunching dry gravel.

"I'll meet you two back here before midafternoon." Vector relieved Larina of the rope. "Don't be late. The last thing we want is to approach the falls in the dark."

"Do you know where I can find someone called Wender?" Larina asked.

The mention of the tailor's name visibly shocked Vector. "Wender? Why would you want to visit her? There are better tailors in Songsbirth than that crazy, old witch."

Witch? Larina frowned. "That's who Quincette told me to look for. My belt's wearing my breeks thin. I was hoping she could mend them."

"Ah." Vector appeared skeptical. "If Quincette told you Wender, I'm not going to dissuade you."

"How do I find this…Wender?"

"Oh, that's easy. Take the wooden walkway as far as you can. When you reach the end, the little shack you come to will be Wender's. Don't worry. You can't miss it."

"Perfect. Thanks." Larina started for the walkway fronting the row of buildings that abutted the base of the cliff.

"Be sure to knock loud," Vector called after her. "The old bird's hearing isn't great."

Without turning around, Larina raised a hand of thanks; crunching gravel marking her passing. Gazing skyward, she didn't like the look of the heavy, grey clouds blowing over the eastern mountain peaks.

Many people were out and about, enjoying the weather. Some wore Songsbirthian Guard grey, but Larina didn't recognize anyone. She stopped at the base of the steps leading up to the *Lullaby Inn*, contemplating whether to say hi to the kind people who ran the place, but Vector's warning about being back before midafternoon got her feet moving again. Who knew how long it would take this Wender person to fix her breeks? If the woman couldn't do it on the spot, Larina had no idea what she was going to do. She didn't own another pair. Until the day came that she was accepted into the Guard, they weren't about to outfit her.

Caught up in the eclectic architecture of Songsbirth—its gingerbread filigrees, wainscoting, peculiar angles, outlandish colours, and wooden and stone gargoyles lurking off building façades, Larina stumbled off the end of the wooden walkway.

She caught herself on the loose scree and looked around, embarrassed. Content no one had seen her mishap, she turned to face the sad looking hovel. The weathered wooden frame of what could only be a one-roomed hut listed to the rear. If not for the support of the wall of rock shooting up behind it, she was sure the structure would have fallen over long ago.

A quick search for a sign that might indicate she stood outside a tailor shop left her wondering if she had gone too far. There was nothing to denote anything of significance except a lichen encrusted statue of a dragon—one of its wings broken and lying on the ground—hidden in a jumble of assorted brambles and weeds as high as Larina's waist.

"You like my dragon, dearie?"

A jolt of fright shot through Larina. Turning around she looked down to see the withered form of a woman so gaunt, had she not been standing and staring kindly up at her and leaning on a bent stick, Larina would have thought she was a corpse.

"He's lurking in the bushes, eh?" The old lady cackled; thin lips parting over a pointed chin, revealing the fact she had no teeth. She pointed at the dragon statue with her gnarled cane. "The last of his kind, that one."

Larina swallowed her revulsion at the strange woman's appearance and forced a smile through her bewilderment. "Um. Yes. Quite, um, ferocious."

The stooped woman leaned close. "Eh? Did you say something?"

Larina recalled Vector's warning, *'The old bird's hearing isn't great.'* "He looks ferocious!" She yelled so loudly, she was afraid the villagers might think she was berating the wisp smiling up at her.

The old woman nodded vigourously. "He can be. He can be. But only if you try to harm her."

Larina frowned—the woman seemingly bereft of her faculties. Fearing she knew the answer, Larina asked, "Um, do you know where I can find Wender?"

The woman cupped her ear. "Eh?"

Larina sighed. Clearing her throat, she said louder than she meant to. "I'm looking for Wender!"

The old woman's wrinkles fell. "There's no need to yell, young lady."

Larina's shoulders slumped. She tried hard not to roll her eyes. "I'm sorry. I need to find someone named Wender. I was hoping that might be you."

The old woman sidled up to her, her small head only reaching Larina's ribs. "What did you say, dearie?"

Larina wanted to scream. Perhaps her breeks would last a little longer after all. Forcing a smile for the woman's benefit, she turned to step back onto the walkway. She recalled passing at least one building that appeared like a tailor's shop.

"You have a good day, dearie."

Larina raised her hand to wave good-bye, but the woman's next words stopped her in her tracks.

"If you ever need something special mended, old Wender's here for you."

Aware that her jaw had dropped, Larina spun on the old lady and pointed. "You're Wender?"

"Aye. Who did you think I was? Queen Quarrnaine?"

Before Larina could respond, Wender lifted a hand in the air before her and the flimsy door on the hovel creaked open, swinging askew on its hinges. Larina blinked and shook her head. If she didn't know better, she might have believed magic had been involved. Vector's words came back to her.

'Why would you want to visit that one? There are better tailors in Songsbirth than that crazy old witch.'

Swallowing her better judgement, Larina followed the old woman into the dark interior but paused as Wender emitted a crazed cackle. Looking around for someone to assure her it was okay, Larina sighed and ducked into the musty shop.

Wender faced her from amongst a cluttered interior—the walls stacked to the roof with strange artifacts covered in dust and strung together by cobwebs. A small table stood at Wender's feet, its scarred surface overflowing with bits of cloth and various types of sewing needles. A lone window on the shop's eastern wall was matted in filth so thick it struggled to let in more light than the warped, wooden walls.

"Don't tell me." Wender put a withered hand to her forehead. "You're the one they call the Lightning Shaft."

Larina's breath caught. Though not entirely accurate, Wender was close. How did the crazed woman know her nickname? She hadn't told anyone she was coming to Songsbirth. She hadn't known herself until Master Caulder had informed everyone over breakfast that today's training had been cancelled.

Vector and Ulk were the only people who knew where she was and neither one could have gotten here before her without her seeing them. She swallowed her misgivings and snatched a quick look at the sunny day outside the listing doorway. She had an uncanny sensation that if she tried to leave, the door would slam shut, barring her escape.

"Um, it's actually, Lightning Bolt." Larina mumbled nervously. She expected Wender to ask her to speak louder, but the old woman nodded, as if confirming her statement.

"Aye. Right you are. But, where's the harm in an errant word, eh dearie?" Wender cackled, her gaze directing Larina to the hoard of odd furniture crammed against the walls, buried beneath bizarre utensils, scattered tomes thicker than Larina's thigh, and corked bottles half-filled with different coloured unguents—all intermingled with the stuffed carcasses of a multitude of animals. Some she recognized, others she didn't—their vacant stares eerie.

Wender's voice rose in volume, drawing Larina's attention back to her as she sat on a low stool and motioned for Larina to sit on the floor on the opposite side of the low table. "Old Wender knows the importance of a misplaced word."

Larina almost jumped. In the centre of the table sat two cups with ornate handles, set on either side of a steaming metal jug—none of which had been there a moment before. Of the cloth and sewing supplies, there was no sign.

"Have a seat, dearie. It's not often Wender gets to enjoy a cup of tea with a living soul."

Larina didn't doubt the creepy woman. She couldn't imagine anyone in their right mind coming anywhere near Wender's hovel.

The door creaked, sending shivers up Larina's back. It banged against the doorframe, shaking dust from the rafters and dropping the hut into semi-darkness. If Quincette hadn't recommended Wender by name, Larina would be long gone by now. "I'll stand, thanks."

If Wender heard her, she didn't let on as she poured the contents of the steaming ewer into the cups and stirred the liquid with a blackened spoon.

"It's okay, dearie. You're the brazen thief Thoril Half-Hand has had his eyes on for years now."

Larina eyes bulged.

"Oh, don't look so surprised. You must have known you were destined for greater things than rummaging through the muck of that backward seaport at the end of nowhere," Wender said, her tone brooking no argument. "Now, do Wender a small service and enjoy a spot of tea."

Everything about the situation screamed at Larina to run. The woman was off her nut, and yet, she spoke of truths not many people other than Larina would know. Curious, Larina couldn't take her attention from the stranger before her. Judging by Wender's words, there was more to the old woman than her occupation of tailor let on. Larina's instincts told her that Wender would not harm her, but it was all she could do to lift the proffered cup to her lips. Sniffing at its pungent aroma, she dared take a sip.

Once it got past her nose, the taste wasn't bad at all. Lemon and eucalyptus mixed with something Larina couldn't identify—its steam making her eyes water as the concoction surprisingly soothed her throat.

"You like it, dearie?"

Larina didn't trust herself to speak. She nodded and sipped, cold hands gratefully cradling the warm cup.

"This pleases Wender." Wender topped up her own cup, and rested her curved spine against the stuffed carcass of a large, black-haired creature.

Larina had never seen an animal matching its description. From what she could see of its head buried beneath a bolt of cloth, it passed for a cross between a troll and a tall bear. Whatever it was, Larina hoped she never had the occasion to come face to face with a live one.

"What brings Larina Chizel to seek out old Wender?"

Larina frowned and tilted her head. "Chizel?"

"Aye, dearie. Your sire. You *are* Larina Chizel, are you not?"

"I don't know who you're talking about. I don't have a last name. My…my mother was a…" Larina felt uncomfortable sharing her past with Wender.

"A woman of the evening," Wender answered for her. "Yes. We know of your mother's profession. Fortuitous for Zephyr she chose that pursuit."

The conversation was growing weirder by the moment. "What would make you say something like that?"

Wender held her hard stare, casually sipping her tea. Putting her cup down ever so carefully, she gave Larina a toothless grin and raised wild eyebrows. "If not for your mother's services to Master Chizel, the kingdom would have been deprived of one of Zephyr's most unpolished jewels."

"Huh?" Larina blurted but the gist of Wender's words sunk in.

"Aye, dearie. You."

"That doesn't make sense." Larina looked around the bizarre hut's interior, noticing for the first time that it comprised more area than its exterior suggested possible. Exasperated, she sputtered, "You're crazy. The whole idea of you claiming to know my father is ludicrous. I never knew him myself." She put the cup down hard, the contents sloshing over its brim and onto the table and turned to leave.

"Of course I know your father. He saved my life."

Larina stopped, her body stiff as she stared at the door.

"Aye. And the life of a special young woman."

Young woman? Larina had no idea who Wender referred to. Her immediate thought was Sadyra. Or maybe Lozen. That would make sense.

"Many years ago. Before you were born. A young woman was taken by the Kraidic Emperor, Krakus Kraken. He originally wanted her as a bedmate, but he was no fool. At least not in the early days of his reign. I fear he's half-crazed at present, but that's a concern for another day. Suffice it to say, he saw the potential in this woman. Much like the Half-Hand sees in you."

Larina turned around, her head reeling, trying to focus on the woman's ramblings. Mesmerized by Wender's claim to possess intimate knowledge of her father—the man Larina had dreamed of everyday while growing up in Storms End—the old woman's revelation shocked her to the core.

"Krakus handed the training of the young girl over to his chief weapons' master. A man who was rumoured to be so skilled in the ways of the blade and the art of subterfuge that most people weren't aware that he existed until they felt the touch of his blade at their throat."

Larina eased herself to the ground in front of the low table, her eyes locked on Wender's wrinkled visage.

"Your father, Antyoche Chizel." Wender paused to let the name sink in. "That's right, dearie. That was his name."

"Was?"

Wender's toothless look of compassion gave Larina the chills. "He was hunted down and killed by the Kraken's men for his complicity in the escape of the emperor's most valuable seer and deadliest assassin." She nodded. "Aye. He facilitated a means for Quincette and myself to flee Kraidic before it was too late."

Pollard

Larina was glad she had been kneeling. Wender's words sapped the strength from her legs. Her backside thumped to the rock floor, almost pulling the little table over. The interior of the hut whirled around her. Whether due to whatever the witch had put in the tea or because of the startling revelation of her father's identity, Larina wasn't sure. She suspected a bit of both.

"Your father was a tinker. A nomad if you will. Tough as rock. He had the reputation of a rusty axe head. If his bite didn't kill you, the infection he left behind certainly would. He hailed from a place known as Clansmen Glen in the heart of the Kraidic Empire. There are many rumours that surround how his ancestors came to live there. Some claim they came from across the Niad Ocean. From beyond the landfall that surely marks the water's distant edge."

Wenders voice dropped low, forcing Larina to lean forward to hear it.

"I've heard it from more than one source at the palace that Antyoche sailed across the waves, not on the deck of a ship, but on the back of a dragon." Wender nodded solemnly and lifted the ewer, topping up Larina's abandoned cup.

Larina grabbed the cup by its delicate handle and raised it to her lips with a shaking hand.

"Careful you don't burn yourself, dearie."

The old woman stared at her from above the rim of her own cup as they sipped, Finally, she put her cup down; her soft eyes hardening. "Tinker, tailor, spy. Together we escaped the tyranny of Krakus Kraken's rule."

With the help of her walking stick, Wender rose uncertainly to her feet. Holding Larina's stunned look, she said, "Who knows? Had Krakus retained the services of Quincette's killing ability, you father's fortitude, and my ability to foresee the future by reading the nuances of mankind, Zephyr may already be under Kraidic control. And that, dearie, is exactly why you and the rest of the recruits have been enlisted. Not to defend Songsbirth *if* another threat to Zephyr arises, but to fight for her very existence *when* the storm hits. The ache in my bones tells me that time will soon be at hand."

Larina stared dumbfounded, hanging off every word. She blinked several times in surprise as the old woman walked down a path between the clutter into the face of the cliff at the rear of the hut.

Larina studied her cup, wondering what the witch had put into it. She would have staked her life on the fact that the passageway and the gap in the back wall hadn't been there moments before.

"Come dearie. Show Wender what you need mending."

The cackle accompanying Wender's words as she disappeared amidst the clutter raised the hair on Larina's exposed skin.

Pollard

Hip Shank

Wender waited for Larina at the back of a spacious cave beyond the rear wall of the hut, its interior less cluttered and surprisingly much warmer. Rushlights flickered from randomly placed iron tripods set around the grotto.

"What do you have for me?"

No matter how she tried, Larina decided she would never feel comfortable in Wender's presence. How had the witch—Larina was sure that's what Wender was—known that Quincette had sent her?

As if reading her mind, Wender chuckled. "No need to fear me, dearie. Only those who need to know are aware of who I really am. To most, I'm a deaf, crazy old woman who does odd jobs for the citizens of Songsbirth. Rumours of my insanity keep regular folk away." Wender smiled ruefully at Larina's expression. "Oh, I still get the odd crackpot who thinks they can match my level of instability, but they soon realize their deranged views of the world are shaken after spending time with Wender.

"Few are those who seek my counsel and that suits me fine for they're the ones who must bear the yoke of responsibility. Rest assured, Master Pul and Master Banebridge are men of honour and integrity. Men who would willingly forfeit their lives in King Malcolm's name."

Larina studied the eclectic decorations adorning the walls and perched atop random tables—most of the relics she couldn't identify.

"Like what you see?"

"I have no idea what I'm looking at, to be honest."

"Ah. Honesty. A good policy, hmm? Even when it leads to heartache?" Wender cackled, struck by a sudden laughing fit. As her mirth died off, her intense gaze bore into Larina. "To alleviate any concern you may have, Quincette belongs in my trusted circle. Now, why has she sent you?"

Second thoughts had Larina wanting to back out of the cave, but she had wasted too much time with Wender. If the witch wasn't able to help her mend her breeks, she'd have to put it off to another day and get back to the dory.

She stopped and fidgeted under the pale gaze of the witch. "My breeks are wearing thin where my belt rests on my hips." She lifted her tunic and pulled up on her belt to expose the worn leather waistband.

Wender shuffled up to her and leaned in close. The witch's posture pretty much put her eye level with Larina's exposed waist.

"Tsk, tsk, dearie. You've got bony hips." Wender's gnarled fingers grabbed hold of Larina's waist band and twisted the material. "You need more meat on you if you wish to survive the winter."

What does the crazed woman think I'm about to do? Larina wondered as she tried to pull away from Wender's icy touch. *Hibernate?*

Wender wrapped icy fingers around Larina's waist and held firm. "You need new britches, young lady. The ones you wear have forgotten their good days."

"New breeks?" Larina flinched in Wender's grasp, her mind racing with the implications. She had no idea what a new pair would cost, but she had come to Songsbirth with the pittance she had received in training pay. She had feared that it might not be enough to cover a quick repair. There was no way she could afford a new pair of leather breeks, and yet, given the nature of the training sessions and the terrain she found herself in recently, she doubted any other material would last. "I don't have money for new ones."

Before she could stop her, Wender latched onto her belt buckle and undid the clasp.

"What are you doing?" Larina snatched the ends of her belt from Wender's grasp.

"You can't try on britches if you're still wearing these." Wender hooked long fingernails inside Larina's waistband and tugged, shaking her head. "Honestly, for someone Master Half-Hand holds out so much hope for, you sure are naïve."

Larina bent at the knees and yanked free of Wender's grasp. Making sure to remain out of reach, she pulled her belt tight and buckled it. "I don't have the ability to pay for them."

Wender rolled her eyes and walked away shaking her head, the action reminding Larina of the way Sadyra reacted to anything she didn't agree with.

Wender stopped but didn't turn around. "You young ones have so much to learn. King Malcolm would never expect payment for something that may save your life."

"Save my life? All I want is for someone to mend my breeks so they don't fall apart on me."

Wender spun faster than Larina would have believed possible, poking her cane into the air between them. "If you wish to survive what is coming, you must prepare to meet it head on. If you actually listen to Master Banebridge's teachings, you'll appreciate the fact that you're only as good as the equipment serving you. Look after it, dearie, and it will look after you."

Larina's head hurt trying to make sense of the witch's babbling. All she wanted was a few stitches to bind her pants together—at least until she earned enough coin to purchase new ones. If she could make them last long enough, she would be given a Songsbirthian Guard uniform, but according to Pollard and Lozen, that day was still a ways off and that was the root of her angst. From what she gathered from the conversations overheard, the real test to become one of the Songsbirthian Guard came in the form of a long journey. If the snows held off, rumour had it they would set out in a few days, but no one knew how long they would be gone. She dreaded the thought of her pants coming apart while on the road.

Something Wender had said about the king not expecting payment brought her whirling thoughts up short. "I don't understand. You're a tailor, are you not?"

"Wender has been called many things. For you, I can be a tailor."

"But I can't…" Larina trailed off, dropping her gaze to the ground.

Wender raised a crooked finger in unison with her unkempt eyebrows. "Master Half-Hand and Master Pul will have what's left of Wender's sorry carcass if she turns away their Thunder Bolt."

Larina sighed, not bothering to correct her.

"Now, slip out of that ratty pair and try these on for size. Consider them a gift from those in the know."

Larina looked up and gaped. A brand-new pair of breeks hung from Wender's age-spotted hands. Where they had come from, Larina had no idea.

Not bashful, she pulled her boots free, hoping Wender's sense of smell wasn't what it once was, and peeled off her old pair.

Wender's gaze seemed to focus on Larina's nakedness more than Larina thought prudent. With a nod of what could only be construed as approval, Wender handed her the flawless, black leather pants.

"Slip them on and let me know how they feel." Wender turned away to rummage through an oily, leather bag resting atop a pile of ratty rugs.

Never been worn before, the leather was tight around Larina's thighs but she appreciated its suppleness. Hitching the waistband into place above her hips, her fingers located something hard buried within the folded hem over either hip.

"Ah, here they are." Wender turned and cast a critical eye on Larina; her hands holding two sets of throwing knives. "They look good on you. How do they feel? Not too big for your lack of stomach?"

Larina laced up the opening that allowed the breeks to slide over her hips. The fit was uncanny. "Its like they were made for me."

"That's because they were."

Larina frowned. "But how?"

Again, the crooked finger. "Wender does the king's work."

The creases in Larina's brow deepened—Wender's explanation not helpful.

"Put your belt on."

Larina did as she was asked. The belt fit fine, as she knew it would, though she could feel the pressure of what ever it was sewn into the waist above her hips. She tried adjusting the belt to sit differently, but no matter how it hung, the hard seams made themselves known.

"Ah yes. Those are the hip shanks you're feeling. Not to worry. You'll forget they're there in time."

"Hip shanks?"

"Aye, dearie. A little invention Wender came up with a long time ago to assist Quincette in her craft." She nodded, raising her brows. "Very useful to an assassin."

"But I'm not an—"

Wender thrust the two leather pouches, each bearing three throwing knives, into Larina's hands. "These are your blades."

"My blades? I don't own throwing knives."

"You do now, dearie. Quincette's request."

Speechless, Larina pulled one of the thin blades free: appreciating its keen edges. If she wasn't careful, she would cut herself. "I don't understand."

Wender's cackles sent shivers through Larina.

"It's not for you or Wender to understand. Quincette is her own woman."

Larina raised her eyebrows at that understatement.

"Deadly if crossed." Wender nodded, her wrinkles transforming into seriousness. "But loyal to a fault. If anyone were to so much as look at Pollard the wrong way, there's a good chance they'd find a blade such as those buried between their eyes."

"Are they…? You know. A couple?"

"Pollard and Quincette? Hah! Neither have time for such weakness." Wender pursed her thin lips as if about to say more, but shook her head and shuffled past Larina, leaving the cave.

Larina turned and watched the old woman hobble between piles of hoarded belongings lining the hut's interior. She couldn't be certain, but she thought Wender mumbled, "A shame that. Their spawn would have become heroes to be reckoned with."

Larina searched the cave for her discarded breeks but couldn't find them. She searched again, thinking she must be going mad, but the sound of clinking porcelain drew her attention to the dimly lit hut where Wender poured two cups of tea. She sighed. Of course. The witch had taken them.

Blinking a couple of times at the relevance, she shook her head and joined Wender in the hut.

"Ah, there you are, dearie. Come sit with me a while. You have time before you rejoin your mates on the beach."

Larina didn't care that her jaw dropped. Wender knew everything.

The old witch cackled and handed Larina a cup. "There you go. Drink that while old Wender explains what else you can do with a hip shank."

Pollard

Storm

Ominous clouds filled the sky between the ring of mountain peaks, blotting out the sun and obscuring the lofty heights of the Muse. A bad storm was coming in.

Far below, a dory bearing three people approached the granite platform abutting the wide brink of Splendoor Falls. Judging by the increasing wind and leaden sky, the boaters had made it back just in time. The front blowing in from the east promised heavy rain as long as the temperature didn't drop.

Pollard sighed. The wound he had received pulsed beneath his bandaged side. If it got any colder, and the storm proved as bad as those from the east generally were, his planned journey to the southlands would be in jeopardy. He knew he should have trusted his gut and cut the training sessions short by a week, but he was a stickler for detail. He ran his recruitment campaign a certain way and was loathe to mess with the effective regimen that rooted out the weak and built on the skills of the stalwart trainees that were left behind. Instilled by his father's values, shortcuts led to mistakes. In the role of a Songsbirthian Guard, mistakes meant death.

He stretched his left side, wincing at the sensation of the poultice plastered to his ribs. If not for his grandfather's trusty cuirass, the troll's claws likely would have raked him from shoulder to hip—tearing his chest open to inflict a mortal wound. Leagues into the Pass of Lost Souls, a wound of that magnitude would have seen him bleed out long before Quincette or Carnoch had found him.

Pollard

He smiled gratefully at the profile of one of the two people he owed his life to. Quincette's dark hair blew about her face with reckless abandon but she never blinked.

Never to be accused of being pretty, Pollard measured her beauty by the size of her heart. Quincette possessed the charisma of an old stump and the personality of a cliff face, but Pollard appreciated her more than anyone else in the world. Were either one of them inclined to be distracted from their duty, he envisioned a future with the fine woman.

He swallowed and followed her gaze beyond the gap in the mountains where Splendoor Falls spilled the contents of Madrigail Lake to the mainland below. His father had foreseen it. Master Pul had foreseen it. A violent storm Wender had predicted accurately twice before was converging somewhere over the Niad Ocean, gathering strength and preparing to unleash its fury on Zephyr and everything around the great kingdom. A storm that the old witch predicted would not be controlled this time. A cataclysm that would rend the land from Cliff Face to Apexceal. From Madrigail Bay to the borders of the desecrated land known by most as the Forbidden Swamp.

If the destruction wreaked by the sorcerer, Helleden Misenthorpe, two years ago was any indication as to the potential of the approaching front that Wender claimed had been but a taste of what was to come, Pollard doubted anyone, or anything, could stand in its way.

"You think she found Wender?"

Quincette never took her eyes from the distant horizon. "Without a doubt. Wender had been expecting her."

Pollard cast Quincette an odd look but she never took her eyes off the gap in the mountains. Staring at her hard features, admiring the beauty beyond her chiselled mien, he bit back what was on his mind—what was always on his mind when in her presence. He couldn't explain the attraction, but something about her twisted his stomach into knots. Not one for small talk, he found he couldn't stop talking whenever he found himself alone with her. Sighing again, he looked east. The distant mountains at the head of the lake were lost in a shroud of what could only be the onset of the storm.

"We'd best get below. It looks to be a bad one coming in."

Quincette met his gaze. Her features softened, but not for long.

In that brief moment of time, Pollard's heart swelled. A sadness filled her green eyes, inviting him to embrace her and ask her to expose whatever it was that lingered along the periphery of their strange relationship. He swallowed and turned away, unable to take that step.

Descending the steep trail of the lower peak, careful not to slip on the layer of crusty snow clinging to the mountain heights, he tried to push aside the pall of regret that assailed him each and every time he dared consider how it might be between him and the older woman if they only gave it a chance.

He smiled despite his mood. Older woman. He suspected there was more to Quincette than she let on. He doubted she was merely human. Like him, he assumed her family heritage came from mixed races. Being half-giant, Pollard's lifespan was three times that of a normal man. If he was right about Quincette, she would outlive most of the people around her as well. That being the case, ten to fifteen years difference in age meant nothing in the great scheme of things.

He paused at the edge of a snowdrift that partially blocked the entrance to the mountain and listened. The most dangerous part of their journey home would happen here. Had one or more of the mountain denizens been aware of their passage through the upper tunnels earlier, there was a good chance they would be lying in wait for him and Quincette to return.

Pollard

Quincette approached with a wildly curved and etched dagger in her hand—its blade so wide at the hilt, it matched the width of one of the swords of his mighty weapon.

He pulled the double-sword free of the twin baldrics on his back and held out a hand. He would never think to have Quincette go first when danger was about. Never think about anyone chancing harm if he were able to prevent it.

She glowered. "Please. You're about as quiet as a troll on fire."

Pollard pulled the half-spent torch he had used on their journey out of the drift where he had stashed it and struck a flint with the edge of his sword. It took several tries before the oily brand flared to life. "Nonetheless, I'm stronger. If something lies in wait, they'll rue the day they met my sword."

"You may think you're stronger." Quincette's pained look of patience wasn't lost on him. She motioned with the angry point of her dagger. "But, by all means. Clear the way."

Pollard ducked beneath the drift and started into the opening. He stopped to do a doubletake at her words. Shaking his head, he slipped into the darkness beyond.

He held his breath as it took a moment for his eyes to adjust from the blinding white snow to the torchlit cocoon of light surrounding him. Experience taught him that it was during these times of transition that he was most vulnerable to the creatures living beneath the ground.

Quincette slipped by him before his vision registered her movement, her own torch in hand and blade ready. She took several steps, careful to avoid the lip of the ledge of the pathway that opened up on one side to expose a fathomless cavern dropping away to depths unknown. Turning her head one way and then the other, she peered back at him. "Well? Are we good to go?"

He shook his head—something he did often in her company—a smirk belying his feigned disgust. He had half a mind to put the insolent woman over his knee.

Pollard

Pollard's premonition about a bad storm proved true. To his chagrin, it was far worse than he expected. The outlying entrances exposed to the elements were buried in snow.

Trips to Songsbirth became impossible until crews cleared the platform beside the falls and dug the boats out of the ice that held them fast in hidden alcoves above the waterline. Freeing up the pulleys and tackle that hoisted and lowered the boats was another matter altogether.

It wasn't often that this end of Madrigail Lake froze over, but it wouldn't take long for the eastern side of the lake around Songsbirth to solidify into dangerous conditions.

A quick foray to the lone exit at the base of the falls confirmed Pollard's fears. Much time and labour were required to clear the ice seizing the edges of the secret door. When it reluctantly rumbled open, a drift of snow fell across the tunnel's threshold. It took a long time to clear the door's track before they could secure it again.

Unless the weather took a drastic turn for the better, the winter snows were here to stay.

Not one to languish on his setbacks, Pollard took advantage of the winter months—determined that this group of recruits would be the best trained yet. In the intervening days and weeks, the relentless pounding and strenuous schedules he and Lozen inflicted upon the trainees proved too onerous for two more of the recruits. During a small break in the winter weather, the despondent male and female were sent to Songsbirth to wait out the winter.

Pollard

By the time the spring thaw allowed them to set out on their final test, Pollard was confident that each and every one of the thirteen recruits who had persevered would have no trouble becoming the newest members of the Songsbirthian Guard.

Pollard

Speechless

When the day arrived to set out for the final trial, Pollard stood outside the entrance at the base of the falls, his suede boots gripping a thick layer of icy snow that refused to melt in the shadows of the towering cliff. Arms crossed, he proudly observed the self-assured men and women that he and his trainers had inflicted countless hours of anguish and pain onto; all in the name of building physically, and more importantly, mentally strong troops who would prove up to the challenges that their new role would throw at them.

A hooded Naiche on her shoulder, Lozen led thirteen recruits from the catacombs they had called home for the last four months—eight males, strutting with chests out and a swagger in their step, and five females who matched their counterparts' cockiness. To a person, they bristled with confidence; exuding a persona that they were now forces to be reckoned with.

Thirteen people of different colour, size, background and personality, all comingling into a fearsome, if yet untried, fighting unit that Pollard wouldn't hesitate to have at his side when the coming storm broke.

Chin in hand, he considered each person in turn as they squinted in the natural light of early morning; as cloaked in shadow as the base of the cliff was.

Nyler with the darkest of skin, his strong, thick limbs capable of bending steel.

ℙollard

Onynx, the redhead with the whitest of skin; tall and gangly—lacking strength but full of stamina and emerging as the most critical thinker of the group.

Larina, Quincette's personal favourite; a ferocious fighter with short blades and emerging as one of the better bowmen of not only the trainees, but of the garrison itself.

On Larina's heels, which was no surprise to anyone, the enigma of the tiger from Fishmonger Bay bounded happily along—her freckled face and cheery disposition an amazing coverup for the tenacity of the ferocious woman the rest of the recruits referred to as Sadie. Cheeky as the day was long, she had endeared herself to everyone—guardsmen and recruits alike. He had feared for her after her run-in with the troll; afraid the incident had the propensity to instil in her an underlying fear, but he had quickly learned that his worries were misplaced. In fact, the auburn-haired ball of energy tried to coax him and anyone else in the Guard who would listen that they should help *her* rid the outlying catacombs of the ever-present threat of trolls. Pollard shook his head. Sadyra's archery skills outshone anyone he had ever witnessed loose an arrow—he idly mused that she might be able to rid them of the troll threat all by herself. In fact, her prowess as someone not to be crossed reminded him of a compact version of Quincette.

An odd sensation twisted his stomach. Admiring how Sadyra bounded carelessly alongside Larina like an excited puppy, he assumed the emotional tug had to be associated with his secret love for the former Kraidic assassin. Shoving aside thoughts of Quincette, he focused his attention on the next trainee in line.

Mikter, the shortest of them all. After his near brush with expulsion all those months ago, his willingness to overcome his fears and his penchant for assisting others to better themselves had endeared him to Lozen, and thus had allowed him to make it this far. Of all of the remaining candidates,

Pollard

Pollard considered Mikter the one who might yet fail to make the cut.

The angular faced Klara strode beside Mikter. Though slight of form, she had proven time again she wasn't afraid to take on any challenge the trainers threw at her.

Ulk swaggered through the doorway; perhaps the biggest paradox of them all. Beefy and without mercy when engaged in combat, he was the gentlest of souls. Had Pollard not witnessed how formidable Ulk was with bludgeoning weapons, he would have never pegged the man with soft blue eyes as someone who might earn their way into the Songsbirthian Guard.

Rync emerged and stretched. A burly fellow, he was the last person Pollard's crew had recruited out of Madrigail Bay before they had sailed to Storms End to gather Larina and Lozen and then onto Thunderhead where they had happened upon Sadyra. The quietest of the group, Rync wasn't one for small talk. Pollard liked that about the brown-haired, scruffy bearded young man who rarely spoke unless prompted. When he did, it was with assured knowledge. Many were the evenings Pollard had strolled past the catacombs' poor excuse for a library and noticed Rync's nose buried in the musty pages of a tome so thick, Pollard doubted Rync could lift it comfortably with one hand.

Bringing up the rear were the last of the recruits. Though Pollard knew them all by name, the female and four males were more nondescript than the rest and kept amongst themselves. He smiled. Those five posed the least of his worries. Adept with their weapons of choice, they had all proven their ability to not only perform the daily tasks of a Songsbirthian Guardsman, but to do so without having to be supervised.

Nodding his satisfaction with the knowledge that each and every one of these fine individuals were up to the final test, he was content that in a few weeks time, the Songsbirthian

Guard's roster would be augmented by thirteen more fighters.

He raised his eyebrows. Or perhaps not.

He had briefly gone over their destination after supper last night. He informed them that they were going to travel to a special place south of the Undying Wall. A place that would test their mettle. When he had mentioned the Gulch, the mouths of those he had recruited from Apexceal and Ember Breath had dropped open. He had left them to ruminate amongst themselves.

His gaze lingered on Quincette as she and Carnoch brought up the rear of the procession, the latter stopping to trip a lever and the thick slab of granite rumbled back into place. Perhaps the journey would give him a new perspective on how to deal with the raw emotions the gruff woman instilled in him.

Leagues of the Olde Gritian Road passed beneath the feet of the contingent from the Splendoor Catacombs at a grueling pace, circumventing the southwestern reaches of the Muse. The speed at which the slowest of the group set was faster than anything Pollard had experienced while cross-training with the King's Guard a few years ago. Albeit, the recruits weren't burdened with the heavy armour the King's Guard employed, but they still bore rucksacks full of rations and supplies and carried at least two weapons each, strapped to their backs or hanging from their belts.

The trip to the home of the Chamber of the Wise generally took five days on foot. Pollard's group crested the northern rim of the Gritian basin before the sun had set on the third. Not accustomed to a forced march from sunup to sundown, most of the contingent's faces were bedraggled as they observed the holy see of the kingdom—most of them for the first time in their lives.

For half a millennium, the monarchs of Zephyr had depended upon the counsel of the wise men and women residing below the Muse, entrusting the security and wellbeing of the kingdom's lower reaches to their capable hands. Barring occasional raiding parties from the Kraidic Empire and kingdoms south, the Gritian militia were more suited as an internal peacekeeping force. The rugged landscape of The Spine deterred most incursions into lower Zephyr from the west, while The Forbidden Swamp to the east, and the elven kingdom of South March abutting Zephyr's southern border, practically eliminated any possibility of threat to the lower mainland.

The Olde Gritian Road had emptied onto Redfire Path, Zephyr's main north to south artery, several leagues back. Before Pollard's group had travelled much farther, they were met by four horsemen draped in the surcoats of Gritian: deep forest green, emblazoned with a brilliant yellow picture of twelve high-backed chairs surrounding a golden eye.

Redfire Path continued south from where they stood taking in the strange sight before them, cleaving the bowl-shaped valley in two. The roadway dropped into a trench at the depression's centre—the walls lining the roadway peppered with doorways on the eastern side and one outbuilding on the western wall close to the midpoint of the trench.

"That's it?" Sadyra gaped at the large barn on a hill to their right and several outbuildings surrounding it. A small guard hut was visible on the southern rim of the bowl, matching the one the group stood beside.

Larina shrugged. "Not very impressive, is it?"

"Let that be today's lesson." Pollard tried to sound authoritative. "Looks can be deceiving. The entire town of Gritian lies underground."

On his signal, Quincette accompanied one of the two guards manning the northern guard hut down the gently sloping rim toward a group of people robed in red who had emerged from the lone structure in the middle of the trench.

Not having to be told, the trainees followed her lead and horsemen fell in on their flanks—more out of respect for the contingent from Songsbirth than to keep an eye on them.

Lozen spoke several words in her native tongue to Naiche who sat upon her shoulder. Removing his hood, she nodded to him and he took flight, winging high over the trench and disappearing beyond the southern rim of the Gritian valley. She started down the road but stopped to wait, raising her eyebrows as if to ask what the holdup was.

Pollard shrugged and gave Sadyra and Larina a questioning look as the two women hung back—his elation at reaching the first stop of their journey dashed. Whenever these two decided to act differently from the rest of the group, it usually meant he had better keep his wits about him. If not for how much he valued their proven worth to the Guard, he would have sent them packing months ago.

He laughed inwardly. Had he taken the time to consider how much trouble they were capable of when he had first evaluated them, he would have thought twice about recruiting them in the first place.

He motioned with a nod of his head. "Are you two not planning to accompany them?"

Sadyra ignored his question. "Who are the cloaked people?"

Pollard followed her gaze to the trench. "Those are members of the council. Some of the wisest men and women in the land. Please don't make me regret bringing you here."

A large man appeared amongst the robed figures. Though draped in Gritian green, it was obvious he wasn't regular militia.

"And that guy?" Larina asked.

Pollard squinted. "That would be none other than High Warlord Clavius Archimedes, himself. The man in command of the king's army."

Pollard

"King's army?" Sadyra searched the grassy bowl. "Are they underground too?"

Pollard sighed. He didn't want to waste time explaining the state of affairs in Zephyr, but short of picking the women up and carrying them under his arms, he knew they wouldn't move until he satisfied their curiosity.

It irked him to no end that they didn't respect his authority the way the others did. Nor did it make sense to allow them to flaunt their free spirits around the rest of the recruits. The example they were setting was one he couldn't afford to let fester. And yet, in their own way, their defiance to comply with the norm was one of the main factors that elevated them above their peers. They had the audacity to think for themselves. A good trait in a leader. Unfortunately, Larina and Sadyra were teenaged women, naïve to the ways of structure and discipline. They had much to learn before they could be trusted to lead others. He cringed at the thought.

"The king's forces were crushed two years ago at the hands of Helleden Misenthorpe. Gritian's personal forces were gravely affected. The local warlord died protecting Queen Quarrnaine."

"Fat lot of good that did," Sadyra mumbled. "She died anyway."

Her words threw Pollard. He fought to keep the edge from his voice. "Ya, well, in order to shore up his defenses, King Malcolm sent the high warlord to watch over southern Zephyr, charging him to reoutfit the Gritian militia while he rebuilt the northern forces from his seat in Carillon."

"Doesn't look like much," Sadyra said. "An out of shape old man if you ask me."

Pollard's face reddened but before he could say anything, Sadyra added, "No offense to the man, but look at him. Greying hair and living in a hole in the ground." She gave Pollard a once over. "And then look at you. Young. Strong. Capable of swinging a sword. You should be the high warlord."

Pollard

Pollard sputtered; words lost to him.

"Come on, Sadie. You're embarrassing Master Banebridge." Larina grabbed Sadyra by the hand and pulled her down the path. Reaching Lozen, she looked over her shoulder at Pollard, a playful smirk beneath dark locks. "Well. You gonna stand there all day?"

Speechless, Pollard rolled his eyes, thinking all the while he was becoming more like the two of them every day.

Pollard

Better than That

Abraham Uzziah was every bit as magnanimous in person as Sadyra had been led to believe—perhaps more so. His regal-bearing, long, white beard that came to a manicured point in the middle of his chest, and angular nose prominent between intense blue eyes, were enough to instil a sense of worthlessness in her while in the high bishop's company.

Abraham mounted a set of exquisitely carved granite steps and strode gracefully across the lower level of a four-tiered platform that had been chiselled out of the rear wall of the massive cavern housing the Chamber of the Wise. A black rope knotted at his waist cinched his voluminous robes tight about his thin frame.

Pollard put the back of his hand against his lips and bent low as he walked down the long aisle in the centre of the cavern—majestic, cylindrical, grey marble pillars, wider than a grown man's arm span and set upon massive rectangular bases of white marble, lined the lengthy expanse of the high vaulted chamber on either side of the walkway. Spaced evenly, the columns supported a natural rock ceiling barely visible in the shadows of thousands of flickering rushlights placed throughout the hall. "The black rope belt denotes Abraham as the head elder."

Sadyra studied the high bishop. "Good thing he's wearing it then. Being the high bishop *and* the Chambermaster."

Pollard glared at her, putting a finger to his lips.

She hadn't thought she had spoken that loud, but looking around, it seemed as if the chamber people walking in

Abraham's wake were staring at her. She swallowed and kept her eyes on the polished stone passing beneath her feet.

The high warlord's boots thumped up the steps, the man making no pretense of humility in the vaunted chamber.

Sadyra tracked the warlord's progress to a set of four, throne-like chairs facing away from the large audience chamber. Red velvet cushions piped in golden thread glittered in the ambience of the rushlights littering the tiered podium.

Clavius took his place beside Abraham in the central two seats. An older female draped in an auburn robe that was snugged together by a spun silver cord took her place on Abraham's far side while another man draped in red, armed with a bejewelled scimitar, sat on the warlord's left.

Pollard leaned his head between Larina and Sadyra as they slowed to await those ahead of them mounting the steps. "That's Vice Chambermistress Arzachel Gruss and Vice Chambermaster Solomon Io with Clavius and Abraham. Their opinion carries considerable weight when important decisions are required of the Chamber of the Wise."

Following the remainder of the chamber people and select members of the Gritian militia onto the stage, Sadyra made sure she didn't step on Larina's heels as they mounted three more steps to the second tier and assumed a seat on the stone bench carved along its length—affording them a view of the incredible Chamber of the Wise. The massive cavern dwarfed that of the Well of Despair. Looking beyond the stage to the seemingly endless rows of stone benches lining the audience hall, she estimated there was room for thousands of spectators.

Pollard squeezed in between her and Larina, his broad shoulders higher than the top of their heads even while seated.

Studying the four people seated on the lower stage, talking amongst themselves, Sadyra said more to herself than anyone in particular, "The high warlord looks like he'd rather be anywhere than here."

Pollard nudged her hard.

"What?" She hadn't spoken that loud. "He can't hear me up here. What is he? A dog?"

Pollard glared.

Snippets of conversation from the main stage reached them above the hushed voices occupying the second tier.

"Who's this Thwart fellow they keep talking about?" Sadyra asked, her attention on Chambermaster Uzziah.

Pollard frowned. "Huh?"

"The Chambermaster has mentioned the name, Thwart, a couple of times now," Sadyra answered, not bothering to keep her voice down. "Is he another one of these religious types?"

"Hardly," Pollard whispered pointedly, as if trying to set an example. "Thwart is the Enervator of Gritian,"

Sadyra stared into Pollard's eyes. "What's an Enervator?"

Pollard took a deep breath and let it out slowly. "Not too many places make use of Enervators anymore. They're like the Inquisitors of the old kingdom."

Sadyra tilted her head. She had no idea what he was talking about.

"An Enervator is the religious equivalent to the person appointed to mete out the king's justice. Someone who carries out the punishment decreed by the high bishop or the responsible prelate of a local order."

Sadyra imagined that the bewildered look on Larina's face matched her own.

"Look, it's not important. Let's just say, the Enervator of Gritian is someone you never want to meet. Never will meet, actually, unless you run afoul of the Chamber or have the misfortune of getting yourselves on the Chamber's watch list."

"Why?" Sadyra leaned in. "What is he, some kind of assassin?"

Pollard

Pollard raised his eyebrows and sat back, his gesture answering the question without having to say as much.

Larina's face lit up in wonder. "Can anyone be an Enervator?"

Pollard gave it some thought. "I don't see why not."

Their attention was drawn by an old man who entered the Chamber and shuffled up the long aisle with the assistance of a staff almost as tall as him. Draped in a hooded, black cloak, a tapered white beard protruded from the cowl hiding his face. He spoke at length with Abraham and Clavius, and then assumed a spot behind the Chambermaster's chair.

Larina took her attention from the main stage. "Even a woman?"

Sadyra could tell Pollard's patience was wearing thin, but to his credit, he shrugged and answered Larina.

"I don't know why someone would want to assume that role, but I can't see why any of my trainees wouldn't be up for the tasks of an Enervator." He looked past Larina, down the row of recruits whispering amongst themselves, and lowered his voice further. "Except, perhaps, Onynx. She's too slight to intimidate anyone. To be an Enervator, you must be ruthless. From what I hear of this Thwart, he's a nasty piece of business."

Sadyra mulled that over. Before she or Larina could grill Pollard further, the white-bearded newcomer's voice got the attention of everyone on the stage.

"Chambermaster Abraham Uzziah welcomes the contingent from Songsbirth."

Pollard nudged Larina and Sadyra. "Listen well. You're about to bear witness to the words of Zephyr's greatest thinker."

Sadyra glanced at Abraham, but her interest lay with the black robed man. She tried to see his face, but his features were lost in the shadow of his hood. Though she had never met one before, the man's outward appearance reminded her of what she thought a wizard might look like.

Pollard

Abraham stood, a seemingly forced smile lifting the corners of his thin lips. His gaze sought out Lozen, Quincette, Pollard, and Carnoch in turn, seated amongst the ranks of recruits. "It brings Gritian great joy to welcome an entourage from our esteemed council from the solitude of the Muse. I trust Master Pul is well."

Abraham held a palm out toward High Warlord Archimedes. "Clavius and I have been discussing the need for the Songsbirthian Guard's continued vigilance. We hope you will take back to the Songsbirthian counsel our belief that, although valiant, the expenditure of resources and manpower to pursue such endeavours as you are about to undertake are sorely misguided during these peaceful times."

Pollard stiffened beside Sadyra, the pride he had exhibited when praising the Chambermaster moments before, gone.

The high bishop's attention honed in on Pollard as he strolled to stand in front of him on the stage below. "Son of Thoril Half-Hand. Though your presence graces our stage, I speak on behalf of the entire Chamber of the Wise. We respectfully request that Master Pul no longer send armed contingents through lower Zephyr. Such displays of strength are neither acceptable nor appreciated during this time of rebirth. The people of Zephyr have endured enough fear these last couple of decades. It's time to change the way we think."

Pollard glared at the man before him. Abraham Uzziah, the high bishop, and head of the Chamber of the Wise, wasn't making sense. Aware that everyone in the Chamber stared at him, he took several deep breaths, his hard stare never leaving that of the Chambermaster. Rising to his feet, he had half a mind to berate the highest-ranking official in the entire realm outside of the royal family.

Pollard

Generally slow to anger, Pollard had to bite back what he wanted to say. He bowed his head. "Your Grace. I'll convey your advice to Master Pul and send word to my father in Storms End."

High Bishop Uzziah held his stare, waiting for more.

Unable to stop himself, Pollard asked, "May I respectfully inquire of Your Grace what's brought on this course of action?"

The bold footsteps of High Warlord Clavius Archimedes echoed throughout the cavern. The large man strolled to Abraham's side, his heavy-set brow a perpetual scowl. His deep voice thundered throughout the Chamber. "As the highest-ranking military authority in all of Zephyr, I decree that nothing good can come from ramping up our military might. Such actions send wrong signals to our neighbouring kingdoms. Refortifying outposts to pre-Helleden levels will be seen as nothing short of an act of aggression. The last thing our depleted garrisons need to contend with is a hostile reaction from the north."

The high warlord's words echoed through Pollard's head—the senseless sentiments so wrong in his eyes. Nor did they sound like anything Clavius would say or promote. The man was born a military leader. To encourage the scaling back of refortifying Zephyr's army was out of character, especially if what Master Pul and his father claimed was coming were true. "With all due respect, High Warlord Archimedes, it'll take years just to replace the people we lost. Surely that can't be misconstrued as *ramping up* our standing army."

Even as he spoke, Pollard was aware of the bitterness in his voice, but he didn't care. He and his cohorts had striven hard to get the Songsbirthian Guard back to the numbers the Songsbirth elders felt were necessary to effectively man the catacombs. The perceived threat of replenishing their ranks, whether real or not, should have no bearing on that effort.

Pollard

The high warlord replied with the even voice of confidence a man in his position commanded. "Master Pul and Captain Holmann may do as they deem fit with regard to the security of their own region, but their influence does not extend beyond the Muse."

The tone of finality in the high warlord's words wasn't lost on Pollard. As much as he wanted to argue the fact that two esteemed elders had expressed a view contrary to that of the Gritian Chamber of the Wise, Pollard was a man of integrity who respected the pecking order in Zephyr's army. He decided it best not to correct Clavius on the fact that the highest military authority in all of Zephyr was actually King Malcolm.

That being said, unless grave circumstances were at hand, the high warlord held sway in everything to do with Zephyr's armies. If he said not to continue with their efforts, then like it or not, it wasn't Pollard's place to argue the point.

Pollard bowed his head. "Very well, High Warlord."

High Bishop Uzziah nodded at the high warlord's words and added, "The Chamber will gladly put you up for the night but come morning, we expect you to lead your people back to Songsbirth."

Pollard tried to keep the colour from flushing his cheeks. He had planned on taking the recruits over the Wall and into the Gulch to complete their training like he did every year. His tone belied the raging emotions that demanded release as he bowed his head again. "Very well, Your Grace."

Watching the two high-ranking officials return to their seats as if nothing untoward had happened, the staying hands of Sadyra and Larina latched onto his wrists; their gentle tugs prompting him to sit. His venomous glare never left the centre of the lower stage.

Nothing that either leader had said made sense. It was like they were up to something. He purposely breathed heavier than usual in an effort to keep himself from saying or doing something rash. His father had raised him better than that.

Pollard

To Go Where No One Should

Gritian all but a bitter memory, Sadyra skipped along the hard-packed dirt of the Olde Gritian Road as it meandered west into the setting sun. It had been a casual day of walking since departing Gritian at daybreak. To the north, the towering crags of the Muse were visible on the horizon whenever the path crested a high hill.

She caught up to Lozen who had recently disengaged from an animated conversation with Pollard and Quincette and was walking by herself near the back of the pack. "So, what now?"

Typical Lozen, she greeted Sadyra with a friendly smile— her falcon nowhere to be seen. "Interesting you should ask. We were just discussing that."

When Lozen offered no more, Sadyra urged, "And?"

"It's not for me to say."

Sadyra rolled her eyes. Biting back words she might regret saying to the woman who had been nothing but kind to her, she stopped walking and waited for Larina and Ulk to catch up. Seeing how the two had gotten along during their trip south, she wondered if there was something going on between them.

"What's the matter?" Larina asked.

Sadyra appreciated how her friend picked up on her moods. "Apparently we're headed somewhere else."

Ulk and Larina exchanged looks.

"Aye. I asked Lozen, but she wouldn't tell me."

"I guess we'll find out when they're ready to tell us," Ulk said, stepping around Sadyra and continuing to walk up the roadway, leaving them to themselves.

Larina stepped to the side of the roadway to allow Nyler and Onynx to go by, her eyes following Ulk.

"You like him?"

Larina blinked, pulling her attention away from the beefy recruit. "Ulk? Nah. He's just a nice guy."

Sadyra winked. "Ya, right. Then why are your cheeks going red?"

Larina's jaw dropped, seemingly at a loss for words. Before Sadyra could grill her some more, Pollard stopped at the front of the procession with Quincette and Carnoch flanking him. Beyond him, the Olde Gritian Road turned north, circumventing a butte of exposed rock.

"Due to circumstances we have no control over, we've had to reconsider how to complete your training," Pollard said as everyone crowded around him. "Quincette, Carnoch, and I have decided that a journey southwest of this point is in order."

Gasps escaped those who were familiar with the region.

Sadyra stopped behind Onynx and Nyler, and exchanged puzzled looks with Larina.

Larina shrugged.

"Lozen, on the other hand, expressed her concern over this course of action, but has agreed to respect our lead," Pollard went on. "With the sun about to set behind The Spine, we're going to need to pick up the pace if we wish to make camp on the edge of the Torpid Marsh before nightfall."

The name of their destination elicited more intakes of breath from most of the other trainees.

Larina shrugged again. "Never heard of the place."

Onynx and Nyler looked over their shoulders, but it was Onynx's faint voice that expressed their shock.

"You haven't heard of the Torpid Marsh?"

"No. Why? Should I have?" Sadyra asked.

Nyler interjected, "I'd say. Of all the places in Zephyr I'd rather not visit, the Torpid Marsh is at the top of my list."

Onynx nodded. "Aye. It has a worse reputation than the Gulch."

Up until the night before they had set out from the catacombs, neither Sadyra nor Larina had heard of the Gulch either, but the discussion that had ensued that night had filled them with visions of ghosts and undead wandering around a mist covered swamp.

Sadyra swallowed. "How can this marsh place be worse than what we were told about the Gulch?"

Onynx raised thin, almost non-existent eyebrows. "Because the creatures of the Gulch are either dead or spirits of the dead."

Sadyra wanted to slap the self-righteous tone from Onynx's voice. "And there's something worse than that?" She asked with a squeak.

"Far worse. The creatures of the Torpid Marsh are not only alive, but they feed on other creatures," Onynx answered as if that explained everything.

Nyler nodded. "Rumour has it, these creatures covet human flesh above all else."

Onynx's skin appeared paler than usual. The gangly woman lowered her colourless gaze and muttered, "Master Banebridge wants us to go where no one should."

Pollard

Torpid Marsh

Larina tried to come to terms with what Nyler and Onynx had told them back on the Olde Gritian Road. Engrossed in keeping up with the others cutting through the rugged terrain of the Gritian Hills, the land giving way to wetter, denser, ground cover, gave her time to dwell on the random thoughts haunting her.

Her gaze fell on Pollard's back as he disappeared over a ridge. She was reminded of his father, Thoril Half-Hand, and the night they had met in the most unusual of circumstances. Every time she recalled that life changing event, a pang of guilt twisted her gut.

Passing over the ridge, her spirits fell further. The Gritian Hills carried on forever. Up one slope of scree covered rock and down the next. Hill after monotonous hill. Her leg muscles protested more with each climb.

A sadness heightened her guilt about her role in stealing the Crusher Scroll. Her dear friend had been a casualty of that debacle. As had many others. Though Sadyra, Lozen, and Pollard had tried to console her over the months since, telling her it wasn't healthy to blame herself for the actions of others, their reassurances were little consolation at the end of the day. Had she not coveted the purse Korwynn and his lackies had offered, Allard might be alive today.

As much as she was glad to be away from Storms End, there would always be a part of her hometown that would never leave her. Fond memories of Bear and his little sister Cassie. Oh, how she missed that spirited, angelic-faced girl.

Pollard

Sadyra grunted close-by, lifting herself over a low ledge as she plodded along.

The sight of her auburn-haired friend helped push away the darkness. The cheeky girl had endured hardships and unspeakable mental anguish at the hands of her parents. Larina couldn't begin to imagine how horrible her friend's upbringing had been. Sadyra's story made her trials with her own mother feel like a fairy-tale in comparison. At least her mother never beat her.

The face of the witch, Wender, jumped into mind. With that image came the solemn knowledge that her dream of meeting her father would never come to pass.

Antyoche Chizel was nothing but a name to her. The silhouette of a man who Wender had praised for being a tough individual. Unfortunately, he had sacrificed his chance at a normal life by angering not just anyone, but the emperor of the Kraidic Empire. She tried hard to picture what Antyoche might have looked like, but every time she did, his face was blank.

A ruckus up ahead pulled her out of her reverie. Climbing to the top of a high ridge beyond the one she had just crested, the members of the group that had already reached the top stared at something below, pointing and speaking in wondrous voices.

Sadyra glanced at her and started moving faster, as if challenging her to a race. She smiled at the one person who had ultimately been responsible for making her life in the Splendoor Catacombs bearable. Taking up the challenge, there was no way she could beat Sadyra to the top of the ridge. Not many in the group came close to matching Larina for pace, but no one was able to keep up with Sadyra running long distances. Pollard's so-called tiger was tireless.

Sadyra reached back to help her up the last few steps of the ever-steepening incline.

The sight that greeted her at the top of the ridge left her gaping. Even in the twilight of the dying day, the lush green and blue of the land that extended outward from the base of the far side of the bluff was a stark contrast to the dull grey brown of the Gritian Hills. The Torpid Marsh sprawled into the distance for as far as the eye could see.

Beside her, Onynx pointed west. "Wow. It goes all the way to The Spine." Her arm swung in front of Sadyra. "And look. It carries on south to the Undying Wall."

Larina followed Onynx's finger to a line of purplish-black crags running along the southern horizon. Overwhelmed by the scope of the Torpid Marsh, she couldn't help feeling insignificant in the grand scheme of the world.

"We'll set up camp here tonight," Pollard announced.

Sadyra frowned and swatted at a bug biting her exposed upper arm. "Huh?"

The crest of the ridge under their feet was not much wider than their shoulders and dropped steeply away on either side.

Apparently Sadyra wasn't the only one who questioned Pollard's directive. They overheard him tell Rync and Klara standing beside him, "You're more than welcome to spend the night down there."

The words no sooner left Pollard's mouth when Onynx and Nyler shrugged free of their packs, shaking their heads and muttering, "Nope. Here's good."

As warm as it had felt while traversing the rugged hills, a pervasive cold crept across the marshland, dropping the temperature as fast as the setting sun and seeping into everyone's bones.

Pollard insisted they weren't to light fires for fear of attracting whatever lurked in the Torpid Marsh, but he changed his mind as a full moon rose into the clear sky from the east and the cold deepened. If he expected the trainees to be alert and thinking clearly in the morning, they required a good night's sleep.

He needn't have worried. For most of the recruits, sleep wasn't happening. Whispered rumours of what awaited them in the marsh kept even the hardiest of them from having a restful night.

Larina's presence comforted Sadyra as they sat halfway down the bank fronting the marsh, staring at the mist rolling across the reedy marshland—obscuring it in an ethereal, moonlit glow. Had she not seen Lozen and Quincette steal from camp in the semi-darkness, she wouldn't have been able to locate them squatted farther down the bank, keeping an eye on the camp. Where Carnoch had gone, she had no idea. He wasn't sitting around the two campfires crackling atop the berm.

Larina had pulled out a set of her throwing knives and absently fiddled with them as they listened to the nocturnal noises emanating from the marsh. "What do you think lives out there?"

Sadyra's nerves jumped, startled by Larina's voice. "No idea. Likely something worse than one of those can bring down."

"Huh?" Larina followed Sadyra's gaze to the blade in her hand. "Ah. Heh. You never know. If I hit them in the right place it'll at least slow down whatever is coming at me."

Sadyra couldn't disagree. She had seen her friend in action zinging the thin blades around. Though she'd never say it to Quincette's face, she thought Larina was better with them than the former Kraidic assassin. She had said as much to Larina once, but Larina had vehemently denied the claim.

A distant screech pierced the night.

Sadyra's skin crawled. She looked at Larina with concern.

Larina smiled for her benefit. Ignoring the night sounds, Larina held up the blade to inspect it in the moonlight. "I'd hate to get hit by one. They're so small, and yet so deadly. If they don't sever something vital, they'll distract a target long enough to take them out with something more substantial."

"Like an arrow through the heart," Sadyra said waving a hand in front of her face to ward off the annoying insects flying around them.

Larina's curiousness transformed into shock.

"What?" Sadyra asked, a sheepish look on her freckled face. "You're the one going on about sticking someone with your knives."

Larina held her gaze for several moments before returning it to the wall of mist crawling up the lower reaches of the bank. Her next words startled Sadyra.

"Have you ever killed someone?"

Sadyra frowned. She had certainly thought about it but had never been brazen enough to see it through. She scratched at her scalp and slapped at the back of her neck. "Not that I know of?"

"What's that supposed to mean? You either have or you haven't."

Sadyra sighed. She should have dealt with her father before she left Fishmonger Bay. "I've killed animals before."

"That doesn't count."

"How about trolls?"

Larina considered that. She shrugged. "Ya, I guess. But I mean, have you ever killed a person?"

"Is there a difference? Have you killed a troll? They're like hairy, angry people if you think about it. They're obviously capable of thinking and communicating with one another."

Larina's face twisted in thought. She nodded slowly. "Hard to say if there's a difference. I guess I won't know until I kill one, but you never answered *my* question."

Sadyra's struggle in Thunderhead came to mind. "Not unless you count that guy I shanked in the market."

"Was he dead?"

"We never checked."

Pollard

Larina's brows came together in thought. "You're right. We left him to bleed out."

A pang of guilt churned Sadyra's stomach. An experience she wasn't used to when thinking about the fateful day that had brought her and Pollard's crew together. She took a deep breath. The man had deserved it. If she hadn't defended herself, they would have dragged her in front of Ivar the Blade. She shuddered. "I'm sure his mates came back for him."

Larina nodded, tapping the flat edge of her blade on an upraised knee. "Do you think you *could* kill a person?"

Sadyra considered Larina's profile; the moonlight illuminating her friend's freckled face beneath a voluminous head of dark hair. It didn't matter how long she had known the young woman from Storms End—she didn't think she'd ever get over how pretty she was. Nor could she forget the stories of how deadly the Storms End Lightning Bolt had been in her previous life on the streets. Killing the baron and a captain of the Watch in cold blood marked her as someone who shouldn't be trifled with.

Thinking about Larina's question, she wanted to blurt out, 'Of course I can,' but something deep inside stopped her. Sitting on the banks of the Torpid Marsh, surrounded by people who were trained to defend Songsbirth to the death, she couldn't honestly answer the question. She stared at the damp grass between her legs. "I don't know."

Larina waved a hand in front of her face and turned her head; the movement prompting Sadyra to look her in the eye. "I was hoping you'd say that."

Sunlight slinking over the land in the wee hours of the morning came as a welcome relief to the weary-eyed trainees and trainers alike. It had been a long, eerie night camped on the banks of the Torpid Marsh.

Mikter and Nyler tended the smoking campfires and served up the morning gruel.

Pollard stretched his arms over his head in a huge yawn, thankful that the temperature had risen noticeably since last night. He accepted a wooden bowl from Lozen and set into the tasteless mush.

"That was quite a night," Lozen spoke around a mouthful. "I hope we don't encounter half of the creatures I heard."

Pollard raised his heavy brow. "Aye. With any luck, they'll have gone to ground with the new day."

"I still have my reservations about doing this."

Pollard smiled, appreciating his friend's concern. Lozen was never one to balk at danger. "I take your hesitation seriously. I've had time to think long and hard on how to go about today. Would it ease your mind if I were to tell you that we will venture into the marsh until high sun and then return back here long before dusk?"

Lozen took her time swallowing what was in her mouth. "Not really, to be honest. Dangerous creatures prowl by day as well. There's good reason the legends claim this place is shrouded in evil."

"Duly noted, my wise friend. We'll be wary. I have the utmost of faith in you and Quincette. A shadow couldn't sneak up on either one of you. Not to mention, Naiche will be warding us from above."

Lozen held his stare, clearly not impressed. "Shadows hide in darkness." She rinsed her bowl with her waterskin, careful to drink the water she used, and walked away to take up a spot on the far side of the camp—her gaze on the mist shrouded marshland to the west.

Pollard stared after Lozen, her cryptic message muddling his thoughts. He shook it off. It would take something catastrophic to cause their party harm.

He slapped at his forearm, irritated by the incessant flying insects that had taken a liking to him.

"Master Banebridge!"

Pollard searched the berm for whoever had called him.

Dodging Onynx and Klara who were sitting on the edge of the ridge eating their breakfast, Ulk ran up to him.

Quincette and Lozen followed in Ulk's wake; shrewd eyes scanning their immediate area. Quincette's blades were in her hands and Lozen stopped long enough to string her bow—an action that took her no time at all.

"What is it man?" Pollard demanded, his hackles rising.

"Rync is missing!"

Pollard

Lozen!

Carnoch shook his head. "No, Master Banebridge. I never heard a thing."

Pollard knelt beside Lozen as she inspected the telltale signs of someone being dragged over the lip of the berm—the path of trampled grass leading into the Torpid Marsh. Her fingers traced the outline of what appeared to be claw marks in the dirt.

"What do you make of it?"

Lozen lowered her face to the ground and sniffed. She looked up and shrugged. "Hard to say. Definitely big enough to be a troll."

Pollard stood, his troubled gaze taking in the hurried preparations of his well-trained recruits as they tore down the camp. Though the Gritian Hills were at his back, he doubted they provided the usual terrain trolls were known to haunt. "We're too far from the mountains. I can't see a troll being this far away from home. They'd never make it back before sunrise."

Lozen straightened and shrugged again. "I have no idea what to tell you. The tracks speak to me of a troll, but there's something unique in its appearance that I've never seen before. Whatever it is, the watch never heard a thing."

Quincette nodded. "I've never seen that particular track either."

Pollard ran troubled fingers through his hair, desperately searching the lush marshland—its fauna so thick it was impossible to tell what might be watching them from beyond the mist at the bottom of the hill. Perhaps he should have listened to Lozen. The Torpid Marsh was not a good choice to travel through.

He sighed. It was too late now. Rync was missing. He wasn't about to leave until he found out what had happened to him.

"We're all set, Master Banebridge," Carnoch declared.

Pollard inspected his group. Thirteen untried trainees…He corrected himself. Twelve untried trainees and three experienced fighters plus himself. None of the faces watching him were able to mask their underlying concern about what lay in wait for them. Even Quincette, perhaps the toughest of them all, glanced around nervously—her fingers clutching and readjusting her grip on the leather wrapped hilts of her curved daggers.

"Then let's go. Swift and alert. Lozen and I will lead. Carnoch and Quincette will bring up the rear." He nodded at his charges. "You up for this?"

Without hesitation, twelve heads bobbed in unison. An underlying fear in their eyes betrayed their brave faces; leery about venturing into the unknown. To their credit, each and every one of them held their shoulders back and their chins high. It was time they proved they were worthy of the title of Songsbirthian Guard.

Once in the marshland proper, the terrain changed dramatically. Soft ground and endless tracks of reed-filled, brackish water made their progress slow and tricky. An overpowering stench of wet rot and musty loam turned up their nostrils while a thick layer of green flotsam coating the water's surface clung to their clothes and skin.

The tracks left by whatever had taken Rync were easy to follow at first. Huge footprints that weren't quite human and yet, weren't like anything Lozen had seen before, left deep impressions in the loam. Tracking through thick grasses as high as their waists, the path was plainly visible for even the most inexperienced of trackers. But, as the ridge separating the marsh from the Gritian Hills fell out of sight behind stands of cypress trees that were surrounded with dead branches jutting out of the water at various angles and shrouded in a dissipating wall of mist, Lozen's skills were tested to their limits.

As the morning wore on, it became increasingly difficult to keep walking on dry ground. On more than one occasion they were forced to jump from one clump of dirt to another, oft times slipping or falling short. Looking back the way they had come, Pollard had no idea which way the berm they had first descended lay.

Lost in their own thoughts, a piercing shriek brought everyone up short.

Lozen turned a worried face to Pollard, her voice little more than a whisper. "I've lost the trail."

Pollard whirled on her. Tired of the incessant insects making everyone's life miserable, his anxiety began to get the better of him. He snapped in frustration, "What do you mean you've lost it? Find it again, dammit!"

As soon as the words left his lips, his shoulders slumped. His reaction set a poor example for the recruits. He looked Lozen in the eye. "I'm sorry. You've done your best. I'm surprised we've made it this far."

Grim-faced, Lozen nodded.

"So, what now?" Quincette called out from the rear of the procession, her eyes darting every which way at once.

Lozen shrugged. "Though I have serious doubts as to the sanity of it, all we can do is attempt to follow a straight line from the last two spots I pointed out. We can't leave Rync to fend for himself."

Pollard knew Lozen suspected what he had right from the outset. Rync was long dead. Devoured by whatever had taken him. He wasn't about to voice it to those depending on him for leadership. Rync had been under his care. Until he satisfied himself as to what had happened to the young man, Pollard refused to give up the search.

Looking to the sky, the position of the afternoon sun sapped what little was left of Pollard's spirit. If they didn't turn around now, there was no way they would make it back to the berm before nightfall. "Where's Naiche? Surely he must have found something."

The worry in Lozen's eyes was answer enough. Her spirit companion hadn't been heard from since she had sent him searching at daybreak.

Onynx crouched on a grassy knoll not much bigger than her head; forlorn, pale eyes staring at the never-ending marshland ahead of them. "We should never have come here."

Pollard glared at her but kept his anger in check. She spoke the truth.

"There!" Sadyra pointed to a small tuft of grass in the distance; an open stretch of green water separating them.

Whatever Sadyra was looking at, Pollard couldn't tell. He pulled his sword over his shoulder, searching the marsh for movement but saw nothing out of the ordinary. "What do you see?"

"The grass is bent slightly to one side."

Pollard squinted but couldn't see what she was looking at.

Lozen splashed into the water, surprise on her face as she sunk up to her waist. Not pausing to worry about it, she made her way toward the tuft. "I see it. They came this way."

Pollard searched for another way to the clump of grass. Not seeing one, he stepped over a half submerged, downed tree and plunged after her, almost losing his balance as the slick muck underfoot gave way, sinking him up to his ankles and sucking at his feet with each step. His wide shoulders swayed back and forth, carrying his unique sword above the water's surface.

Pollard

Splashes sounded behind him as the rest of the group followed.

By the time Lozen reached the tuft of grass, she was shoulder deep in the putrid water. She pulled her chest onto the spit of land and ran her hands through the grass. Pulling a hand back, she stared at her fingers. Wide-eyed, she faced everyone. "Blood."

Lozen lifted her head higher and stiffened; pointing to a place ahead of her that no one else could see. "There!"

Without waiting for the others to catch up, Lozen slipped into the water and waded around the tuft.

Pollard forced his way through the thick water; his skin and clothing covered in the debris floating stagnant upon the water's surface. Rounding the tuft where Lozen had spotted the blood, his heart skipped a beat.

The prone figure of a brown-haired, scruffy-bearded man lay contorted in angles a body shouldn't be able to achieve, atop another spit of land little bigger than the last.

Lozen swam in water that Pollard surmised was over her head toward the spot where Rync's vacant stare looked back at them. Plodding through chest deep water, Pollard could see that the young man's throat had been ripped out.

"Lozen, wait!" Pollard called out, searching the area around Rync's body, fearing for her safety.

A high-pitched cry from overhead drew everyone's attention. It took Pollard a moment to find the grey missile diving headfirst from the sky, seemingly aimed at Rync.

Naiche had spotted something, his urgent call unsettling as he plummeted at an incredible speed.

A guttural roar turned Pollard's blood cold. Rising out of the water on the far side of Rync's body, a hairy, black beast, bristling with dagger-sized claws, lifted its long arms above its head and hovered over Lozen.

The shaggy beast hesitated for the briefest of moments, yellow eyes locking on Pollard, before it roared again and lunged.

Pollard

Pollard tripped over something hard and fell face first into
the murky water. Straining to get his feet planted firmly
beneath him, he hoisted his sword clear of the water and
cried out, "Lozen!"

Pollard

The Evil Darkness Brings

Sadyra half swam, half jumped through water up to her neck, pulling her filleting knife free. Cries of dismay and frantic splashing marked the progress of the rest of the group—pandemonium breaking out as the reality of what was happening slammed into them. This was no training exercise.

Beyond the rushing bodies of her fellow recruits floundering in the deepening water, a beast larger than the trolls she had tangled with, fell upon a helpless Lozen.

She looked to the sky as an ear-piercing shriek rose above the din. At the last possible moment, Naiche broke out of his dive and hit the beast between its wide shoulder blades—the sound of impact audible from where Sadyra struggled to keep her head above water.

Shorter than most of the others, Sadyra's next step landed her in water over her head. Larina charged past, her arms in the air with a throwing knife in each hand.

Sadyra swam for all she was worth. All the years of fishing the rough waters off the coast of Fishmonger Bay served her well. As heavy as the water soaking her clothes made her progress difficult, she made up for it by dipping below the water and pushing off the bottom every now and then, concerned about the strange objects she trod upon.

Something bumped against her thigh so hard it shoved her sideways. She yelped and tried to see which of her companions had hit her. Other than Larina who was too far ahead to have done so, there was no one else near her.

Frightened by the encounter, her hands and legs moved quicker than ever.

Off to her left, one of the males from the clique of quieter recruits cried out in despair. His terror-filled eyes met hers for the briefest of moments. Searching the water around him, his shoulders gyrated as if he were fighting something below the surface. A scream ripped from his throat just before he disappeared beneath the scum covered surface. Ripples and bubbles churned the water where he went under, ominously trailing deeper into the marsh.

Sadyra started after him, but whatever had taken the man, swam much faster than she did. She swallowed; her eyes blurred by more than swamp water.

She forced herself to give up on him and focused on what lay ahead. The spit of land where Rync's body now hung half suspended in the water was visible amongst a flurry of activity.

Pollard latched onto Lozen's suede jerkin and pulled her from harm's way.

The ferocious beast that had risen from the depths roared in fury, its paws clawing furiously at Naiche as the falcon flapped and pecked at its face without mercy.

Quincette took carriage of Lozen but immediately unhanded her. The warrior woman from the Altirius Mountain Elk tribe demanded to get back into the fight.

Another cry for help sounded on Sadyra's left—emitted by a second male from the clique. His plea was echoed by his female companion who was trying to help him.

Sadyra gaped. In unison, the man and woman were jerked beneath the surface, their demise marked by two currents trailing away.

"Look to the waters!" Sadyra half choked out the words, half spitting a mouthful of green water.

Larina suddenly disappeared.

Pollard

Sadyra screamed. Her arms flailed in a whirlwind of action, her knife almost stabbing Larina in the shoulder as Larina broke through the surface, her hands empty.

Sadyra wrapped her arms around Larina's neck and the two of them struggled to keep above water. Their faces touching, she asked, "What happened? How'd you get free?"

"I don't know. Something latched onto my leg and pulled me under. I stuck it with my blades and it let go." Larina's head slipped beneath the surface momentarily. When she came back up, she brandished new throwing knives.

Screams sounded from their left. The last two males of the clique thrashed in the water, trying hard to keep their heads above the surface. One of them jerked out of sight. The second cried out and dove after him.

It didn't take long for Sadyra to realize that neither one was coming back up—trails of swirling flotsam marked their departure from the area.

She exchanged a terror-filled glance with Larina and swallowed hard. Nudging her friend away from the place the others had disappeared, they made their way to where Pollard had engaged the beast on the far side of the spit of land, the water now only up to his thighs.

The sight of Quincette and Carnoch engaging a second beast sent chills up Sadyra's spine. "Where did that one come from?"

She and Larina swam up to where Onynx, Klara, Mikter, and Nyler were gaping at Rync's mutilated body. "What are they?"

"Bear trolls," Onynx said, never taking her eyes from Rync. Tears streamed down her cheeks.

The first beast roared.

Pollard's mighty sword bit into its side.

It latched onto Pollard's weapon embedded in its hide, seemingly not caring that it had been cut.

Pollard's body contorted, trying to wrest his sword from the beast's grasp but it wouldn't let go. Its strength easily matched the half-giant's as it twisted Pollard back and forth, threatening to rip the sword from his hands.

Larina pushed past the paralyzed recruits, screaming, "Why aren't you helping them?" She never stopped to listen for an answer.

"Carnoch told us to stay here," Mikter said, his arms wrapped around the clump of land to keep his head above water.

Sadyra frowned and shook her head. "And you listened? Where's Ulk?"

As if in answer to her question, she saw him struggling to reach something floating in the water close to where Pollard and the beast squared off.

Ulk scooped Naiche from the water and held the falcon against his chest. A rapid series of squawking protests escaped the bird's beak. It pecked and struggled in his grasp, one of its wings badly mangled.

Free of the clump of land, Sadyra started swimming again. Halfway to where Pollard fought for his life, her feet touched down.

The beast leaned forward, twisted, and stepped to one side. With a mighty wrench, it ripped Pollard's sword from the half-giant's wet hands and threw it.

The heavy sword spun twice around and splashed into the swamp, disappearing from sight.

A moment of shock passed between the beast and Pollard at the relevance. The two goliaths locked stares.

The beast bared fangs longer than Sadyra's fingers and attacked.

Lozen thrashed in the water, closed on the combatants, and raised her dagger, lunging at the bear troll. Her blade dove into its thick fur but did little to slow the beast.

Sadyra was torn as to who to help out first. Off to Pollard's right, blood poured from a nasty gash on Quincette's forehead. She had wrapped her thick arms around the second bear troll and was trying to wrestle it off its feet.

Pollard

The beast thrashed, snapping its jaws at her head.

Alongside Quincette, Carnoch grabbed onto one of the bear troll's arms in a futile effort to help subdue it. The beast lifted him out of the water and threw him through the air.

The soft muck of the marsh bottom made movement difficult. Passing by the jagged end of a rotting stump, Sadyra pulled her bow over her shoulder, jammed its end into the rotten wood and bent it around what remained of a branch. Bow strung, she lifted her head and pulled an arrow free with her left hand.

The bear troll confronting Pollard swiped at him, almost taking his face from his skull.

Pollard stumbled backward and fell into the water, holding his hands above his head. Lozen fought to pull her dagger free of the beast's matted fur. She drove her shoulder into its ribs trying to keep it from falling on Pollard, but its momentum pushed her back as if she wasn't there.

The bear troll roared and reached for Pollard. Its momentum stopped—its head snapping backward; an arrow buried between its eyes. It staggered sideways and emitted the strangest of growls before it splashed into the water and disappeared.

Lozen rode it under, wrapping her hands around its throat and holding it beneath the water's surface.

The second bear troll roared and swiped a massive paw at Carnoch who had rushed back to assist Quincette.

Carnoch's head snapped to one side in a spray of gore— his flailing body creating a great splash of green water. Not moving, he sank out of sight.

The bear troll tore free of Quincette's hold and turned on her. Oblivious to the lightning-fast jabs she inflicted with her daggers, it stopped in mid-stride and straightened up, its yellow eyes staring at Larina—the end of a throwing knife embedded in its cheek.

A second knife flew into its neck. It flinched and stepped sideways, grabbing at the offending blades.

Pollard

Quincette steadied herself and prepared to drive her daggers home but as she raised one overhead, an arrow buried itself in the beast's chest.

The wounds inflicted by the throwing blades forgotten, the bear troll clutched at the fletches of Sadyra's arrow, trying to pull the offending shaft from its body.

Two more throwing knives dove into its face, the second blade taking it in the eye.

A horrendous roar burst from its mouth.

Sadyra's skin crawled. What did they have to do to take this thing down? She nocked another arrow but held back, fearful of hitting an enraged Quincette as the woman savagely drove her blades into both sides of the bear troll's neck.

The former Kraidic assassin disappeared, driving the thrashing beast beneath the water's surface. The water churned and bubbled, erupting with flashes of fur and leather armour, and then went still.

Sadyra followed in Larina's wake, converging on the spot of the battle but before they could do anything, Quincette's head broke free of the surface, gashed and bleeding profusely.

The stocky Songsbirthian Guard's green eyes regarded Larina and Sadyra for a moment before they rolled back in her head and she sank out of sight.

Mikter and the others rushed past Sadyra and dragged Quincette back to the surface.

"Come on!" Nyler hammered on the back of Quincette's shoulders with the palm of his hand. "Spit it out!"

Quincette coughed and hacked, spewing a mouthful of water, her large body dead weight in Mikter and Klara's hands.

Onynx located Carnoch's body. She struggled to pull him up from the marsh floor. "Help me!"

Larina reached her first and together they lifted him out of the water. His mutilated head lolled to one side.

Pollard

Sadyra reached them. "Is he alive?"

The grim look Larina gave her was all the answer she needed.

An eerie silence descended over the marsh.

Pollard swayed on his feet, obviously in shock, blood seeping from wounds to his shoulders and arms. He inspected Quincette to make sure she would be alright and then took charge of Carnoch's body.

Lozen accepted Naiche from Ulk, giving him a silent thank you. She cradled her spirit companion to the top of her breast, careful not to bend his broken wing, and cooed softly. Turning a dark glare on Pollard and Quincette, she said, "This is the evil darkness brings."

Pollard

The End of All Things Good

Huddled on a patch of dry land, the survivors of the skirmish in the Torpid Marsh shivered the night away.

Lozen's dark demeanour reminded them they weren't out of danger yet.

Onynx and Mikter spent most of the night wrapped in each other's arms, sobbing.

Ulk stared into the darkness the way they had come, his face frozen with disbelief.

Nyler and Klara kept to themselves but helped Larina and Sadyra tend to the wounds suffered by Quincette, Pollard, and Lozen—the latter unusually subdued.

Haunted by the recent skirmish and the extreme tension their locale instilled within them, they jumped with every nerve-rattling noise that pierced the darkness. Pestered by the never-ending buzz of insects they never knew existed, the bleary company got no rest.

The darkness had noticeably lessened in the predawn twilight as Larina stared at the mound they had dug on the sprit of land they sheltered upon. Carnoch and six trainees would not be going home—the remains of five of them never to be seen again.

Larina had endured the fall-out of many battles in the streets of Storms End but nothing had prepared her for the savage ferocity of the bear trolls and whatever lurked beneath the waters. The distant stares of her companions left her hollow and numb.

Pollard

Pollard didn't have to tell them. The disheartened giant solemnly stowed his gear and slung the rucksacks containing Carnoch and Rync's few possessions as he prepared to start for home.

Everyone followed his lead. With a last look at the mound, they bowed their heads, muttered whatever comforting words meant something to them, and waded into the stagnant stench of the Torpid Marsh's brackish waters.

It wasn't lost on Larina that Pollard had his sword in hand—the fact that they had been able to find it still amazed her. Nor did she miss the tension that had risen between him and Lozen—the latter barely speaking two words to him as she pointed them in the direction they needed to take in order to clear the marsh.

Carefully tucked in a swaddling of cloth, Lozen cradled her spirit companion in her arms.

To everyone's relief, they cleared the Torpid Marsh without further incident aside from lesions and welts inflicted by slips and falls, and the relentless bugs infesting the region. The sight of the Olde Gritian Road did wonders to lift their spirits.

Pollard and Quincette spoke quietly amongst themselves, as did Klara, Mikter, and Nyler. Lozen and Ulk remained quiet during the days it took to reach the familiar forested area surrounding the base of the Muse.

It hadn't taken long for word to spread throughout the catacombs. Captain Johnnes Holman and second in command, Guardell Caulder, had dispatched guardsmen to relieve the company of their physical burdens long before they entered the tunnels.

Pollard

Fed and allowed to rest, they were escorted topside to provide a full account to the Songsbirth Chamber of the Wise.

Master Pul listened patiently to their individual accounts; inviting each and every member of the expedition to tell the story from their point of view. When the last person had spoken, the elder councilman sat back in his chair and stared at the Chamber's ceiling.

The tapers flickering on the table had burned low by the time he sat forward to address them. "That is indeed quite a tragic tale. One that I'm not surprised to hear when speaking of that vile place." He squinted to peer directly at Pollard. "A valuable lesson to be learned by all, I suspect."

Pollard nodded, lowering his gaze to the tabletop.

"Do not berate yourself, Pollard Banebridge. With the reins of leadership come heavy responsibility. Decisions made for the good of all can unfortunately lead to repercussions for the few. Hindsight is a valuable teacher going forward but does nothing to mitigate the damage done by decisions gone awry."

Master Pul smiled for the benefit of everyone seated at the table, but his toothless grin turned into one of compassion as he gazed upon Lozen. "As for you, my dear friend from the Elk Tribe, I fear your time with us has come to an end."

Pollard looked up; his shock overshadowed by that of Lozen.

"During your absence, Wender has sensed a profound change in the otherworldly dimensions she dabbles in. The storm we have foreseen is almost at hand. Wender is of the opinion that your peoples will have great need of you in the near future. She has asked to accompany you so that she may watch your peoples and learn their ancient ways. You have demonstrated to us that we can learn much if we just take the time to listen."

Pollard

Everyone around the table sat up straight, the dull ache of loss and failure transformed into complete attention and concern.

"Aye. That's the response we need if we are to live long enough to come out the other side," Master Pul said gravely. He turned his attention on Quincette. "As such, I'm asking you, my steadfast bastion of strength, to escort Lozen and Wender. Our way of thanking our esteemed colleague and her Elk Tribe for the priceless lessons and knowledge they have enlightened us with. See they have everything they require for the long journey." He stared deeply into Quincette's hard eyes. "I am trusting you will be the one who stands in the face of the wind."

Quincette held his stare, pride evident in her bearing. "It would be my honour, Master Pul."

"Excellent. Then it's settled." Pul dropped her intense gaze and scanned his attentive audience. Using his gnarled cane, he refused Pollard's offer to help him to his feet.

Once standing, the master of the Songsbirth Chamber of the Wise leaned his cane against the table and put his hands together. "Though not as formal as we usually do these things, I think it a fitting time to announce that every one of you has earned the right to call yourself a Songsbirthian Guard."

Pul allowed his proclamation to settle in.

Stunned expressions turned into happiness and relief. The former trainees looked at each other, unable to contain their emotion.

The Chambermaster let them congratulate themselves before his thin smile faded. "Don't get too excited. The easy part is now behind you." He nodded to Pollard. "From this day forward, the leaders of the Songsbirthian Guard will demand from you a sacrifice I doubt any of you had prepared to give. Stay strong. In body as well as in soul. The kingdom's future lies in your hands."

Pollard

Standing outside the exit at the base of the Splendoor Catacombs, Pollard knew he wasn't successful at hiding the emotion that was ripping him apart. He shivered in the morning breeze, absently thinking how different it felt when he wasn't wearing his brass cuirass.

He stretched his back muscles. The lesser weight of the simple great sword strapped to his back reminded him that his favourite double sword was in the care of the Catacombs' smith to clean it up and retune its edges after the battle with the bear troll. The beast's rock-hard hide had taken a surprising toll on one of the sword's keen edges.

Almost the entire contingent of the Songsbirthian Guard had assembled at the base of the cliff to bid farewell to Wender, Quincette, and Lozen as they emerged from the lower tunnel. The Guard had formed two lines on either side of the exit, creating their own tunnel beneath the bare branches of early spring. Scattered amongst the regular Guard were the beaming faces of the Songsbirthian Guard's newest members. Ulk, Klara, Nyler, Onynx, Mikter, and the two women he, Lozen, Quincette, and Carnoch had placed the most hope in—Larina and Sadyra.

A bittersweet sadness made his eyes well over. Carnoch wasn't here to take part. He swallowed. He knew in his heart that his loyal friend looked down on them, a great smile on his face. Carnoch's body may have left the world of the living, but his spirit would carry on forever in their hearts. He had died performing the duty he loved. Pollard was sure Carnoch wouldn't have wanted it any other way.

Wender stepped away from the end of the line of well-wishers and hobbled up to Pollard, having to bend over backward to take in his face.

Pollard

Out of respect for the aged woman, Pollard took her frail hands in his huge mitts and squatted. He forced a smile, though his lower lip trembled. "It has been an honour to have known you, young lady."

"Bah, sonny. Always the flatterer," Wender admonished. "It's a little late to be making a move on old Wender."

Pollard laughed despite his melancholy. He squeezed Wender's hands, careful not to hurt her. "You take care of yourself. You'll be in good hands. The best."

"You mean they're in the best of hands, I think." Wender cackled and leaned in, stretching up on her toes to kiss Pollard's cheeks.

Reaching into a fold of her tattered clothing, she pulled out a necklace fashioned with beads that held a dark blue, bear troll's tooth Pollard had extracted in the Torpid Marsh and brought home to honour the sacrifice of his friend, Carnoch.

He bowed his head and waited patiently as her shaking hands struggled to secure the clasp.

She patted his bare chest and let the necklace settle into place. "You're on your own now, Master Banebridge. Carnoch's spirit will be forever with you."

She stepped back and directed her gaze to Sadyra and Larina near the end of the receiving lines. She winked. "I pass your safety into their hands. Ward them well. You three will have great need of each other in the days to come."

Pollard smiled and nodded, distracted by the approach of Quincette. "I will, Wender. You take care of yourself."

Quincette stepped in front of Pollard. Her watery eyes stared into his, imparting an unspoken message.

The lump in his throat threatened to cut off his air supply. Much to Quincette's surprise, he wrapped her in a warm embrace, holding her tighter than he had ever held anyone in his life. If only they had met under different circumstances.

He eased the strength of his hug but didn't release her. Staring into her hard eyes, he found himself at a loss as to what to say. In his heart he knew she felt the same way about him. Tears rolled off her cheeks, matching his own, and that almost choked him completely. This was good-bye. Something in his gut told him he would never see her again. Not caring what anyone thought, he grabbed her by the cheeks and planted a long, hard kiss on her lips.

Quincette fought at first but wrapped her muscular arms around his neck and pulled him in tight.

When they finally released each other, Pollard knew his flaming cheeks matched hers. Without a word, she looked shyly at the ground and stepped aside to allow Lozen to come forward.

His breath caught. The special bond he and Lozen had formed over the few years she had graced the Songsbirthian Guard had been precious to him. The patient, caring, nurturing way she had with everyone under her care was second to none. So many good people were saved as a result of her intervention. Mikter being the last of a long line of recruits who had been on the verge of expulsion from the training classes. They were kept on as a result of Lozen's insistence that in order for their true mettle to shine, they needed to be polished in a special way.

Lozen's role in saving Larina from certain death at the hands of the Storms End Watch had been instrumental in providing the Songsbirthian Guard with one of the most promising prospects it had seen in a long while—since the day they had discovered Carnoch begging on the streets of Carillon.

As was Lozen's role in convincing Sadyra that the Songsbirthian Guard offered her a home where people appreciated her for who she was. Where people valued her skills. A home where she was loved.

Staring into Lozen's intelligent brown eyes, it felt like the end of all things good. As much as he loved Quincette, his love for Lozen was deeper—founded on a mutual respect that transcended the normal bonds joining special friends.

Pollard

Lozen liked to speak of spirit companions, but Pollard had taken that premise one step further when it came to the special woman staring up at him. Lozen was the sister he never had. Someone with whom he could share his deepest, darkest feelings without fear of judgement. Lozen was an extension of himself.

The emotional pain he had been experiencing since the battle in the Torpid Marsh had gutted him. As much as the deaths of Carnoch and the trainees had affected him, the sense of betrayal he felt that had grown between him and his dear friend had left him barely able to function. He had no appetite, no longing to get up in the morning. His usual lust for life had left him wallowing in the depths of self-pitying despair. He had ignored Lozen's warning and people had died as a result.

His eyes focused on Naiche resting comfortably in an open-topped basket that hung off Lozen's shoulder. It took him a couple of attempts to force the words past his constricted throat. "Is…Is he going to be okay?"

Lozen, true to form, didn't sugar coat her response. "Time will tell. Will he ever be the bird he once was?" She shrugged. "Maybe one day, but I doubt it. I have the feeling Naiche will depend on me for the rest of his life."

Pollard didn't know what to say. His best friend was leaving with the only woman he had ever truly had romantic feelings for and all he could do was wallow in the shame of an ill-timed decision. Perhaps he wasn't born to lead after all.

He forced a bleak smile, not knowing what to say.

Lozen glared at him for what felt like an eternity. Just when he thought she was going to walk away, she sighed and wrapped her arms around his waist, holding him close. Face pressed against his chest, she said softly, "Do not lament what happened. You acted with the best of intentions. In the end, I control the destiny of my spirit. I could've refused to follow you."

Pollard

Pollard's eyes widened. The relief that washed through him threatened to sap the strength from his legs as he listened to her soothing voice. So absorbed in her words, he stared straight ahead, unable to focus on anything but the feel of his best friend holding him.

"Carnoch, Rync, and the others died doing their duty. They did it out of love for the Guard, but more importantly, they did their duty out of love for their leader." Lozen's soft voice and the message she conveyed tingled his skin with goosebumps. "There is no higher honour than to have someone lay down their life in support of another's beliefs."

Lozen released him and gazed into his eyes. "As much as Naiche is my spirit companion, Pollard is my spirit warrior. I would follow you to the end of the world and throw myself off its edge if you asked."

Pollard could barely see through a fresh wave of tears. He picked her up as if she weighed nothing and hugged her head against his own. "I would throw myself off first to break your fall."

Pollard

Spring Equinox

Sadyra waited patiently near the end of the line of fellow guardsmen. It felt strange to consider herself one of the elite fighters of Zephyr. She didn't dare think to lump herself in with the likes of Pollard or Quincette, but just the thought of being accepted made her heart happy.

It appeared as if Pollard and Lozen had mended the rift between them—the two were clasping hands with Quincette and talking amongst themselves. Guardell Caulder seemed to be keeping close to Lozen as if they had shared more than a casual friendship during her stay with the Songsbirthian Guard. Hovering around the leadership group, the old hag Larina referred to as Wender also took part in their private discussions.

The faces of many men and women Sadyra hadn't seen before while training were mixed with those she was more familiar with. The sheer number of Songsbirthian Guard was impressive to say the least. Fighting a mischievous urge that she hadn't known since the Torpid Marsh, she nudged Larina. "Hey. You were right."

Larina frowned. "About what?"

"Your throwing knives."

Larina's frown deepened.

"You said that if they didn't sever something vital, they'd distract a target long enough to take them out with something more substantial."

Larina shook her head. "I have no idea what you're talking about."

"On the hill overlooking the marsh. Remember?"

"Sure, I guess." Larina shrugged. "What of it?"

"Nothing really. Watching Pollard and Lozen reminded me, that's all. During the battle, your knives distracted the bear troll and my arrow took it out."

"More like Quincette decapitated it."

Sadyra thought about that. "Ya, I guess you're right. In the end she did, but had your knives not thrown it off, and my arrow not staggered it, Quincette would be lying with Rync and Carnoch…"

Her mind drifted to the other five trainees she had never really gotten to know and the creatures that had attacked them from beneath the water's surface. "Or worse."

The formal receiving line had disbanded, and people milled about. Some waiting to escort Wender, Quincette, and Lozen to the dock at the end of the forest trail while others disappeared into the gaping hole at the base of the cliff.

Sadyra followed Larina into the tunnel, thinking about Lozen's parting message to her as they had said their good-byes. *"You are unique, Sadie. Your skill with a bow is unprecedented. I'm honoured to pass the title of best Songsbirthian Guard marksman onto you. While searching for Rync, you also proved your skill as an elite tracker. You spotted something in the terrain that had escaped me."*

Sadyra remembered thinking that perhaps it might not have been a good thing. Had she not discovered the trail leading to Rync, things may have turned out differently.

The mention of her tracking skills had been bittersweet. Scruff had originally taught her how to track. Other than his betrayal in the end, she had fond memories of the first man that had given her stomach flutters.

Accepting a hand up into the next tunnel, she plodded along beside Larina.

"What are you so happy about?" Larina asked.

"Huh? Oh, nothing. Just something Lozen said."

Pollard

When she didn't elaborate, Larina shook her head in disgust. "And?"

"Huh? Oh. Well, you know. She said nice things."

"Nice things?"

"Ya. Like how good of a bowman I am. And how good of a tracker I am." She shrugged, her mischievous grin a warning that Larina should beware of what was to come. "But she really wanted to point out how I need to be careful of the trouble *you* can bring."

Larina stopped and gaped.

Sadyra laughed and kept walking, awaiting her turn to pass through the hidden doorway into the third level tunnel that ran in one big circle. "Don't worry. It's nothing I can't handle."

Larina scrambled to catch up. "Wait. She didn't really say that, did she?"

Sadyra winked as someone from above hoisted her through the ceiling. The look on Larina's face made her laugh out loud. Without waiting for her friend to be hoisted through the gap, Sadyra skipped up the tunnel.

The galley was full to overflowing as most everyone involved in the send-off had gathered for the midday meal. Half of those crammed into the mess hall belonged to the Songsbirthian Guard stationed in Songsbirth, but Sadyra and the rest of the new members were respectful enough to allow the tenured guards the limited seats available.

Finding Larina against a side wall with the rest of the new guardsmen, Sadyra carried her wooden platter over to them and snuggled into a spot next to Larina so she could set into the delicious fare of pheasant and root vegetables. She flashed Larina a brief smile, but her friend was pretending to be mad at her because of their earlier conversation. At some point she'd have to tell Larina she was only joking, but decided it was fun to let her stew some more.

Sitting against the wall, her eyes followed Onynx and Nyler as they walked past. She smiled to herself at the nickname Larina had labelled the pale-skinned woman with. Ox. What a silly name for the skinny girl. She shook her head. The things that came out of Larina's mouth.

Onynx laughed and replied to something Nyler had said. "The spring equinox was yesterday. I've heard about rituals…" her words trailed away as she and Nyler kept walking.

A jolt of cold shot up Sadyra's spine. The mention of the spring equinox made her shiver—the relevance hitting her hard.

Images of the Mating Festival that would be well underway overpowered her thoughts. She could only imagine the state of drunkenness her parents would be in. The weeklong festivity provided them an excuse for a seven-day bender.

Larina's voice startled her back to the mess hall.

"What do you think they have planned for us now that we're full-blown guards?"

Sadyra tried to shake off the icy sensation chilling her soul. "No idea."

"Hmm. Me neither. Oh well. Wherever it is, it should prove interesting." A great smile lifted Larina's freckled cheeks. "Just think. We're full-fledged Songsbirthian Guards."

Sadyra returned her smile but wasn't feeling the happiness. Her mind was preoccupied. The spring equinox. Through everything that had happened lately: the rigourous training, the attention to detail, the trip south, visiting the Gritian Chamber of the Wise and meeting the High Bishop of the land, coupled with the unfortunate events that followed in the Torpid Marsh, the date had flown from her mind.

Pollard

The sudden shock of realizing the spring equinox was upon them shook her emotional foundation to the core. Had she remained in Fishmonger Bay, she would be married to Bano Shell. More importantly, if things had progressed like her father had intimated, she would have met a horrible death on the end of Bano's sacrificial dagger.

As sobering as that was, her fear for her sisters shook her so hard, her plate tumbled forgotten into her lap.

"Hey clumsy." Larina's hand flashed out to grab the plate before it rolled onto the ground. Staring into Sadyra's eyes, she asked, "What is it?"

Onynx and Nyler spun to see what the commotion was all about.

Ulk appeared out of the crowd and stared down at her. "What happened?"

Sadyra said nothing, her eyes wide with fear.

Larina shrugged. "One minute she was fine, the next…"

Vector stepped up beside Ulk. Seeing Sadyra's state, he knelt and looked her in the eye. "What is it, Sadyra? You look like you've seen a spectre."

Sadyra swallowed. She shook her head.

The people closest to where Sadyra and Larina sat against the wall had stopped what they were doing and watched on.

Realizing she was making a spectacle of herself, Sadyra shook her head and tried to get to her feet. "Its, um…nothing."

"Some nothing," Vector grabbed one of her hands and assisted her to her feet. "Come on. Let's get you out of here."

Larina stood with them and grabbed hold of Sadyra's arm. "It's okay. I got her. She needs some air."

"Alright, people. False alarm," Vector said, ushering everyone back so that they could pass through the crowd.

Larina nodded her thanks to Vector as she gently escorted Sadyra from the mess hall. "She's not feeling well. Probably something she ate. I'll watch her."

Pollard

Had Sadyra's mind not been reeling with the horrible visions the mention of the spring equinox evoked, she would have thanked Vector for his quick thinking. As it was, she could barely concentrate on keeping herself upright. She was vaguely aware of leaning on Larina, thankful that her friend hung onto her.

Larina stopped in the hall and grabbed her by both hands, looking into her crazed eyes. "This has something to do with why we found you in the Thunderhead marketplace all those months ago, doesn't it?"

Larina's voice spoke to her through the fog clouding her mind. She wasn't sure if she nodded or not.

Larina squeezed her hands. "You don't have to say anything unless you want to. I'm here for you if you need to talk." She nodded to the faces watching with concern from the doorway. "We're all here for you. Whatever it is, it can't hurt you now."

Sadyra wanted to scream. To tell Larina she had no idea what she was talking about. The fear crippling her could indeed hurt her. In a more profound way than Larina or the others could ever know.

Guilt added itself to the soul crushing emotions threatening to overwhelm her. With her departure from Fishmonger Bay, her sisters would be the ones to feel the wrath of their parents—especially Sable.

She swallowed. What had she done? She had abandoned them. Left them to fend for themselves against the tyranny of the dark secret that tormented their parents. Some nonsense about a dragon witch.

Her father's words rushed back to her—spoken when he had confronted her in Gitch's warehouse. *"It's time to exorcise the burden of the Ors' legacy and send you to the nether world."*

The fear he had instilled that day was as poignant as ever. It was as if he were right there in front of her now.

Pollard

"Bano's parents have committed Bano to offer his unsullied wife as a sacrifice. Thus, we shall appease the dragon gods and lift the family curse from our generation."

The proclamation had shocked her to the core back then and the hurt had never really diminished. Everyone and everything she had believed in, all of it, had been nothing but a pack of lies—a ruse to keep her confused until the Mating Festival of her twenty-first birthyear.

"Typical Sadyra," her father had snarled. *"Always making things difficult. According to legend, we're supposed to wait until your twenty-first name year, but I don't think your mother or I can take it that long. We'll just have to take our chances with Sable."*

She had originally thought that her father meant they would do the same to Sable that they had done with her—wait for Sable's twenty-first birth year. Now that the day had come and gone, something deep inside whispered, *What if you're wrong?*

She spun out of Larina's grasp and clutched her best friend by the shoulders, her eyes wild. "I have to go!"

Larina winced as Sadyra jerked free of her grasp. "Ow! What the—?"

"I need to get out of here," Sadyra said, her voice shrill. Her eyes flicked from person-to-person as if she were afraid of them.

"Sadie. Calm down. You're scaring me. What is it?"

"Where's Pollard?" Sadyra started up the tunnel toward the sleeping quarters but stopped. Changing direction, she pushed past her concerned peers spilling into the passage, and broke into a run toward the Well of Despair.

Larina called after her. "Sadie. Wait!"

Her friend's plea barely registered. She needed to get home. If the launch that had been sent to carry Lozen and the others hadn't left yet, she could steal a ride downriver.

Pollard

Under her hand's pressure, the wall separating the tunnel from the Well of Despair grated open. She pushed through the gap as soon as it was wide enough.

Dashing across the Well of Despair, careful to give the darker stone around its centre a wide berth, she burst from the cavern and ran headlong into Pollard.

The surprised giant had no choice but to catch her in his arms or be run over. "Whoa, lass. Where're you going in such a hurry?"

Sadyra punched at him and twisted in his grasp. "Let me go, you big oaf. I have to go!"

Larina's voice echoed in the cavern, "Hold her! She's gone mad!"

Punching and kicking, Sadyra struggled to break free. Frustrated, she screamed, "No! Let me go! I have to get to the launch! I need to save Sable!"

Pollard struggled to keep a hold on her. "Easy lass. You need to calm down."

Sadyra squirmed and twisted, contorting her body unnaturally. She bit the hand holding her upper arm and stomped down on Pollard's foot.

"Ow!" Pollard released her.

Sadyra sprinted up the tunnel.

"Sadie, stop! It's too late!"

Sadyra's mind reeled. Too late? How did he know it was too late? Sable might still be alive, or did he know something she didn't?

Scruff and Captain Gitch's betrayal slammed into the forefront of her mind. She stumbled. Could Pollard and everyone else be part of the same deception?

Catching herself against a wall, she had arrived at the first transition doorway. Swallowing her rising terror, she triggered it without having to search for the release. Slipping through, she released the opposite latch and the doorway ground shut behind her, closing off the cries of those giving chase.

Pollard

The spring equinox was at hand.

It was as if the catacombs were caving in around her as she ran.

Pollard

Where Darkness Thrives

"**Leave** her to me," Larina cautioned Pollard and the others who had accompanied them on their frenzied flight through the Splendoor Catacombs.

They hadn't been able to catch up to Sadyra in the tunnels, nor did Larina think they would. Sadyra had proven many times over that there wasn't a person in the Songsbirthian Guard who could match her pace over any sort of distance. Sadyra was tireless. Driven by her crazed determination to return home, only Naiche would have been able to keep up with her, but sadly, their feathered friend had left with Lozen.

The sun had dropped low in the western sky by the time they had emerged from the forest and converged on the dock jutting into the Madrigail River.

Immense relief filled Larina. Sadyra was crouched on the end of the dock, her long, auburn hair blowing around her hunched form. She had missed the boat.

Larina approached quietly and knelt behind her, placing her hands on Sadyra's trembling shoulders. Gently turning her friend into her, she hugged Sadyra's head into her shoulder and stroked her hair, cooing ever so softly.

Pollard clomped up behind them, a grave look on his face. "I tried to tell her it was too late."

Larina could tell that the poor man thought this was all his fault. Somehow connected to the debacle in the Torpid Marsh. Her chin on top of Sadyra's head, she smiled for

Pollard's benefit and shook her head, motioning for him and the others to give Sadyra room.

Though she didn't know the whole story of Sadyra's past, her friend had been reluctant to say much about it during the time they spent together, Sadyra had told her enough.

Beaten and mentally abused by parents who cared little to nothing for her welfare, Sadyra had endured a hard life growing up in what she called a backwater, fishing village. She had hinted her parents weren't the only ones who had wronged her, but Larina didn't know who the other people were. From what she could surmise, one of them had been a man Sadyra had romantic feelings for. There was also a prearranged marriage mixed in there somewhere, but Larina didn't think the two individuals involved were connected.

Wracking shivers shook Sadyra's body. Given the unusually warm day, Larina struggled to hold back her own tears. Her friend was suffering horribly, and she was helpless to prevent it. All she could do was hold her tight and reassure her that she was there for her.

The sun had lost its grip on the land before Sadyra looked up at Larina—her face a mess of tears, snot, drool, and smeared dirt. Larina smiled, biting back the words that came to mind. As cheeky as the two of them were with each other, it wasn't the right time to tell Sadyra how awful she appeared. In fact, the haunted look in Sadyra's wide-eyed, faraway stare, scared Larina.

Ever so carefully, she helped Sadyra to her feet and half-carried her to a log beside a community firepit built off to the side of the dock. The temperature had fallen rapidly but Pollard had seen to it that a large fire crackled in earnest.

Larina searched the area and frowned, wondering what had happened to all of the others who had given chase.

Pollard gestured with a thumb over his shoulder and mouthed, "I sent them back."

Pollard

Darkness enveloped the land, rapidly dropping the temperature. Resigned to the fact that they would be spending the night under the stars, Pollard informed Larina that he would check in on them from time-to-time. He wanted to make sure they weren't set upon by trolls. Every time he returned, he brought with him an armful of wood and restoked the fire before slipping into the cold night air.

If Larina caught any sleep during the night, it was in short spurts. Sadyra lay against her like a newborn babe nuzzling her mother. She never made a sound other than to sniffle.

Sadyra groaned and rolled her head to look into Larina's eyes, a sad smile on her face. She swallowed and sat up. Pushing away from Larina, she whispered, "I'm sorry."

"No need to be sorry, Sadie." Larina nodded toward Pollard who sat on a rock, tending a turkey he had roused out of the undergrowth last night. Bits of charred feathers littered the edge of the firepit. "Master Banebridge and I will always be here for you. Neither one of us can imagine what you've gone through…Are going through."

Sadyra frowned. "You told him?"

"You didn't leave me much choice. Taking off crazed like you did, you scared everyone. Master Banebridge deserves to know the truth. He needs to know what's happening to you."

Sadyra's hard glare softened. She dropped Larina's gaze and stared at Pollard's stick stirring up the embers. "I guess you're right. I apologize, Master Banebridge. I don't think I'm up to all this guard stuff. I have to go home."

Larina exchanged a worried glance with Pollard. She put a consoling hand on Sadyra's forearm. "Don't be so silly. You're the best damned archer this place has ever seen. Lozen told you that."

Pollard

Sadyra shrugged off her touch and turned a bitter stare on her friend. "You don't understand. I *need* to go home." She appeared poised to say more, but instead, she returned her gaze to the fire.

Larina's patience was running thin. It had been a long night. "Then help us to understand," she said a little more vehemently than she meant to.

Pollard shoved the stick into the fire and let it go. "Sadyra. Look at me."

With a resigned expression, Sadyra met his gaze.

"We're family now. You, me, Larina. Everyone in the Guard. As a part of the family, we look out for each other. If someone hurts, we all hurt. If someone's in trouble, we band together and deal with it as a family." He looked up, as if beseeching Larina for help. Heaving a heavy sigh, he added, "I guess what I'm trying to say is, we can't help you if you don't allow us in."

A long while passed but Sadyra didn't offer any more.

Pollard carved the pheasant and served it on pieces of bark he had shaved clean sometime during the night.

The morning meal done, Pollard smothered the fire and readied himself to leave. Looking pointedly at Sadyra, he asked, "Are you coming?"

Larina feared Sadyra would say no, but breathed a sigh of relief as her friend nodded and got to her feet.

"Come on." Pollard smiled. "Let's get you cleaned up."

The early spring day was rife with wildlife scampering about the forest floor and flitting amongst the barren branches overhead. Pollard led them to the left of the catacomb's entrance and took them to a wide catch basin of turbulent water at the base of the falls. Giving Larina and Sadyra privacy, they bathed in one of the calmer side pools carved into the rock around the basin's edge and dried themselves off as best as they could.

Pollard

Pollard returned a short while later looking much cleaner himself. "Much better," was all he said as he made for the trail that would lead them back to the catacombs' entrance.

Sadyra's plea stopped him. "Wait!"

Pollard did as he was asked.

Sadyra appeared on the verge of tears again. "You're right. I'm ready to talk if you're willing to listen."

Larina said at once, "Of course we are."

Pollard nodded emphatically and led them to a recently downed tree partway up the trail.

When Sadyra spoke, they had to lean in close to hear her over the distant roar of the falls. She started slowly, filling in snippets of her early years. She couldn't recall a time she never had the semblance of a bruise somewhere on her body. By the time she finished her story, Larina and Pollard stared at her, stunned. She hadn't left anything out.

Birdsong filled the air and the annoying buzz of insects kept them swatting as they shared a tender moment embraced in a collective hug, each of them trying to come to terms with what was just revealed.

As sad as Sadyra's story had seemed to Larina before, the stark reality of her friend's past was so much darker than she had let on. How she had coped with it for so long was a mystery.

Larina considered how she would have handled it had it been her in Sadyra's position. She was sure she would have ended her father's life a long time ago. Perhaps her mother's as well. What that would have done to their family, Larina had no idea, but to constantly live in terror of abuse that one knew was coming was incomprehensible. Sadly, she conceded that perhaps she wouldn't have handled it any better than Sadyra. To grow up not knowing any different, how could she?

The slow burn of anger that had been simmering since last evening while she held Sadyra close, feeling deeply for her friend, was fanned to a raging inferno by Sadyra's story.

Pollard

Though she'd never really appreciate what her friend had endured, Sadyra's plight reminded her of the injustices she herself had fought so hard against in a losing effort to help the vulnerable souls of Storms End.

She released Sadyra and Pollard and stood. "Get up. Both of you."

Sadyra and Pollard released each other. Wiping their faces on their shoulders, they stared at her.

"Let's go. Now!" Larina put her hands on her hips. "We have two precious girls to save."

Sadyra's face transformed into one of awe while Pollard frowned in consternation.

"But how?" Sadyra asked, her voice breaking. "We missed the boat. There won't be another for a fortnight."

"On foot if we have to," Larina declared. "I'm sure Master Banebridge's authority will be enough to conscript horses when we come across a farm or town."

"Seriously?" Sadyra looked from Larina to Pollard. "You would do that for me?"

Pollard appeared taken aback by the suddenness of the new course of action, but he surprised Larina when he lifted his chin and said, "Of course. It's time to extricate your sisters from the darkness."

Larina started up the trail toward the catacombs' entrance.

"Where are you going?" Pollard asked.

"Back to the trail that leads to the Olde Gritian Road."

Pollard waved a dismissive hand. "That'll take us out of our way. We need to cross the Madrigail and pick up the northern route from there."

Larina walked back, confused. "Where do you suppose we cross? This section of river is far too rough. We can cross at the boat launch."

Pollard raised his heavy brows twice in quick succession. "Not if you know where to look."

Larina frowned. "I've been up and down the south shore many times during training. I defy you to show us a safe place to cross. The gap between the rocks are too wide, even for a big oaf like you."

A slight smile lifted the sadness from Sadyra's face.

"Follow me, ladies." Pollard spun about and strutted up the trail toward the waterfall basin. Before long, he turned off the trail and stopped, his path blocked by the cliff face.

Larina and Sadyra watched in amazement as a thin doorway revealed itself.

"I never knew about this tunnel," Larina said, eyes wide taking in the area around them in the hope of remembering where to find it in the future.

"Ha! There are many secrets concerning the Splendoor Catacombs that you may or may not become privy to during your stint as a Songsbirthian Guard. There are things about the labyrinth that none of us has discovered." Pollard reached inside and grabbed a torch from a metal basket. He set it ablaze and nodded for them to precede him. "After you."

The tooth rattling rumble of grating rock filled the close confines of the passageway behind the falls. Small stones popped under the weight of the slab of granite moving along its hidden track. Though she had no way of knowing, Larina suspected the tunnel hadn't been used in a long time.

Navigating the meandering passageway in the faint light of the torch wasn't easy. "Do many people come this way?"

"Not that I'm aware of. Other than Holmann and Caulder, we might be the only ones who know about it." The tunnel was so narrow that Pollard walked sideways to keep his wide shoulders from brushing the roughly hewn walls.

"Here," Pollard said and gave Larina the torch as he squeezed by.

It took longer than usual to find the trip mechanism. As the door rumbled open, he relieved Larina of the torch, snuffed it, and placed it in a thin metal basket. Leading them out of the cliff, he said, "It's best you be ready for whatever comes."

Pollard

The granite slab slipped back into place behind them as Sadyra pulled her bow over her shoulder and strung it, and Larina unsheathed her dagger.

Pollard stared at the rugged landscape before them. "It's time we go where darkness thrives."

Pollard

Over the Edge

Horses' hooves pounded the hard-packed roadway two days north of The Forke. Riding in single file, Larina and Sadyra's mounts easily kept pace with Pollard's larger destrier. Six full days out of Millsford, where Pollard had conscripted three horses and sent a message back to Songsbirth about where they were going, they rode hard, stopping frequently to rest their mounts. Their pace had slowed considerably as the road they followed ventured deeper into the Spine. Though the Storms End Route generally kept to the valley floors that separated individual mountains, their route continually climbed higher, turning west toward Storms End.

Larina had never travelled down the Storms End Route. Had never been outside of her old city until recently other than to wander the moors atop the fjord on occasion. With nothing to look at except wondrous hills, deep blue lakes, and water tumbling from jags of bare rock that reached for the partly cloudy sky, her eyes fell on the necklace Wender had given Pollard.

It was as if a switch went off. She recalled her visit to the witch's shop in Songsbirth. Behind her little table in the middle of Wender's cluttered hovel, Larina remembered wondering about a large, stuffed animal that had been half buried behind the old witch. A bear troll! Where the crone had acquired such a nasty thing was a mystery.

While restocking their provisions in The Forke, Pollard had informed them it would be a three-day ride to Storms

End in good weather. So far, the conditions had been favourable, if a little cool. With a mountain crossing ahead of them, Pollard had the foresight to acquire warmer clothes and leather gloves for the last leg of their journey.

With the mountain pass far behind them, Pollard slowed his mount at the top of a steep, snow-covered rise and stared over a wide valley. The Storms End Route continued along the side of the valley, dipping to the shores of a large lake— its deep blue surface reflecting the sky and hills around it. "Not much farther now. The highland moors lie on the far side of this valley."

"And this road will lead us to Thunderhead?" Sadyra asked, her distant stare filled with a craving to get home as soon as possible.

Larina sighed, feeling for her friend. Admiring the view, it dawned on her she knew this valley. It marked the boundary of her travels while in Storms End. She had spent many days frolicking through the tall summer grasses above the lake, playing and laughing with Cassie. It looked different from this angle.

Pushing the memory from her mind to quell the powerful emotions the valley evoked deep within her, she coaxed her mount into a trot, and led her friends over the last few leagues into Storms End. It would be bittersweet to see the city again. With any luck, she'd get to visit Bear.

"Where are you going?" Pollard called after Sadyra who had urged her horse into a gallop and was quickly putting distance between them. He stared down the left fork of the road to where he could just make out the edge of his father's estate at the top of the fjord.

If Sadyra heard him she never slowed.

Pollard looked at Larina. "I thought we agreed to spend the night at Banebridge Manor?"

Larina raised her eyebrows and shrugged. "I doubt she's thinking straight anymore. She's worried about her sisters."

"She'll be no good to them when she gets there if she runs herself ragged. If what she said about her father is true, I doubt she'll be welcome home." Pollard sighed, turning his horse off the path into Storms End and starting after Sadyra. "We'd better go after her."

It was dark before they caught up to Sadyra. Unable to safely ride their horses over a rough stretch of the roadway running along the north rim of Thunderhead Fjord in the dark, they decided to set up camp.

Pollard estimated it was a full day's ride to Thunderhead from their present position and at least another day before they reached Fishmonger Bay. The coastal route joining the two centres wasn't kept in good repair as most people preferred to travel the waves along the rugged west coast of Zephyr.

They clattered into Thunderhead at sundown the following day, stopping briefly in the marketplace to restock and were off again. If the fight Sadyra had been involved in when they had first met phased the auburn-haired woman, she never let on.

Sadyra had withdrawn into herself, barely acknowledging her companions when they spoke to her.

They camped two bays north of Thunderhead on a thin strip of beachhead. As soon as it was light enough to see the next morning, Larina and Pollard were hard-pressed to keep up with Sadyra along the twisting, coastal trail.

"Sadie, wait! Pollard's horse can't carry him that fast!" Larina called after her receding form, but it was no use. Charging up the mountainside, Sadyra ignored her.

Larina left Pollard to follow along as quickly as his horse would allow, but before long, she could only snatch glimpses of Sadyra in the distance—her waist length hair billowing out behind her. By midday, other than fresh hoof prints that confirmed Sadyra still followed the trail, Larina couldn't see her anymore.

Pollard caught up to Larina on the crest of a high ridge as the day's last rays glinted off a distant peak north of their position. He pulled up beside her and pointed to the snow-capped summit. "Fishmonger Bay lies at the base of that mountain."

Larina considered the darkness rapidly covering the land. "Do we dare keep going?"

Pollard raised heavy eyebrows. His heart urged him to keep moving but common sense warned him against it. "This is a treacherous trail. It'd be foolish to go any farther tonight."

"I thought you said Sadyra's village was only a day's ride up the trail?"

Pollard shrugged. "I guess I was wrong. These mountain trails twist and turn all over the place." He exhaled a long breath and scanned their surroundings. "I wish Sadie would've stopped at Storms End. We could have taken one of my father's boats."

"What?" Larina gaped. "Why didn't you say something?"

He slapped his hips in frustration and shook his head. "I didn't think about it at the time."

Larina gave him an exasperated look. It was obvious she wrestled with her conscience. As if sensing her mood, her horse stamped back and forth, looking like it yearned to continue up the trail. "You know she won't stop?"

"Oh, I know. You don't have to tell me." Pollard sighed. "I'm willing to walk my horse all night if you are."

Larina didn't hesitate. "Absolutely." She leapt from the saddle and grabbed her horse's reins, leading him into the deepening shadows of the next valley.

Pollard joined her on the ground, mumbling to himself, "I hope we don't miss the spot where Sadie's horse carries her over the edge of a cliff."

Pollard

Dead Reckoning

If Sadyra lived to see another say, she silently promised her horse that she would pamper him long and hard—the magnificent creature had without hesitation carried her along the treacherous route between Thunderhead and Fishmonger Bay. He had slipped and stumbled several times throughout the night; twice throwing Sadyra into the undergrowth. The resulting bruises and scrapes she had picked up as a result hadn't deterred her from continuing on in the least. Fixated on what she might be walking into, nothing else mattered. She would either recover from her injuries or she wouldn't. She didn't care. Her sisters needed her and that's all that mattered.

Her eyes felt as if they were filled with sand by the time the snowy summit of Peril's Peak glistened in the light of the new day.

The Mating Festival would be over—nothing more than a raunchy tale for those who had partaken in the weeklong gala of debauchery and hooliganism—the likes of which would turn the Thunderhead brothel district's cheeks red. How a quiet, hardworking village could transform itself once every three years into a wild carnival mecca was mind boggling. She could just see the crowds that had travelled to the small village from Thunderhead and beyond. The bay would be so thick with boats that a person could walk across the water by leaping from one to another.

The path leading up to the summit of Peril's Peak passed by on her right. The inference of what it represented made her breath catch in her throat. She stopped her horse and gazed up the trail, the path faint in the early morning twilight.

She had experienced something special up that way, on the edge of the canyon that ran along the mountain's western flank. For the briefest of moments, she thought she had found out what love was all about. Scruff's musty scent had filled her senses as he took a handful of her hair and ran it through his fingers—a tenderness she had never seen in his eyes. Thinking back, she wondered what she could have done to have encouraged that moment into something more magical.

Her eyes hardened. Scruff had been no better than the others. A snivelling, self-serving boor who had played with her heart to perpetuate the lie he and everyone else in Fishmonger Bay had taken part in.

She stared up the last stretch of trail that would take her into Fishmonger Bay. Not caring about the tears spilling down her cheeks, she urged her horse forward. It was time to face those responsible and expose the dark secret that had been hanging over her head for the past two decades.

The edge of town came into view, most of its buildings in dire need of repair. At the base of the cliff that rose up from the rocky strewn spit of land the village was built upon, the *Witch's Cauldron* lay in the early morning shadows next to the temple. Hidden beyond the house of worship, she envisioned the village mercantile, most of its trappings too expensive for one of her ilk.

Across the gravel commons lay the largest building in the village. Gitch's warehouse. She stared hard, grinding her teeth at what the building represented—a false bastion full of men who would sooner slit her throat than spend another day in her company.

She firmed up her resolve. If she survived her encounter with her parents, she would return to the village and deal with them. The bastards had it coming.

Pollard

Thankful for the hooded cloak Pollard had got for her during their brief stay in The Forke, she pulled the cowl over her head and walked her horse across the village centre, bowing low over the horse's neck.

It was early morning. The only danger of encountering anyone at this time of the day would come from the direction of the warehouse. Gitch was a stickler for hitting the waves at first light.

Sure enough, the sound of men's idle banter echoed off the cliff as Gitch's crew prepared their boats. Sadyra kept her horse as close to the *Cauldron* and the temple as possible. Relieved, she realized the crew had tied off to the rickety old jetty last night and wouldn't see her until she approached the break between the two houses backing onto the steep hill at the north end of the village.

Rounding the temple steps and passing in front of the mercantile, her heart skipped a beat. The distinct squeal of the warehouse door pierced the early morning air. A bald-headed man with an oft broke nose emerged from around the far corner of the warehouse and watched her. She swallowed and slunk deeper into her hood, keeping her head turned away as best she could.

There was nothing that should give her identity away, but she couldn't help thinking that Captain Gitch had recognized her.

Her left hand found the hilt of her filleting knife. She should ride over and gut him where he stood. The surprise on his face as he realized who had disemboweled him would be worth the risk of being hunted by his crew. But not yet. She had to get to her hut on the hill. The home of the Dragon Witch.

Not wishing to alert her parents of her approach, she tethered her horse to a tree behind the buildings flanking the trail entrance and started up the hill on foot. Reaching the top of the main trail she hesitated. What if she was wrong?

Pollard

What if everything was okay and her presence only exacerbated her sisters' grief?

She debated turning around. She had been gone for half a year. A lot could have happened since she fled. Perhaps with her gone, her parents' malady might have corrected itself.

Her eyes found the two gravestones in the barren undergrowth at the foot of the path that led to her family's cabin. Headstones of people who had lived hundreds of years ago if what Bano Shell claimed was true.

A bitter laugh escaped her. As if. The lecherous man was no better than the rest of them. Bano would have to be held accountable as well.

She sniffed her derision and glared up the path—the roofline of the dilapidated hut visible through the bare branches of trees lining the thin, dirt track. If anything had happened to her sisters, there would be a dead reckoning in the Ors family homestead.

Quiet as a shadow, she padded up to the hut. Looking around, unsure how to continue, she slipped around the side of the building. Keeping her back close to the wall, she constantly scanned the shadows clinging to the bushes and trees around the hut. It would be just like her father to be waiting for her. He always ruined everything.

Crouched below the hut's only window in the middle of the rear wall, she took a deep breath. It was time to stand up to her parents—her father in particular, and rescue her sisters from their tyrannical ways. Something she should have addressed long ago.

Ever so slowly, she rose and twisted to peer into the hut's interior. It was too dark to see anything. From where she stood, her parents would be off to the left and her sisters on the right. Cupping her hands against the grimy windowpanes didn't offer her anything better.

Beads of perspiration dripped off her face. Heart racing, she crouched again and beseeched herself, "Think, Sadie, think."

Pollard

Knowing her parents, they would be dead to the world. If she could sneak into the hut without making a noise, she might be able to sneak Sleena and Sable out without waking their parents. From there it would be an easy task to put them on her horse at the base of the hill and ride them out of town.

Not knowing what else to do, it made the most sense. Her desire to kill her father hadn't changed one bit, but as she shivered in the early morning chill, she knew she was fooling herself. Being on the cusp of a confrontation with the people who had caused her so much grief, her resolve had abandoned her. There was no way she could see herself attacking them, especially Tural—even in self-defence. She shook her head, angered by her ineptitude.

It made no sense. She had battled with Gitch's crew, killed two trolls, fought with dozens of men and women while training with the Songsbirthian Guard, and had been partly responsible for taking down a bear troll—a feat that she had been told not to take lightly. Yet, when it came to Tural, icy tendrils of fear pulsed through her veins—rendering her incapable of doing anything but suffer whatever punishment he wished to inflict upon her.

Nodding to herself, she knew what she had to do. If her sisters had any chance of a better life, she must sneak them away from Fishmonger Bay. She briefly considered waiting until she knew her father was elsewhere, but the thought of Larina and Pollard's imminent arrival precluded that option. Their presence in the Bay would evoke questions that eventually led to her. If her parents suspected why she had returned, she doubted she'd get another chance.

The shadows had lifted noticeably as she rounded the hut and stepped softly onto the warped boards of the front porch. She managed two steps before one of the boards protested beneath her weight.

She cringed; her body going still. Listening, she didn't dare move for some time before she hazarded another step. The offending board creaked again as she took her weight off it; causing her to freeze.

A cool breeze swept up the path from the ocean, raising goosebumps—her garments soaked with perspiration. Daring to move again, she put a hand on the door handle and winced even before she gently pulled the door open; anticipating the squeal of its hinges. Although it made a noise, she opened the door so slowly that it negated the worst of it. It took just as long to pull the door closed.

Her eyes went to where her parent's pallet was built against the right side of the hut. Other than a dark mass, she couldn't tell if anyone slept there.

Tiptoeing around the dinner table, she almost cried out as her toe caught the leg of a stool and scraped it on the hardwood floor. Cursing her clumsiness, she held her breath, but no sound reached her except for a soft snore from where her parents would be.

She made it to the back corner of the hut and squinted, trying to see her sisters' heads poking above the blanket she knew they would be sharing. She thought she could make out one of them against the wall, but that was it. The other must be buried beneath the blanket.

Her leather pants creaked as she knelt, the dead silence making the noise sound so much louder. Crawling across the spread of blankets, she quietly patted the area before the splay of hair against the wall but didn't find anyone else. She could tell by the size of the lump beneath the blanket that it was Sleena.

She frowned. Poor Sable. Sleena must be hugging her—protecting her from the fear the darkness always held for their youngest sibling. She fought off the guilt threatening to immobilize her. She should have been the one comforting Sable. Comforting both of them.

Putting a hand on Sleena's thin shoulder, she leaned in close and whispered, "Sleena. Wake up. It's me, Sadie."

A confused face turned in the faint light to stare up at her—Sleena's eyes growing wide as it dawned on her who knelt beside her.

Sadyra put a finger to her lips, shushing Sleena louder than she cared to. She looked over her shoulder, fearing the inevitable, but no one stirred.

Hoping Sleena had recovered from her initial shock, Sadyra whispered, "Where's Sable?"

Sleena's eyes grew wider.

"What is it? Where's your sister? I'm here to take you away from here."

Sleena shook her head, terror in her eyes.

"It's okay. I have friends coming. We're going to take you away from all this." Sadyra looked over her shoulder. The longer they fussed in the corner, the greater chance her parents would waken.

Sadyra leaned over Sleena and went to feel the space between her and the wall but Sleena sat bolt upright and tried to push her away, her head and shoulders thumping against the log wall.

"It's okay. It's me, Sadie. Your sister, silly," Sadyra's whisper was louder than she felt prudent, but she couldn't help it. She swallowed and glanced at where her parent's pallet lay across the hut.

A sinking feeling chilled her to the bone. Something was dreadfully wrong.

Pollard

The Demon Within

Pollard had given in to Larina and remounted shortly after dark. Against his better judgement they rode as fast as they dared through the night; stopping to walk quickly with their horses at various times when the trail became too hazardous.

Larina had gone down once, but Pollard's warhorse was nimble for its size and sure of foot. The horseman from Millsford had certainly trained his horses well.

The sun was rising in the east, but it would still be a long while before it crested the mountainside rising on their right. He had hoped they might overtake Sadyra, but in his heart he knew that short of errantly charging off a cliff, there was no way the woman with the heart of a tiger would be put off. He pitied anyone who stood in her way.

Larina stopped her horse at the junction of a trail that meandered up the side of the mountain. "Which way?"

Pollard rode up beside her and followed her gaze. "I've never been to Fishmonger Bay before but if I had to guess, I'd say we keep along the coastal track."

He jumped from his horse, thankful to stand and give his bruised butt some respite. Both trails were composed of flat rock and hard packed dirt making it difficult to find evidence of a horse that may have turned off and followed the path up the hillside. Several steps along the coastal trail, he knelt and found what he was looking for. "She went this way."

He had no sooner spoken than he had to move off the trail to avoid being trampled by Larina's mount.

Pollard

She gave him a grim smile and urged her horse to a trot. Pollard heard her say to the wind, "We're coming Sadie."

Sadyra sensed the new presence in the hut before she saw it move.

Rising from where their parents' pallet lay, a thin, angular silhouette struck a flint twice in quick succession, igniting a flame to a handheld sconce. In the flickering glow of the struggling flame, Areeza Ors' haggard face regarded her from across the cabin.

"Who goes there? Tural? Sleena?"

Her mother hadn't seen her yet, but that wouldn't last long. It wasn't lost on Sadyra that her mother hadn't mentioned Sable.

Sadyra grabbed Sleena's hand and lifted her to her feet, the two of them facing the advance of light. She pulled her dagger free of its sheath and knelt to look Sleena in the eyes. "Where's Sable?"

Sleena shook her head rapidly; the light from the sconce exposing tears streaming down her cheeks.

"Sadyra?" Areeza gasped and stopped halfway across the cabin, squinting.

Sadyra released Sleena's hand and stepped toward her mother, filleting knife clutched firmly in hand. Fearing to find Tural on the pallet behind her mother, she demanded, "What have you done with Sable?"

"Ah, so it is you? Come back to haunt us, have you?" Areeza's tone was acidic.

Sadyra brandished her blade between them. "Where's my sister?"

Areeza shook her head; disgust registered on her sour face. "Gone. Banished to a place we should have sent you years ago."

Sadyra staggered, grabbing the rounded bulk of one of the logs comprising the wall beside her to keep from falling over. "What do you mean, gone? Where is she?" Even as the question lingered in the air between them, she already knew the answer.

"Where do you think, witch? We sent her back to your devilish ancestors. Her blood has ensured they'll no longer cast their shadow over us."

The filleting knife clattered to the dirty floorboards as Sadyra cupped her face with shaking hands and dropped to her knees, her mind struggling to comprehend her mother's horrific words.

Never taking her eyes off Sadyra, Areeza sidestepped to the counter below the window and snatched up a wide-bladed carving knife. Putting the sconce on the edge of the dinner table, she started forward, the knife blade glinting in the flickering light. "It's time you joined her."

Frozen with terror, Sadyra could only watch as her mother came for her. It was true. Everything she had feared had come to pass. And, it was all her fault. By fleeing her predetermined fate, she had sentenced her dear sister to death. Although her mother's intentions frightened her, it was nothing more than she deserved.

"Sadie!" Sleena wrapped her arms around Sadyra's head, her little body protecting Sadyra from their mother's blade.

A hideous cackle escaped Areeza. "When Tural gets back, he'll be ecstatic to know I have rid him of both of you." She hoisted the blade to her shoulder and dove in for the kill.

Sadyra's shoulder hit the floor, the impact sending a jarring pain through her neck. She extended her arms, throwing Sleena away from where their mother stumbled into the space where the girls slept.

"Run, Sleena! Get out of here!" Sadyra screamed, wild eyes locked on Areeza—their mother's image blurred by tears.

"Why you little…" Areeza growled and spun on Sadyra.

Pollard

Acting on instinct alone, Sadyra slammed a palm against the underside of Areeza's knife bearing arm, driving it out wide. Her other hand shot out to clutch Areeza by the throat and drive her against the wall; their feet getting caught up in the blankets underfoot.

Her knife arm pinned to the wall, and her neck squeezed in Sadyra's death grip, Areeza croaked, "It's too late, witch. Sable has been sacrificed to the dragon gods. Our generation's burden has been exorcised."

Sadyra gritted her teeth, resisting the urge to smash her mother's insolent face with her forehead. "You're the demon within our family. You and father. You murdered your own child!" Sadyra pulled pack on her mother's neck just enough to slam Areeza's head against the unforgiving log behind her.

Spit frothed at the corners of Areeza's mouth. "You wait until you have children. You will be the one to bear the burden of the curse." She puckered her lips and spat in Sadyra's face.

Temporarily blinded, Sadyra didn't see her mother's hand shoot up and grab her long hair. With a violent tug and a head butt that cracked Sadyra between the eyes, Areeza broke free and violently shoved Sadyra across the room.

Sadyra backstepped as fast as she could, trying to keep from falling, but she tripped over a stool at the end of the table and went down in a heap.

Sleena squealed. Items crashed to the floor in the darkness.

Sadyra scrambled to her feet, trying get her bearings; her head reeling from her mother's vicious attack. The blur of her sister racing along the front wall caught her attention—their mother closing in on Sleena with her knife raised.

"Get back here you little—"

"No!" Sadyra cried out, hoisting the stool in the air and flinging it across the cabin.

The rickety piece of furniture exploded against Areeza's shoulder, knocking her into the wall and tripping her up. She tumbled in a flurry of grunts and curses; shards of splintered wood covering her frail body.

Sadyra wasted no time. Sprinting toward the door where Sleena quaked; wide eyes staring at their mother as the older woman untangled herself from the wreckage and shakily pulled herself to her feet—glaring death at her and Sadyra.

As much as Sadyra's adrenaline begged for her to finish Areeza, she knew she had to get Sleena away from the village before their father returned. Clasping Sleena's hand, she dragged her from the hut; the poor girl barely able to keep up without falling.

Off the porch and down the trail they ran. A horse awaited them at the bottom of the hill. All they had to do was get there.

The cabin door squealed.

Sadyra looked over her shoulder into the crazed eyes of someone who had claimed to be their mother.

Sleena's scream made Sadyra trip.

Snapping her head back to see where she was going, desperately trying to keep from tumbling face first to the ground at the end of the side path, Sadyra ran into the open arms of Tural Ors.

Pollard

Cursed

Fishmonger Bay wasn't nearly as impressive as Larina had thought it might be. For some reason, even after listening to Sadyra's stories about how oppressive and backward the village was, Larina had expected something more than what greeted her as she and Pollard emerged from the trailhead and clopped across a wide common area between a sour smelling warehouse and buildings lining the base of a cliff—its sheer face eventually sloping out of sight.

Her gaze drifted from one hut to another, from a larger cabin to a building sporting a placard that read: *Witch's Cauldron.* She exchanged glances with Pollard. "What now? She could be anywhere."

"I thought she mentioned she lived in a hut on top of a hill?"

Larina scanned the cliff behind the village and shrugged. If Sadyra's hut was up there, she had no idea how to access the heights. She thought of the path they had passed a little while ago. "Perhaps we should have taken the path."

Pollard glanced back to where the southern trail disappeared within a tunnel of trees as he walked his horse past a long flight of wooden steps fronting what appeared to be a temple.

Larina urged her horse after him. Passing the temple, she spied a mercantile with a large storefront window displaying fineries.

Pollard

"This way." Pollard guided his horse between the temple and the mercantile; stopping in front of a small smithy that existed beneath an overhang at the rear of the shop.

A middle-aged man with a pepper-grey beard that was dangerously long to be working the forges looked up at their approach. He brought a heavy looking hammer down on a long piece of orange-glowing steel several times before flipping it and repeating the process. Holding it up for inspection, he nodded and slid the metal into a vat of water, the action emitting a loud hiss amidst a burst of steam.

Doffing oversized mitts, he stretched his back and stepped to the edge of the overhang—his curious face taking the measure of Pollard. Arms thicker than Pollard's, he crossed them over his barrel chest. "Good day, stranger. What can I be doing for ya?"

Larina studied the man's reaction to her friend. Pollard was an intimidating man while on his feet, but on horseback, he was doubly so. Still, the blacksmith didn't appear the least bit worried.

"Greetings, my good man." Pollard slipped from his horse and offered the smith a handshake. When the smith stared back at him, keeping his hands to himself, Pollard cleared his throat. "I'm looking for a lass who lives in these parts."

The smith furrowed his heavy brow, looking at Pollard as if he were daft. "There's many a missuses in these parts."

Larina rolled her eyes. "We're looking for an auburn-haired girl named Sadyra."

The smith's reaction to the name wasn't lost on her. He grunted, "She got a last name?"

Larina looked to Pollard.

He shrugged.

She looked back at the smith. "She never gave us her last name."

The smith ran his tongue along the inside of his mouth, mulling that over. He turned and spat on the ground. "Then I'm afraid I can't help ya. If she don't care to share her name with ya, I ain't to be divulging her whereabouts. Have a good day."

The smith turned to re-enter his forge but Pollard's huge hand on his shoulder stopped him.

The smith's soot-smeared face visibly darkened as he stared at Pollard's hand. "I don't care how big you are mister. If you don't take your hand off me, you'll be losing it."

Not waiting for Pollard to respond, the smith latched onto Pollard's wrist and spun faster than Larina would have believed possible for such a thick bodied man. Using his momentum, he followed through with a lightning-fast punch with his free hand.

Larina gasped at the suddenness of the smith's movement, but she needn't have worried. Pollard's response left the tough man gaping.

Pollard sidestepped, clasped the smith's punching arm, and twisted it behind his back. Moving in behind, Pollard reefed on the man's arm, forcing him to his toes, grunting in discomfort.

Pollard snarled. "We're not here to cause trouble. We're looking for a friend who might be in danger. We don't have time to be messing around. You get me?"

Larina thought for sure the smith's arm would break as Pollard emphasized his words by forcing the man's thick arm higher up his back.

Purple faced, the smith appeared ready to spit horseshoe nails. He struggled to break free of Pollard's grasp, but a further wrench of his arm convinced him to stop. "Yes! Alright already. Unhand me or I won't be saying no more."

Larina nodded for Pollard to do so.

Making sure he made his point, Pollard shoved the smith's arm up just a little bit higher, making him dance on his toes and cry out, before being shoved away from the forge and any chance of retrieving a weapon of opportunity.

The smith rubbed at his pained arm. "Who is Sadyra to you?"

Pollard

Pollard stepped toward him, clearly unhappy.

The smith held up thick hands. "Easy, lad. I need to know if you mean her harm. Cause, if you do, you might as well break my arm and be done with it."

Pollard clenched his fists.

"Look." The smith beseeched Larina. "I ain't no squealer. Sadie's a member of Gitch's crew. It'd be suicide for me to give her up to someone who means her harm. You ain't from Ivar the Blade's crew are ya?"

Pollard frowned. "Ivar the Blade?"

"He's the brute Sadyra said she provoked in a bar one night. Apparently, Ivar wants to hurt her," Larina said, recalling the story. The fact that the smith had called Sadyra by her nickname struck a chord.

"Aye! That's her," the smith agreed. "They tore apart the *Cauldron* to get at her."

"Where is she now," Pollard demanded.

"I don't know. She fled the Bay last summer. No one's seen her since. Why? What's happened?"

Larina held a hand up to interrupt. "Yes. We know. She's been with us, but she returned here last night. Do you know where she used to live?"

"She's back?" Concern clouded the smith's face. "That's not good." He took a hesitant look at Pollard before he ran into his forge and plucked a large headed hammer from the back wall. "Come on, follow me. If Tural catches her, he'll kill her."

Sadyra tried to scream but nothing escaped her lips. Her father's sudden appearance and iron grip paralyzed her with fear.

Pollard

Tural wrapped her in a bear hug, squeezing the air from her lungs. His hold was so tight she feared he was going to break her ribs.

Movement up the path drew her attention. She shook her head frantically. Their mother stormed down the path toward Sleena.

With every bit of courage she could muster, Sadyra screamed, "Sleena! Run!" Her voice echoed off the heights, mocking her. She should never have come back.

Her mind numb with the realization that by leaving last year she had doomed Sable to what she could only imagine was a horrific death, Sadyra thought she was about to throw up. By coming back, she had sentenced Sleena to death as well.

Tural was right. She was cursed.

Examining the horse at the bottom of the hill, Pollard followed Larina's gaze as the smith pointed up the trail. "At the top of the hill you'll find a path that leads off to the right. Sadyra's cabin is at the end of that path."

A scream echoed off the heights, shattering the tranquility of the bay area.

Pollard's blood ran cold. "That's Sadie!"

"Quickly," The smith urged. "I'll get help and meet you up there. Hurry! Her father's insane."

Before Pollard could react, Larina was already running.

Pollard

Banish the Demon

Areeza latched onto Sleena's elbow and yanked her off her feet.

Sleena whimpered, her eyes filled with terror.

Blind rage replaced Sadyra's capacity to think straight. Knowing her parents, her sister had undoubtedly witnessed what the butchers had done to Sable. Losing control of herself, Sadyra twisted, kicked, elbowed, and thrust her head back and forth trying to hurt the demon who was her father.

It was all Tural could do to hang on. He adjusted his grip, wrapping his arms around her neck and squeezing tight. He snarled through gritted teeth, "You little witch. You've been a nettle in my britches since the day you were spawned."

Unable to breathe, Sadyra's instincts took over. Her training with Gitch's crew all those months ago came back to her without conscious thought. She grasped his forearm with both hands and dipped her chin. Dropping to her knees, her weight shift caused Tural to bend overtop of her. She dipped her shoulder to the side and rolled onto the ground.

He released his chokehold to catch himself. Hitting the ground hard, he twisted and reached out to grab her, but she was too quick.

His fingers brushed her back as she scrambled to her feet and ran at Areeza, reaching for the handle of her knife. Determined to end the evil woman who claimed to be their mother, a cold dread broke over her. She had dropped her knife inside the hut.

"Grab her!" Tural shouted.

Areeza reached out with one hand but Sadyra slapped it out of the way and ran past.

Sadyra hit the porch in a dead sprint, the wall breaking her headlong charge. The flimsy door slammed against the jamb as she staggered into the dimly lit interior. She grabbed the sconce on the edge of the table and made her way to the sleeping area she used to share with her sisters.

The cabin door had no sooner banged shut behind her than it was ripped open again. "I've got you now!"

Sadyra tripped as she spun to face the monster that instilled terror within her. She went down on one knee, her eyes wide with fear—barely hanging onto the sconce.

A sneer lifted the corner of Tural's mouth. Not bothering to walk around the furniture, he flung the table aside and kicked a chair out of his way.

Sadyra dared take her eyes off him, desperately searching the area near the back corner of the hut. She spotted her knife beside the scattered blankets.

Looking back, Tural had pulled out a long dagger of his own.

He pointed it at her. "This is something I should have done as soon as you drew your first breath."

Sadyra put the sconce on the floor and scrambled on hands and knees, snatching her dagger and rising to her feet in a flurry of motion.

Tural lunged but she side-stepped along the back wall, banging into the cabinet where her mother stored tallow and wax candles. She threw the cabinet to the floor, hoping to slow Tural's advance.

The cabinet shattered, spilling its contents.

Her father stepped back to avoid being hit. His dark eyes followed her, an inherent evil glinting in the dim light of the sconce balanced precariously on the edge of the central table. He took a step toward the door to negate any chance she had of bolting for freedom, but he needn't have bothered.

Areeza's haggard form darkened the threshold.

Sadyra gaped. Sleena wasn't with her.

"You've got nowhere to run," Tural's flat voice announced.

Sadyra ignored him. She leaned forward to yell at her mother, "Where's Sleena? What have you done with her?"

Areeza stepped inside the hut, pulling the door closed. "You should be more worried about what we're about to do to you. We'll deal with her soon enough."

Sadyra swallowed, tears streaming down her face—her chest falls heavy. Grabbing a small stool that her mother used when working the ancient loom, Sadyra threw it at the lone window on the back wall. Not caring about the shards that clung to the window frame, she put one foot on the overturned cabinet and jumped headfirst through the gaping hole.

Tural's dark glare appeared in the window. Finding her sprawled amongst the overgrowth in the backyard, he nodded and disappeared from view.

The sharp pain radiating from her left thigh told her that she had gashed herself on a piece of glass but she didn't have time to worry about it. She bounced to her feet and faced the spot she knew he would come. She had spent many long hours in the backyard of their family home wondering if she would ever recover from the beatings her father had laid on her.

A metallic squeal pierced the air—the significance making her breath catch. Her mind screamed at her to run. She was faster than him. He would never keep up.

She swallowed. A faint sensation of finality seeped into her. It was time to face the incapacitating fear that had crippled her for as long as she could remember. It was time to banish the demon or die in the attempt.

Stepping around an old stone bench overgrown with weeds near the back of the hut to put it between her and the back corner, she held her knife in a trembling hand and waited—

constantly peering over her shoulder in case Tural or Areeza decided to come around the cabin from the far side.

No matter how much she thought she was ready, nothing could have prepared her for the sight of her father as he strolled into view. It was all she could do to maintain a grip on her knife. If she saw anything registering in his eyes other than absolute hatred toward her, it was perhaps a touch of surprise.

Tural's gaze didn't miss the fact that her knife shook out of control. He nodded at it. "Aye. You know you can't use that on me. It's time you came to your senses and accepted your fate."

She stared wide-eyed at his approach, her resolve slipping. "No father, *please*. Don't make me do this."

"I ain't making you do anything. You're the one responsible for the curse."

She shook her head. "I don't know what you're talking about. I haven't done anything."

He nodded. "Yes, Sadyra. You have. In you lies the curse of the Dragon Witch."

She swallowed. He had said as much before, but it had never made any sense. She wasn't a witch. She had never done anything that remotely suggested she possessed magic. "I don't know what you're talking about. Please, father. Stop."

A grim smile flitted across his face. Two more steps and he would have her.

"Father, no! What have I done to deserve this? Tell me!"

"You were born," Tural snarled and stepped around the bench, his dagger poised to strike.

Movement from the corner of the cabin behind Tural caught Sadyra's attention. Areeza Ors appeared—the limp form of Sleena draped in her arms.

Locking eyes with Sadyra, Areeza nodded with an ominous smile.

Tural's knife plunged at Sadyra.

Pollard

Distracted by Sleena's lifeless body, Sadyra caught her father's movement out of the corner of her eye. She stepped back and twisted sideways, pirouetting on the spot. Her knife swung around and bit into Tural's shoulder—slicing through his thin leather jerkin, exposing a deep gash.

Tural yelped and leaned over the bench to escape the path of another wild swing; his legs spread wide.

Sadyra took advantage of his vulnerable position. The toe of her boot connected between his legs, followed closely by an open-palmed hand to his chin as he bent over in pain.

Tural's head shot backward under the force of Sadyra's blow. He fell over the bench and landed heavily amongst the weeds. He had no sooner hit the ground than he raised his hands in front of him.

Sadyra didn't hesitate. She threw herself on top of him with wild abandon. The sensation of her knife cutting through flesh, muscle, and fat was a curious one.

Adrenaline surging, her knife struck again and again, scraping bone and making the sickest of sounds as it dove in and out, warm blood splattering her as she opened up wound after fatal wound, screaming incoherently and pummeling her living nightmare.

A white light flashed in her head.

The toe of Areeza's boot had struck her in the face, lifting her from the gory remains of Tural Ors.

Areeza gasped and dropped beside Tural, her features frozen in shock. She looked at Sadyra. "Look what you've done!"

Sadyra rolled into a sitting position and fingered the cut her mother's boot had delivered to her cheek. Driven by an insatiable need to avenge her sisters, Sadyra didn't hesitate.

Areeza tried to stand to defend herself, but she never got her feet under her before Sadyra slammed into her and drove her knife underneath her mother's ribcage.

The stunned look on Areeza's face as she came to realize her demise was oddly satisfying. Straddling the woman who had brought her into the world, Sadyra shoved the blade deeper and snarled, "*My* curse is lifted, *witch*. You can rest assured you and father will rot in an unmarked grave."

"Sadie!"

As the life left her mother's eyes, Sadyra looked up to see Larina run around the corner of the hut, dagger in hand. Her best friend in all the world stopped beside her, stunned—staring at the carnage.

"Oh, Sadie," Larina's voice trembled with heartfelt emotion. She fell to her knees between Tural and Areeza and wrapped her arms around Sadyra, holding her tight.

Numb, Sadyra couldn't return the embrace. She stared straight ahead, shaking uncontrollably, oblivious to the gore around her. She had killed her parents.

She swallowed. What a horrible child she had turned out to be.

Someone else was in the backyard.

Her thoughts disjointed, she turned her head, and tried to focus on Pollard who knelt at the corner of the hut, his attention on something in the grass.

Her mind reeled. Goosebumps riddled her skin. Going limp in Larina's arms, the last thing she saw was Sleena wrapping her little arms around Pollard's thick neck.

Pollard

Captain Gitch held Sadyra's hands over the table in the back corner of the *Witch's Cauldron*, compassion softening his hard features.

Notified by the local blacksmith, the captain had led the charge up to the mysterious cabin on top of the hill with Slim and Slick right behind him.

Had Larina not held her back, Sadyra would have shanked them as well. It had taken a long time to calm her down but getting to hold Sleena and smelling her skin had eased the rage coursing through her veins. She had held her sister for a long time after that, refusing to acknowledge the villagers that had wandered up the hill to see what was going on.

It had been Bano Shell's presence that had finally got her moving again. As soon as they locked stares, the young man's face turned ashen. He turned and ran. Sadyra had started to give chase but Pollard scooped her off the ground. Feet kicking and fists pounding, Pollard was hard-pressed to hang on. When she had finally settled down again, he hugged her close and convinced her to leave the hilltop and accompany a few of her old friends down to the *Cauldron*.

Gitch squeezed her hands, his mug of ale forgotten. He lovingly stroked the edge of the laceration Areeza's boot had opened on Sadyra's cheek. Tears streamed down his face as he hung his head, shaking it and muttering, "We had no idea, dear Sadie. Oh, how I wish we hadn't left you alone in the warehouse that night."

Pollard

Sadyra cried along with him. She had thought her tears were all spent, but she was wrong. How could she have doubted the man sitting across from her? He had been upfront and straight with her from the very beginning. It had taken a bar fight and wrestling with a naked sailor to help convince the rest of the crew that she was okay, but *his* faith in her had never faltered. Looking back, her attempts at fitting in with the crew had been an unforgettable adventure.

She absently noted the stooped-shouldered healer, Henga, slip through the exit. The kindly old woman had tended to her injuries and assured her they would heal in time. It had taken a while before Henga was satisfied she had dealt with the deep gash to Sadyra's leg.

Sadyra returned her attention to one of the only people in in Fishmonger Bay who had bothered to give her a chance. She grasped one of Gitch's hands and caressed it with stained fingers. "It's not your fault. It's mine. I jumped to a conclusion that wasn't fair to any of you."

Gitch smiled sadly. "There you go again. Taking the blame for everyone else. Oh, Sadie. You are such a blessing. How can I convince you to remain here with us?"

Sadyra held his stare, not sure what to say. Other than Sleena, there was nothing holding her to Fishmonger Bay anymore. She gazed around the bar, searching for the one person who might change her mind but there was no sign of him.

Pollard and Larina sat at the table behind her, chatting up Sleena. Pollard's zany antics, a side of the man Sadyra had never seen before, made her sister laugh. The joyous sound made Sadyra's tears flow anew. She couldn't imagine the horror Sleena had endured since the ritual involving Sable that first night of the Mating Festival. Gitch had apologized until he was hoarse that he hadn't known what was happening until it was too late.

Sleena's future was all that mattered to Sadyra now. If that meant she had to give up the Songsbirthian Guard, so be it.

She searched the many grim faces hoisting tankards around the barroom, their gazes ultimately coming to rest on her and Sleena.

Sadyra heaved a heavy sigh and released Gitch's hand. "Where is he?"

Gitch frowned but his face softened. "Ah. Scruff." He nodded and forced a smile. "The night you left was a time I will rue for the rest of my life. I not only lost you, I also lost my best friend."

Sadyra grabbed his hands and pulled them close. "Why? What happened?"

"It's a long story. Let's just say that Scruff went after you that night. Many of the crew followed, but no one could keep pace with him. He was delirious with concern over your welfare. He almost caught up to you, but lost sight of you when you slipped up the fjord in the early morning light. He searched Thunderhead from top to bottom, harassing people until he was purple in the face looking for you. By the time he finally found you, *he* had also." Gitch nodded at Pollard.

"And?"

Gitch raised his eyebrows. "I think I told you before that Scruff was no ordinary man. I had always known that one day he would leave me. Watching you board the *Crusher*, the light that you had brought into his life, left him." He nodded at her gaping stare. "Aye, my gruff enforcer had a soft spot for you."

Gitch wiped the renewed tears welling up. In a hoarse voice he continued, "I spoke with him briefly before he headed inland. Said he had to speak with someone in Storms End before he went on his way. Someone missing a hand, or something like that. Anyway, he left me scratching my head when he said he had done his job and had to be on his way." He shrugged. "Something about a coming storm."

Pollard

A last inspection of the ransacked contents of her cabin had confirmed in Sadyra's heart she could no longer live with the dark memories the place instilled in her. Gitch had assured her the crew would deal with Bano Shell in the severest of ways. Satisfied, she agreed to leave Bano to them, knowing full well that Bano's days were numbered.

With only two horses, she had clung to Larina as they rode to Storms End on the back of her friend's horse. Sleena had ridden with Pollard, sitting between him and his horse's neck. Hearing Sleena's small voice full of wonder as he pointed out different aspects of nature along the road was the tonic she so needed to lift her out of the darkness her confrontation with her parents had left her in. No matter how she tried to forget about what had happened, Sable's death continued to cast her tormented soul in shadow.

Back in Larina's hometown, they had met up with Thoril Half-Hand and Bear. Thoril had insisted she and Larina were the only ones he could depend on to keep his son safe in the days to come. Sadyra had balked at the idea at first, but Bear had stepped in and insisted that he be allowed to be Sleena's caretaker. With much coaxing from Larina, assuring her that Sleena could not be in better hands, and an eye-opening talk with Pollard's father, Sadyra decided that her destiny did indeed lie with the Songsbirthian Guard.

With a heavy heart, she left Storms End a few days later, following Larina and Pollard into the mountains.

Standing at the aft rail of a swift sloop as it whisked them upriver from Millsford, Larina and Pollard discussed what they had learned from the residents of Fishmonger Bay while Sadyra was being treated by the village healer. Totally unbeknownst to their troubled friend, it was the resident's belief that Sadyra had descended from someone they called the 'Dragon Witch.'

According to legends handed down over many generations—five hundred years' worth, if what the villagers reported could be trusted—Sadyra's relatives had borne the burden of a dark heritage. Back then, during the end of times that folklore claimed dragons used to fly the skies of the land, a twenty-one-year-old woman had gone mad and thrown her lot in with the dangerous beasts. Many people from the bay area had been killed as a result. The *Witch's Cauldron* had derived its name from a dark event that dated back to the Dragon Witch's time—the villagers had risen up and burned a witch inside her house on the very spot that the *Cauldron* had been erected.

When questioned by Pollard, no one really knew what had become of the Dragon Witch. The blacksmith had spat and told them he had heard that she had simply disappeared from the land, leading the dragons across the Niad Ocean, never to be heard from again.

Years later, a family came to Fishmonger Bay claiming to be direct descendants of the Dragon Witch and had come in in search of their heritage. The villagers had banded together to demand a sacrifice, hoping to dispel the rampant superstitions accompanying anyone associated with the Ors' family name.

A warm feeling flushed Larina, goosebumps riddling her skin. It had made her heart glad to see Bear again. Sleena couldn't be in better company.

She swallowed. Sleena's sister was the one who needed saving now.

She glanced to the bow where she knew her troubled friend would be.

Pollard

Sadyra rested her elbows on the junction of the starboard and port rails, overlooking the bowsprit of a leaping fish with the upper body of a naked woman.

Sadyra's distant gaze lingered on the mountain peaks rising high overhead and the colossal waterfall that tumbled thousands of feet to the source of the Madrigail River.

"We'd best get ready to disembark," Pollard said. "Not much farther now."

He made to start forward, but Larina put a hand on his forearm. "Best we not mention all that talk about the Dragon Witch, huh?"

Pollard looked from Larina to Sadyra and back again. "Ya, you're probably right. She has enough on her mind."

Sadyra was thankful for her new friends. She wasn't sure what she had done in life to deserve the devotion of such amazing people, but she was grateful. Pollard and Larina were special. They never questioned her when they had stepped off the sloop and she said she needed to visit the base of the falls before returning to the catacombs. It had been a long couple of weeks for everyone, but they had simply nodded and let her lead the way.

Facing the thunderous roar at the base of the falls, Pollard and Larina stood behind her, respecting her need to be alone with her thoughts.

Tears dripped from her freckled cheeks—her throat thick as she tried to come to terms with the loss of Sable. A large teardrop splattered the face of the little cornstalk doll she held in her hands. Dolly had been Sable's dearest friend.

Nobody in Fishmonger Bay had been able to help her locate her sister's remains. As a result, a hollow pit of despair had threatened to suck her into the depths of its darkness ever since. Consumed with the guilt of her sister's death, she could think of nothing else.

Sable was dead. There was nothing she, or anyone else, could do to change that. Standing at the base of Splendoor Falls, the most beautiful spot in all the world in Sadyra's reckoning, she couldn't think of a better place to be laid to rest.

Dropping to her knees, she used her hands and knife to dig a small hole. Holding Dolly over the shallow grave, she tried to be brave—tried to be the strong big sister Sable had needed in the end. Her remorse prevented her from uttering the words her sister deserved. Swallowing hard in an effort to breathe, her shoulders shook violently, making it difficult to place Dolly in the ground.

She felt Pollard's hand on one shoulder and Larina's on the other as they knelt at her side.

Together, they smoothed the dirt over the spirit of Sable's new resting place.

Her palms on the tiny mound of dirt, Sadyra looked to the heavens, beseeching forgiveness.

She followed the erratic flight of a butterfly fluttering above the churning pool at the base of Splendoor Falls as the sun broke through the clouds, casting a rainbow on the towering mist.

Envisioning the soul of her dear sister embodied by the beauty of the butterfly, it was as if the weight of the world had been lifted from her shoulders.

The End

of what led to the most beautiful of friendships.

Thank you for reading *Pollard*. I'd be grateful if you would take a moment to leave a review.

Available now!

Keeper of the Jewel, book 1 in the Highcliff Guardians

Something dark is creeping across the elven kingdom of South March. Something so sinister, that if it is allowed to thrive unchecked, will lead to the end of dragonkind and quite possibly the termination of life as a whole.

The only thing standing in the way of the pervasive evil is a privileged young woman who wants nothing to do with her high standing in life, nor the oppressive responsibilities that accompany the title: Heir to the Willow Throne.

Book 2—Dragon Sect: Coming late 2021

To keep up with everything going on in the Soul Forge
Universe, please visit my website at:
www.richardhstephens.com

All books are written within the Soul Forge Universe.
There are two, loosely written stand-alone prequels, that I
published first so I could understand the publishing side of
writing. Though loosely written, fans enjoy the back stories
about the main characters in the Soul Forge Saga.

The Royal Tournament
Of Trolls and Evil Things

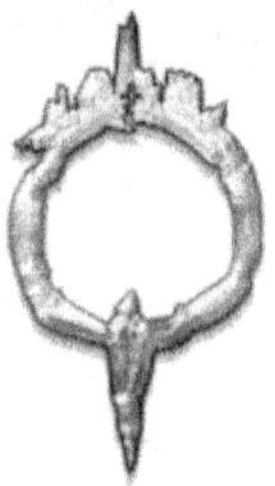

I offer personalized, signed, paperback copies, complete
with bling!

A discount is offered on the purchase of a trilogy.

If you wish to order: richardhstephens1@gmail.com

Books by Richard H. Stephens

Soul Forge - The Epic Fantasy Trilogy

Soul Forge – Book 1

Haunted by the murder of his family, a forgotten hero embarks upon a perilous quest fraught with demons both real and imagined.

Silurian Mintaka only wants another drink, but when the people of Zephyr need someone to save them from an evil sorcerer, he agrees to put aside his bitterness and wreak his revenge.

Deception, betrayal, and fantastic beasts stand in his way. With the fate of the kingdom in the hands of a homicidal lunatic, the only thing left to do is pray.

Legends of the Lurker Series

Reecah's Flight –Book 1

Everyone knows dragons are dangerous, but to hunt them is insane.

There is something strange about the woman living on top of the hill and the people of Fishmonger Bay leave her alone. At least until the day she visits the village witch.

Her life spinning out of control, Reecah must decide whether to slay the dragon or risk becoming a victim of her people.

Can Reecah find the key to unlock her family heritage or will she fall prey to the secret so many have died to protect?

Reecah's Gift – Book 2

The appalling mannerisms of those entrusted to protect the kingdom are shocking.

Braving the perils of a cutthroat city isn't what Reecah envisioned when she sought out a better place.

Can a ruthless giant equip her with the skills she needs to confront the king, or will his unorthodox ways end up being the death of her dreams?

Is an alliance with a murderous elf and a sly dwarf the best way to avert the plight of the dragons? And what is this *Gift* everyone seems to know about? Everyone, except Reecah.

Find out how the machinations of the evil prince and a traitorous wizard turn Reecah's quest on its head in this epic, second installment of the Legends of the Lurker.

Reecah's Legacy – Book 3

The culmination of the Legends of the Lurker trilogy.

Reecah Windwalker comes into her own as she finds peace with her past and bravely sets out to fulfill her legacy.

Keeping a promise to a dead witch, Reecah seeks those who can help her learn the ways of her dragon magic as she embarks on a desperate journey to save the last of the dragons from the dark heir.

The races come together, but their combined strength may not be enough to prevent the high king's dragon slayers from eradicating the beauty from the land.

Banebridge Companion Novels

Larina – Book 1
(A story from the Soul Forge Universe)

Growing up on the streets of Storms End, Larina knows the only way to survive is to take matters into her own hands.

Skulking about the seedy alleyways and taverns of a once great city that has fallen from grace, survival has become a game of steal and lie, or die.

Larina uses her ill-begotten abilities to help the vulnerable, less fortunate souls abandoned by life. An act that fills her with a sense of purpose and pride.

That all changes when the man with the black warhammer comes to town. Now the Storms End Lightning Bolt must decide whether those she has fought so hard to protect will be better off if she ends up dead.

Sadyra – Book 2

(A story from the Soul Forge Universe)

Living in the shadows to avoid the brutality of parents harbouring a dark secret, Sadyra must force a violent confrontation if she is to keep her younger sisters from harm's way.

Begrudgingly accepted to work alongside a hardened group of sailors, Sadyra learns how to survive in a ruthless world.

To save her sisters from a fate worse than death, Sadyra goes against everything she feels is right, and life as she knows it will never be the same.

Pollard – Book 3

(A story from the Soul Forge Universe)

Called together to prepare for the defense of the kingdom's most sacred resource, the son of Thoril Half-Hand sets out to train the realm's most promising fighters.

To keep the recruits performing as a cohesive unit, Pollard is unprepared to deal with the eclectic personalities of those entrusted to oversee the future defence of Zephyr.

A dark secret assails the band of warriors and their very existence is threatened by creatures they are sworn to protect.

The Royal Tournament

(A story from the Soul Forge Universe)

The Royal Tournament has at long last come to the village of Millsford.

For Javen Milford, a local farm boy, the news couldn't be better.

Finally, Javen can perform his chores on the homestead and partake in the biggest military games in the Kingdom, hoping beyond hope that just maybe, he might catch the eye of the king.

Javen enters the kingdom's flagship tournament only to discover that in order to win, one must be prepared to die.

Of Trolls and Evil Things

The (standalone) prequel to the Soul Forge Saga series!

Travel down an ever-darkening path where two orphans battle to survive upon a perilous mountainside, evading the predators and prowlers preying upon its slopes, and within its catacombs.

When the dangers they face force them from their mountain home, they end up in the cutthroat streets of Cliff Face plying their hands as beggars to survive.

Strange circumstances spin their lives out of control, forcing them onto the nefarious slopes of Mt. Gloom in a desperate effort to escape the unpleasant reality looming over them; only to discover their worst nightmare awaits them with open arms.

 Born in Simcoe, Ontario, in 1965, I began writing circa 1974; a bored child looking for something to while away the long, summertime days. My penchant for reading The Hardy Boys led to an inspiration one sweltering summer afternoon when my best friend and I thought, 'We could write one of those.' And so, I did.

As my reading horizons broadened, so did my writing. Star Wars inspired a 600-page novel about outer space that caught the attention of a special teacher who encouraged me to keep writing.

A trip to a local bookstore saw the proprietor introduce me to Stephen R. Donaldson and Terry Brooks. My writing life was forever changed.

At 17, I left high school to join the working world to support my first son. For the next twenty-two years I worked as a shipper at a local bakery. At the age of 36, I went back to high school to complete my education. After graduating with honours at the age of thirty-nine, I became a member of our local Police Service, and worked for 12 years in the provincial court system.

In early 2017, I retired from the Police Service to pursue my love of writing full-time. With the help and support of my lovely wife Caroline and our five children, I have now realized my boyhood dream.

If you wish to keep up to date on new releases, promotions and giveaways, please subscribe to my newsletter by checking out the contact tab on my website.

www.richardhstephens.com

Facebook: richardhughstephens
Twitter: RHStephens1
Instagram: richard_h_stephens
YouTube: bit.ly/2NKpOhn